Hope's Truth

Hope's Truth

Stuart Olds

TRICORN
BOOKS

Tricorn Books

Hope's Truth

by Stuart Olds

Design © 131 Design Ltd
www.131design.org
Published by Tricorn Books
www.tricornbooks.co.uk

Typeface: Baskerville
ISBN 978-0-9567597-2-6
Published 2011 by Tricorn Books,
a trading name of 131 Design Ltd.
131 High Street, Old Portsmouth,
PO1 2HW

Printed and bound in Great Britain by
CPI Cox & Wyman

Inspiration

Part of this book from page 225 - 250 is pretty much a word for word account of the manic episode that happened to me:

"Steady now young man," said the Policeman, with one hand outstretched to grab hold of Bill's arm. Frightened by the physical gesture, Bill pulled away and ran past him. The driver of the Police car had got out and blocked the way to the gate. There was a puddle on the drive and Bill saw the water, which reminded him of the swim Rafievn had had with Sanluin. He sank to his knees and patted the water looking at the drips fall from his hand. He pulled his shirt off, which was almost in rags from the hammering it had already taken, and tried to swim in the puddle.

Some might say that being locked up is the last thing that can be inspirational but in my case it was the exact opposite.

About the Author

To wind the clock back about three weeks prior to the cell door being slammed, will give the best account of events. I had been working in the building industry since 1986 and the squeeze of stupidity was creeping into management by the week. I was desperate to get out and the opportunity to run a pub came up. To me it had massive potential, and my mind was spinning with ideas. I slipped into what has now been diagnosed as bi-polar disorder but it felt normal to me. I had not slept for about eight days and was pumped full of energy, everything was flat out, full speed. Go back in the book to page 229 and that is word perfect as to what happened to me for real. To be honest, the euphoria was immense and the trip my mind went through was beyond belief. I was lucky that I was able to remember it all, as most manic episodes are forgotten by the victim. The biggest victim of this was my wife, who witnessed first hand what looked like complete and utter supercharged madness. The police had their hands full too, but to their credit they were gentle, or perhaps scared to death by my outburst of lunacy.

It took a few months to try to work out why the episode had happened to me. I had experienced bouts of depression since I was seven years old but I just thought that it was feeling bad or miserable, as I did not know what else it could be. This depression developed into what I now have.

After this manic episode the idea of a book flooded my mind; the hairs all over my body stood up and within a few moments I had the bones of *'Hope's Truth'* ready to write. The rest they say, is history. I have pushed my condition to get what I can out of this other dimension; the doctor said it can be dangerous but wait for the next book!!!

To all with mental health problems, just think - they may not always be problems.

Contents

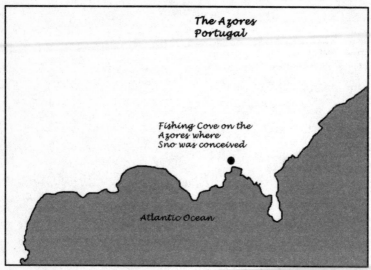

Planetician, (Earth) where Hope landed

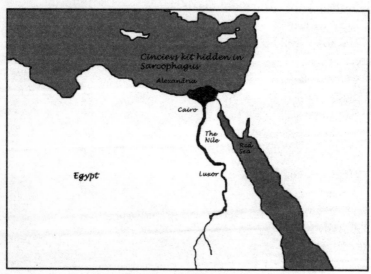

Egyptian coast where Cinciev was left

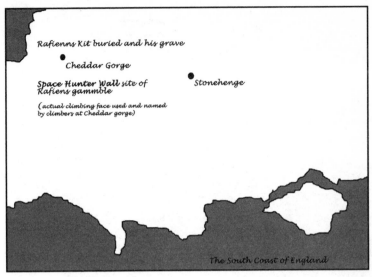

Rafievn's Gamble - *Planetician* (Earth)

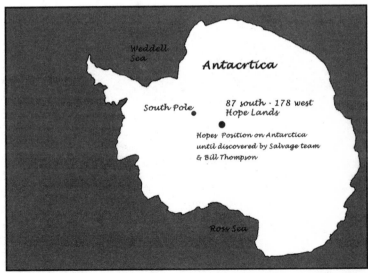

Hope's resting place

1,800 years b.c. Two months from Earth.

The four crew of the space-ship Hope are two months from what we know as Earth; the crew have not seen Earth or know it exists yet. Their own planet is the same size as earth; everything is the same, - they have religions, different languages, which more or less the same as on Earth, they are more technologically advanced but, all that does not mean they will succeed in the simple task of survival.

The Past

A near perfect technology has been created,and a whole human civilisation has become totally reliant on it. The balance of nature has been altered with the help of human greed, and the new technology itself is on the brink of collapse. The architect of the near perfect technology has one survival plan. He knows that a planet exists that can sustain human life.

The Present

Within some of us lay a dormant gene; it was planted in our ancestors by a mirror species. The gene will be activated and the process of inoculation will begin.

The Future

We are developing a technology so powerful we will be almost totally reliant on it. No matter how righteous the human race thinks it is, we are greedy. Literacy, a new belief and acceptance, will be our inoculation.

Chapter One

The interior of the craft slowly comes to life; the navigation point had not shut down for five years, not since it was set when Hope took off from Atronia, the planet that had everything to support life for an eternity. It's only downfall was the life that evolved had developed to a point where it's own technology overtook the need to survive from the planet's resources; artificial life had become the new greed of man. They had become reliant on it.

Nano-technology was producing everything from clothes to food to machinery; even people were upgrading their own genetic make-up with nano-programmes. They could be programmed to be more intelligent and too many were losing their humanity, they were slowly creating a two tier human race. Negative feelings were being blanked from peoples' memories to try and create the perfect life. People with wealth were upgrading their speed of thought with nano-programmes, which were implanted into their genes. People were even changing the way they felt; they would have no depression or low feelings, almost like a permanent high. Because there were no natural lows, people were needing artificial highs, this was all from programmes they could buy, and only available to the rich. The programmes could also enhance physical strength and speed, athletics was non-competitive, only very rarely would the odd natural human beat a nano-being. Basically the better programmer won. Team sports had more competition, as talent could not yet be programmed.

People less fortunate became sub-standard; they were slowly becoming slaves to the nano-beings, which ruled the world. Selected humans who had no wealth were employed by the nano-beings and sometimes used as personal slaves, these were only the very attractive ones though. Sanluin being a natural beauty was highly valued, but worth nothing as it often meant losing a lot of your freedom to a nano-being. Sanluin could have left the company she was working for but had to stay as she was gathering information for her father. The non nano-beings were used mainly for pleasure and to amuse and cater for every whim that the nano-beings required.

Sanluin was working for the director of the Siunc Corporation, Mr Aliik. He and his company was one of the main sponsors for building the Explorer ship and Sanluin's father, Dr Viuuv was heading the project to build the Explorer. He was also building Hope, this was a smaller ship that was so secret only a handful of people knew about it. It was built from the parts he over ordered for Explorer and then upgraded. Sanluin's role was to get information from her boss Mr Aliik. She got most of this when he was using her for his own pleasure; he seemed to talk more freely when he was amusing himself with her naked body. She hated every second of it, but deep down she knew the importance of her whoring. She blanked it from her mind knowing that the quicker Hope was built the quicker her misery would end as she would be one of the crew. Dr Viuuv knew that eventually the Explorer would be built; he could only delay it so much without being caught.

All Explorer's crew would have the nano-programmes in them, their loss of humanity included. Any planet they found which would suit them would inevitably be ruined, just as they have done with Atronia. Dr Viuuv always thought of everything. He planted a nano-virus in Explorer's ventilation system that he could activate using a pulse from Atronia. The nano-virus would be released in a vapour and enter the lungs of the crew, before passing into their blood stream and causing a reaction with their own nano-system, which would make them fall asleep. The Explorer ship would need communication from the crew in the early stage of flight, but as they would all be sleeping, the ship would automatically switch to autopilot. Dr Viuuv programmed the course for this. Explorer would collide with the nearest planet or moon. The Corporation on Atronia would receive false communication, fooling them of the intended catastrophe. As far as they would know, their ship Explorer would still be on a course for the nearest Galaxy.

This was a drastic move but it had to be done as Explorer would be a lot faster than the smaller ship Hope. They could find Hope, and the whole mission that had taken years to plan would be ruined and along with it the chance to get away from Atronia's slavery and inevitable destruction.

The organic life forms on Atronia were at risk, the eco-system was breaking down, everything was being made artificially and for some people this was not how they wanted to exist, as they knew that a virus could either develop itself or be developed by scientists that could wipe out the nano-beings. An underworld of scientists grew however, they had little chance to change their world as the main ruling power was far too strong and any mention of reverting to a life working with the planet and what it had to offer would mean imprisonment or mind alteration. They would be arrested and mentally altered so that any rebellious feelings they might have would be eradicated from their memory. The only advantage that normal humans had was that natural flair and talent could not be created from technology. Most scientists got sucked into the artificial world but some didn't; they could develop a super virus that could one day spread through the nano-beings, who would slowly be finished, taking normal humans with them as the planet's eco-system had broken down beyond repair and it could not sustain or produce food for the population. The nano-beings and their Corporations produced the food, leaving normal humans in a Catch 22 situation. If they developed the virus they would inevitably be destroying themselves; it would take decades but it would happen. One way or another the time on Atronia was running out. Their only chance was Hope, the brainchild of Dr Viuuv.

They built their ship Hope right under the noses of the ruling power; it was risky, but to leave an existence which was heading for its own destruction was worth every risk - survival is worth every risk. If you know one way is to lose, the only other way is to risk as this gives you hope.

Awakening

Sanluin's senses were slowly starting to kick into life. The deep sleep that she and the crew had been in takes a while to wear off and as Sanluin was the crew member in charge of hyper sleep, she had arranged for herself to wake first. Hope would start to wake the crew if she found a suitable planet for them to inhabit. Sanluin purposely programmed her hyper sleep to wake her a couple of hours before the rest of the crew, to give her time to be alone when they were in a galaxy that might have a planet they could inhabit. As she lay in her pod, she kept thinking of what would happen back on Atronia. Would Dr Viuuv be caught? Would Explorer find them? Sanluin was sad as she knew they were never again to see the people who loved them, they would only be a memory. The reality of their mission was coming home to her now.

When they had left Atronia they were all very tense as the Siunc Corporation watched Hope launch, it was supposed to be a test for the Explorer. Dr Viuuv was testing new engines in the ship for Explorer, and Hope was thought to be crew-less. When Hope was out of Atronia's atmosphere a dummy explosion was fired. This was to fool the Siunc Corporation into thinking the engines had failed, causing the ship to explode, which would also delay the building of Explorer.

Sanluin's mouth was dry and she could not swallow. As she opened her eyes for the first time her vision was very blurred, she couldn't make out any of the ship's interior. She closed her eyes again and slipped back to sleep. She started to dream, it was very vivid, her mother who had been dead for 20 years seemed so real she could touch her. She was stood with Sanluin's father Dr Viuuv; they were watching Sanluin collect her medal for swimming. It was her first race; they were so proud and so in love.

again and she realised it was the
...e was seeing much better now. She
...ne pod, reached across and pressed it.
...ly. She stretched her arms forward; this
...high and buttock muscles, which was also
...gy bit, to get up. She slowly turned onto
...omething slid across her chest, she caught
...hatever it was with her right hand. Relieved,
she rea...   r swimming medal. Was it the reason for her
dream? Maybe.   was then she remembered bringing it with her
for good luck. She took a big breath and sat up slowly, the feelings
of nausea swept across her, dizziness was causing her to sway. She
seemed to be sat there for an eternity. As her head became clear
she touched her feet to the floor, her toes felt numb at first but soon
started to tingle as the blood reached them. She stood up straight
for a while and stretched fully, standing on tiptoe. Her body was
enjoying this as much as her mind. She crouched low and started
to stretch her back pulling her head into her chest. Then, she lay
on the floor face down and pushed her body up leaving her hips on
the floor, rolling her head at the same time. She stretched all of her
muscles; it felt so good she could do this forever.

Her bladder was full so she started to walk to the bathroom,
turned on the cold water and washed her face. It felt so refreshing
to feel water on her face for the first time in five years. She was so
hungry but also very excited to see what sort of planet they might
land on. Before she went to the Bridge of the ship she decided to
shower, this might relax her a bit from her excitement. She washed
for a long time as her body had missed the feeling of hot water.
She went to the loo in the shower; her urine was very pungent her
kidneys needed flushing through after the long journey. Being in
hyper sleep the body is shut down and all normal functions are put
on hold except the essential heart, blood and brain functions.

Dressed in the standard suits they had packed, she looked

in the mirror. Her complexion was pale and her hair was dry but still in its original style. It was cut short and was very blond, all in all not too bad for not seeing a brush in 5 years. FM1 Sanluin was stitched on her collar. Each crew member had their own name stitched on their collar to remind the rest of the crew what they were called, as none of the crew had known each other until they took off. This was to prevent any risk of being caught by the Corporation. As Sanluin walked to the Bridge she looked at the other crew still asleep. MF1 Rafievn was next to Sanluin's pod, he was very handsome tall and muscular. Sanluin had got acquainted with Rafievn for about an hour before the launch of Hope and Sanluin was attracted to him immediately. She could see he was dreaming by his eye movement and looked down his body and imagined what he was dreaming about when she saw his crotch and the bulge beneath the fabric. Was she in his dream she wondered to herself, she definitely hoped so. MF2 Cinciev was next to Rafievn; he was shorter with darker skin. The last of the crew was the pilot MF3 Tehkin, who was much older than the other two and reminded Sanluin of Dr Viuuv with his grey hair and leathery skin. The fifth crew member was a droid. The crew named him Nn, which was short for nice-nano. He was on board for emergency, and for company in case anyone was on the ship by themselves for any length of time.

Sanluin wondered if she should look at what Hope had found or satisfy her hunger as she was so very hungry: hunger won. She went to the galley and processed a meal; this was to be their diet for a while. It looked like paste but had all the nutrients they needed, whilst the taste was just bearable. They could choose their flavours - for what it was worth. For a meal of paste it still took a while to eat. This was meant to prevent the crew rushing their food and it gave their digestive systems' time to get back into working order.

Washed and fed Sanluin was ready to see if Hope had found a suitable planet for them to inhabit. Dr Viuuv always used to say there was every chance there was a similar galaxy to their own or a parallel universe as he called it, and had programmed Hope to find a suitable galaxy, even though the crew would still be asleep. The Bridge was semi-lit; this also needed time to wake up just as the crew did. Sanluin sat at the main computer and logged in. FM1 Sanluin, she punched into the keypad. The screen typed back.

"FM1 Sanluin, welcome from your sleep. Hope has found a suitable planet for you. Would you like to switch to voice communication?"

"Yes, please do Hope." She put the earpiece into her ear and adjusted the mic to her mouth. "Hope, how long have we been on autopilot?" asked Sanluin.

"Just under five years," Hope replied.

"Have we travelled through many galaxies?"

"Yes Sanluin, we have been through four since leaving Atronia, they were all unsuitable for your needs, you didn't miss anything." Sanluin was surprised to hear how long they had travelled but also laughed out loud as her father had programmed his voice to be the voice of Hope. She wanted to call the ship Dad, but to all of the crew he had given them hope, so she kept it as Hope, and also it wouldn't make the rest of the crew feel as if Sanluin was special to the mission.

"Can you give me the statistics of the planet? How far are we from it?" asked Sanluin.

"We are two months from the planet. This is a safe distance, as we don't want to be picked up by any intelligence from the planet - if there is any that is. Remember we don't know the development of the life forms yet," replied Hope.

"What type of life is there?" she asked.

"All life forms are organic from the readings, there are vast oceans, land masses and polar caps. You wouldn't have seen a polar cap as Atronias' melted four centuries ago. You would have read about them in your history books. The Planet seems to be much younger in development; there is no reading of pollution, only volcanic activity."

"What is its size? Will there be a problem with gravitational change?"

"Size and density are very much the same, we will know more when we get closer."

"How long will that be Hope?"

"The rest of the crew will need to be ready first, it will take a week or so for you all to get fully acclimatised from your sleep."

"OK Hope, Sanluin off."

"Goodbye Sanluin."

Chapter Two

The crew of Hope were still too far away from this new planet to get a good visual on the screen. Sanluin wanted to wait until the other crew had woken up. They had a lot of talking to do if they would be spending the rest of their lives together and as they had only met for about an hour, this would take some time. MF1 was beginning to wake, this was Rafievn. He would be feeling the same as Sanluin was about two hours ago, so she got him some water for his dry throat. His pod opened, he slowly put his hands to his face. He rubbed his face and then stretched his arms above his head yawning as he did so. She remembered how good this felt for her. She stood over him grinning all the time as she watched him wake.

"Hello Rafievn, how are you feeling?" Sanluin asked.

"Sanluin, is that you? I was dreaming about you for some reason," he said. Her thoughts were right, he was thinking of her in his dream; this made her feel wanted and excited.

"Don't sit up too quickly Rafievn, you may faint. Take it easy, here have some water." He drank it slowly, which was a good thing as it would be hard to swallow in one go. "Try to sit up, but do it slowly, here let me help you." She put her arms around him and helped him up.

"Stop, stop, I'm going to faint, Sanluin. Hold me."

She held him close to her chest, her left knee was resting on the side of the pod. As he steadied himself his hand held onto her leg at the top of her thigh, this sent a shiver of pleasure up Sanluin's spine. She could feel a chemistry between them; she had not felt this for a long time, as her life on Atronia was owned by Mr Aliik. She had been his slave for so long, the feelings she was having now were like they were for the very first time.

"Rafievn, don't worry I did this on my own a couple of

hours ago it will pass."

"OK, I'm feeling better now, my head is not spinning so much." He opened his eyes, his vision a bit blurry, but he could still make out the beauty of Sanluin's face. When they met before the launch of Hope he was amazed by how beautiful she was. She had a very athletic physique, her eyes were a piercing blue with a sparkle that seemed to dazzle as she looked at him. Rafievn did not know anything about her except that if she had been chosen for this mission she would be very aware of what fate was in store for Atronia. When he went into hyper sleep he could remember seeing her through the pod; what a lasting view for him as they would be asleep for along time.

"Sanluin, how long have you been awake?"

"About two hours Rafievn. I have logged into the computer, we have found a planet or should I say Hope has found one for us. It seems perfect, the same size and density as Atronia. It has organic life, vast oceans and polar caps; polar caps like we have never seen."

"It sounds amazing, how advanced is the life on the planet?"

"We don't know yet, Hope is going to wait until we are all awake and recovered from our journey before we go any closer to the planet."

"Are any of the other crew awake yet?"

"No, just you and me so far."

"How long before the others are awake?"

"They will be awake in about two more hours. I sent them off to sleep for a while longer as I thought this would give us time to get to know each other while we would be alone."

As Sanluin said this she gave Rafievn a very warm look. He was eager to know everything about her, having already made love to her in his dream, he felt this may be a reality sooner than he had hoped.

"Shall I run a shower for you Rafievn?"

"Yes please, Sanluin, I will be up and about in a minute."

11

Sanluin walked off into the washroom, Rafievn stared at her figure as she walked and his lust for her grew even more. Rafievn got up and walked around stretching himself from head to toe, this felt good. He thought his muscles would be un-toned from the sleep but they felt surprisingly good, considering. Their state of sleep prevented them from deteriorating.

"Rafievn, your shower is ready," Sanluin called out.

"OK."

He walked into the shower room that was full of steam, took off his sleep gown and threw it on top of the door. The water felt so invigorating as it washed over his body. He looked for wash gel but couldn't see any.

"Sanluin, is there any wash gel around?" he asked.

"Yes Rafievn, one minute." Rafievn turned to face the door, which was open and saw Sanluin. She stood there without a stitch on, holding the wash gel.

"I don't mean to be forward but I knew you were dreaming about me, I saw how your body was reacting and only wished it was for real. We have about an hour and a half before the others wake. I would like us to be alone - if you want?" Still in awe with her beauty, Rafievn could not speak, he pulled her to towards him and kissed her softly on the lips.

"Does that answer your question?" he replied in a slightly croaky voice. She smiled as she poured some wash gel into her hands and began to wash his body, starting with his chest, slowly moving down his stomach and taking his breath away as she reached his lower abdomen. When she crouched down and washed each leg with both hands, Rafievn just stood there soaking up each second of extreme pleasure. Washing Rafievn's body was as pleasurable for Sanluin as it was for him. She stood up and looked deep into his eyes. He put his hands to the side of her head and kissed her passionately, his tongue exploring her mouth. She clenched his buttocks and pulled him close to her, his manhood was hard and felt huge against her stomach. She was desperate for him to be inside her and pulled away from him to lie on the shower floor in front of him.

"Rafievn, make love to me, please make love to me," she urged. He got to the floor and lay on top of her, one hand holding the back of her head, while the other felt her breasts. Sanluin let out sighs of pleasure as he caressed them so gently. She took hold of his manhood and guided it into her body, which was aching for him so much. As his full erection entered her, it felt as though her whole body was receiving all this pleasure at once. She let out a sigh of enjoyment and he replied in the same tone.

"Rafievn!" She wanted to tell him that she loved him but an orgasm ripped through her body, almost preventing her from breathing.

"Sanluin, kiss me." She kissed him hard on the lips as he was beginning to orgasm, he couldn't hold back anymore and exploded into her. They lay for a few seconds, totally tensed, their bodies locked as if one. She relaxed her legs and he lay beside her, they both looked up as they caught their breath, the hot water splashing on their bodies.

"Wow Sanluin, what a way to wake from a hyper sleep," he said and she laughed.

"You don't think bad of me Rafievn?"

"Of course not, I wanted the same, I'd been dreaming of it for what seemed an eternity."

"That's OK then. Would you like me to prepare you some food?"

"Yes, I'm starving. I'll just finish my shower."

"I'll put your clothes on the rail by the door."

"Thanks Sanluin." As Rafievn washed himself he thought how well things were going, he had made love to the girl of his dreams and they had found a planet they could live on. He thought back to Atronia, what had been her fate? Rafievn had no loved ones there, none who were alive anyway. He was on the mission for his survival skills, if they needed them that is.

"That smells interesting, what is it?" Rafievn asked as he walked into the galley area.

"Until we get on the planet it is our staple diet. It doesn't look much but it will fill you up and has all the nutrients you need."

"If you say so. Hmm, it tastes OK for paste. So what has Hope told you so far?" he enquired, changing the subject.

"We must stay at this distance from the planet for about a week, just to be on the safe side. We don't want to be spotted by any intelligence, if there is any."

"Have there been any signs from the planet?"

"No, we are too far away for a visual of the planet but it is definitely suitable for us to live on. When the others are awake we can take some more accurate readings."

"I wonder if that ship the Siunc Corporation were building has taken off yet."

"You knew about that? Who told you?"

"Dr Viuuv. He told me at the last meeting I had with him before we left on Hope. He is one clever guy, a bit eccentric though."

"Sanluin are you OK? You have gone very pale."

"I'm fine it's just that it hadn't sunk in that I won't ever be seeing him again."

"Seeing who?"

"Dr Viuuv."

"What are you getting at, you two weren't…"

"No, he was or still is my father." Sanluin broke down in tears, Rafievn felt awful but he wasn't to know.

Everything about the crew had been kept from them so as not to risk being caught by the Corporations. Rafievn went over to Sanluin and comforted her. He put his arms around her, told her that her father would be fine and that he would see his life-time out on Atronia, as long as he kept bluffing that Explorer was still searching for a planet.

14

"Thanks Rafievn, you are right. He wanted me on this mission to set me free."

"Free, free from what or from whom?" Sanluin looked into his eyes, a look of relief and happiness came over her.

"Free to be with you, and give a beautiful planet a chance to evolve for ever." She didn't tell him what she was set free from, she would let him know in her own time. "The others will be waking soon, we should help them, remember how we felt Rafievn?"

"OK, but they can shower alone."

She laughed out loud, the noise echoed around the ship, which seemed to make it feel warmer. The ship needed human noise.

Chapter Three

Sanluin went off to the pod room to check on the others. Rafievn went to the Bridge and logged onto the main computer. He punched his name into the computer and a welcome from Hope came up on the screen.

"How are you Rafievn. Are you feeling well from your sleep?"

"Yes, very well thank you. Can you tell me about the planet you have found?"

"It is perfect for your future existence. There is a huge variety of life on the planet that appears to be organic, from my sensors. There are no forms of communication coming from the planet, which would indicate that it is not yet evolved anywhere near where Atronia's had," Hope replied.

"When will we get a visual on the screen?"

"When the whole crew is awake, we can get closer to the planet and then once there is no chance of detection, we can get close enough for a visual."

"With the size of their Sun what would the temperatures range from?"

"According to my readings, the two poles would be as low as -60° or much lower and in some of the deserts it may reach as high as 50°+. There are many regions that have a much more compatible temperature range."

"Can you tell what sort of life and how advanced it is there?"

"From this distance it is just coming up as organic on the sensors, we will know in good time Rafievn."

"OK Hope, I'll just have to wait until then."

"Goodbye Rafievn."

Rafievn went into the pod room where Sanluin was, she was checking the monitors for Tehkin who was coming round. "Rafievn, can you fetch some water for Tehkin please?"

"OK." When he got back into the room Tehkin was already sat up. "Here Tehkin, have some water, but sip it slowly."

"Thanks. What is your name, I can't recall?" asked Tehkin.

"Rafievn," he replied.

"Ah. I remember now, sorry about that it must be my age."

"How do you feel?"

"Groggy and really stiff. What do you suggest to get me feeling normal again?"

"A good stretch and a long hot shower. It did it for us." Rafievn looked at Sanluin, she was blushing so much she looked away.

"OK. How long have we been sleeping for?"

"Just under five years," replied Sanluin.

"Has Hope found us anything?" Tehkin asked.

"We are two months from a planet that is perfect for us. We'll wait a while and get everyone on their feet. Hope needs to make sure there is no intelligence from the planet that might detect us. There are no signs yet but we need to be sure," said Rafievn.

"The way I'm feeling, the longer the better before I see any action. I'd better take that shower. "

"I'll fetch you some towels," said Sanluin.

"Thanks Sanluin."

Sanluin took Tehkin to the shower room and Rafievn went across to see if Cinciev was stirring. He wasn't much taller than Sanluin and had dark skin, with very dark hair, going a bit grey on the sides. Rafievn had only met him for about twenty minutes before the launch, so he didn't know much about him. They were told that their fellow crew members would be as committed to the mission as Dr Viuuv was, which meant they were willing to put their lives on the line for a chance to carry on the survival of their race. Cinciev was waking; Rafievn fetched him some water and sat by his pod. The lid opened and Cinciev yawned out loud and stretched his arms up, rubbing his eyes before opening them. He looked up at Rafievn with a confused look.

"Who are you? Where am I?"

"My name is Rafievn, you are on the ship Hope, do you remember?" Cinciev went totally blank, the colour fading from his face as he then got up quickly and shouted, "where am I?" No sooner did he get to his feet, he fell down, the blood rush to his head causing him to faint.

"Sanluin, come quickly Cinciev is in trouble." Sanluin came running into the pod room, Cinciev was still on the floor but coming round again. He stumbled to his feet looking at both of them in total shock, as if they were going to kill him.

"Cinciev it's Sanluin, don't you remember?" she asked.

"No, get away from me, you work for the Corporations, what have I done?"

"We don't, we are on Hope, we are your friends, please calm down, you have done nothing wrong," said Sanluin.

"I don't believe you, where are my clothes? You have altered my mind you bastards." Cinciev turned and ran towards the door. He ran straight into Tehkin who had just dressed from his shower. Tehkin went flying back and hit his head on the wall of the ship. Cinciev fell to the floor after hitting his head on Tehkin. Rafievn grabbed hold of Cinciev whilst he was dazed from the clash.

"Quick Sanluin, get a sedative." She scrabbled in the medic cupboard and grabbed a syringe.

"Hold him still Rafievn." Sanluin injected Cinciev with the full dose. Rafievn felt Cinciev go limp in his arms.

"I'll take care of Cinciev, you check on Tehkin," said Rafievn. Tehkin was out cold on the floor, Sanluin put him into the recovery position and checked his pulse.

"How is he?" asked Rafievn.

"His pulse is OK but he might need a stitch in the back of his head," Sanluin replied. "We need to get Cinciev into a sick-bay and strap him down, we don't want a repeat of what just happened when he comes round."

"Tehkin won't be a problem, I'll let him come round on his own. His cut seems to have stopped bleeding now." Rafievn and Sanluin managed to carry Cinciev to the sick-bay. They laid him on the bed and strapped him down.

"We need to get his memory back to when we were getting ready to leave Atronia, he was fine then. I'll be OK now Rafievn, you go and see if Tehkin is coming around." As Rafievn was walking back, Tehkin was just starting to wake up.

"How are you feeling?" asked Rafievn.

"Not good; my head hurts, what happened, anyway?"

"Cinciev woke up from hyper sleep and just freaked out, he thought we worked for the Corporation. He ran straight into you and you fell back, hitting your head on the wall. You were out for a couple of minutes. Here, let's get you up into a chair." Rafievn helped Tehkin to his feet and they went to the living area of the ship. "Rest on the couch for a while old boy, I'll fetch you something sweet to drink."

"Thanks Rafievn and less of the old!"

"Sanluin, are you alright in there? Do you want a drink?" Rafievn asked.

"I'm fine, but you could bring me some tea, with sugar, please, Rafievn."

"OK."

Rafievn made some tea and walked into the sick bay and saw that Sanluin had put a head cap on Cinciev.

"What are you doing with that head cap Sanluin?"

"It will read his memory right back to when we left Atronia, he was fine then. I can read through his thoughts and see where he went wrong when he woke. These thoughts can be changed and then re-programmed back into his memory. When we wake him up he should be fine."

"That's pretty spooky, have the Corporations done this type

of thing to many people?" asked Rafievn.

"They did it to everyone who was in prison, anyone who had anaesthetic for operations and basically anyone they thought to be a risk."

"Well, I'm glad when I was on Atronia that I was a good and healthy boy."

"I'm happy to hear it Rafievn. Now go and tend to your patient but before you go..." Sanluin took the tea and kissed Rafievn, "thanks for the tea." She winked as he walked away; he felt his feelings for Sanluin becoming stronger by the minute. He was falling in love with her.

"Here you go Tehkin, some sweet tea and a tablet, it will clear your head."

"Thanks Rafievn."

"What did you do on Atronia before you took on this mission Rafievn?"

"I was in the Army. We were the only unit left with survival skills. We would live for months without supplies, as we did not have any nano-boxes to make food. The unit was going to be disbanded but our commanding officer insisted that survival from the land was essential in case the nano-boxes ever failed. The Corporations knew the boxes were fail proof. Our commanders just wanted us to be like the old school soldiers for posterity perhaps. How about yourself?"

"I was in the Air and Space Corporation. I flew mostly short flights to Luuse, the mineral moon, it was being mined for the metal ore they were building the Explorer ship with."

"How did you get contacted for this mission?" asked Rafievn

"Dr Viuuv, who was building Explorer knew me from years back. I test flew a lot of his earlier ships, he knew that I didn't care much for the Corporations ever since they started to make it compulsory for all pilots to have nano-upgrades. I didn't want some machinery in my genes, especially after Dr Viuuv warned me that we could be wiped out with the push of a keypad button."

"Did you leave many people behind who really meant a lot to you?" asked Rafievn.

"My wife had died from cancer 12 years ago, she didn't want any treatment as she knew the Corporation would read her mind and they might find out something about this mission."

"So she know about this too?" asked Rafievn.

"It was her who persuaded me to go in the first place. Dr Viuuv told her before me. He knew how persuasive she could be. Ever since our son had become involved with the Corporation at a high level we started to lose him, he had upgrades. The change in him was frightening, we became obsolete to him. My wife disowned him and wanted to have some sort of revenge against the Corporation, this mission was that revenge. She blamed her cancer on the whole episode with our son. When she died her last wish was for me to take this mission. So to answer your question, if I left anyone behind the answer is no, not really." Just then Sanluin came into the room.

"Cinciev will be out of it for a while, his mind seems pretty confused," she said.

"Maybe it was the realisation of the mission and the fact that we really would never see Atronia again," said Rafievn, "that, or the fact his ex-wife left him for one of the directors of the Siunc Corporation. He must still have feelings for her."

"He has left someone behind he still loves," said Sanluin.

"How did you know that Sanluin?" asked Rafievn.

"The information comes through from the head cap, it comes up on the screen like a book," Sanluin replied.

"How long will he be out for?" asked Tehkin.

"About two hours, then he will need twenty minutes to come round. When the information from his mind has been scanned it will rearrange his thoughts so that when he wakes we should have no repeat of the last time," said Sanluin.

"Lets hope so," said Rafievn. Tehkin, Sanluin and Rafievn stood looking at Cinciev with bated breath, as he started to wake.

"What are you three looking at, have you never seen a Ciption before?" said Cinciev. Ciption was his ethnic origin, they were darker skinned than most on Atronia. All three laughed.

"We were concerned, that's all. When you first woke up you fell from your pod and knocked yourself out, that's why you are in the sickbay," said Tehkin They did not want him to know that he had had his mind read as this may raise suspicion in Cinciev as mind reading was only used by the Corporations.

"Are we near a suitable planet then?" asked Cinciev.

"We are two months from a planet that is perfect for us. We can't get a visual on the screen yet, we are too far away," replied Sanluin.

"Are you hungry Cinciev?" asked Rafievn.

"Now you mention it, I'm starving. What's on the menu?" Rafievn looked at Sanluin and they said 'paste' simultaneously, while helping Cinciev to his feet.

The next week on Hope was very routine. The crew were checking the equipment that had been sent with them. It was all lightweight and compact as all travelling on the new planet away from Hope would be on foot. There wasn't enough room for a land vehicle on Hope. Readings were coming in all the time about the new planet, all the information pointed to an environment similar to Atronia's but an Atronia that was 4,000 years younger. It was exciting for the crew to know that the planet was suitable for them but would there be any advanced life forms there? Atronia's history had a missing link to its chain. The human race there was very close genetically to certain animal species but had evolved to build civilisations. No one could ever explain fully why man had developed away from other animal species on the planet.

If you stood back and looked at the planet, all animals and their habitats looked natural but something happened to man somewhere along the line. They started to build civilisations. They looked totally alien compared to the rest of the planet. Some claimed that an alien people visited them and that had started the change in man, it could have been the missing link that had always been elusive. The reason the missing link couldn't be found is that it wasn't there anymore. Maybe the planet had been visited by a more advanced race that left a genetic change in one of the species, which in turn started their human race. Their downfall started centuries before nano-technology was invented. When money was first used, it took hold on mankind. It definitely took the 'kind' out of mankind and added feelings of greed and envy. It seemed every new technology had its negative side. This was so true for nano-technology, the ultimate technology. It carried with it the ultimate downside. It's strange that they were running away from a technology that had helped them get to this new planet. If only the people on Atronia had not been greedy in their evolution.

The signs from the new planet were very promising, there seemed to be no communicating by any form of radio signal, anywhere on the planet. This meant that Hope could get closer without chance of detection. To be sure, Tehkin took Hope to within two days of the new planet. They could now get a good visual up on the screen, the planet looked beautiful. The blue oceans and the swirling cloud masses but the most exciting place Sanluin wanted to visit was the polar caps. Atronia's had melted long before she was born, she couldn't wait to be out on them and experience their vastness and cold.

"Tehkin, how close can we get to the planet's moon?" asked Sanluin.

"We can get as close as you want, the gravitational pull is a sixth of what the new planet is," replied Tehkin.

"We can use this moon as a satellite, leaving a pulse send and receive unit on its surface. It will give us communication if we are ever separated on different parts of the planet," said Cinciev.

"We don't need to land on the moon, we can land the unit by remote, it should work indefinitely with its solar energy cell," said Tehkin.

"I will go and get the unit ready, we can send it tomorrow," said Cinciev.

"Do you think we are safe enough to enter the planet's atmosphere in a couple of days Tehkin?" asked Sanluin.

"Once we have tested the moon as our satellite, we can continue to enter the new planet's atmosphere," Tehkin replied.

"What will entry be like?" asked Rafievn.

"Well, with an atmosphere like this it will be hot but this ship is well built and will withstand massive heat temperatures on its hull."

Sanluin couldn't wait to smell fresh air again, not like Atronia's, which wasn't very fresh due to the pollution. The crew were all very nervous about the new planet, they didn't know what to expect but the fact there was no life that had evolved the same as their own, was promising. They could have a fresh start and having learnt from their own mistakes back on Atronia, this planet would stand a much better chance to survive.

The crew on Hope were all sleeping. It had taken them quite a while before they could get to sleep as they were very excited. The next day they would be the first people in their own history to see another planet that could sustain life. Tehkin was first to wake. He checked the moon once more, to see if the probe they had sent would pick up messages. Everything was working fine; Cinciev had done a good job. It was a job similar to what Cinciev did on Atronia. He worked on the oceans looking for new minerals such as oil and gas; often he would land a probe on the seabed by remote control. Landing one on this moon was just the same but without the water.

"Tehkin, are we ready for entry then?" asked Rafievn, as he handed Tehkin a hot tea he had just made.

"All systems are in order, the receiver on the moon works fine. It is just down to us now, are we ready?" he replied looking at Rafievn with trepidation.

"I'm ready, just nervous that's all," replied Rafievn.

"I will start entry in about one hour. See if the other two are OK and we will start to pack things away in case of a rough entry."

"OK Tehkin." Rafievn went back to the others who were in the galley having some breakfast. Both Sanluin and Cinciev looked nervous but full of excitement at the same time. It seemed that they couldn't wait for the entry of the new planet to begin but at the same time, they were keen to check and double check everything, as they were nervously apprehensive at the thought of seeing another planet much the same as their own. They would be the first people ever to witness the reality that there was a parallel universe. All the beliefs that had evolved on their own planet Atronia would be proved wrong. The wars that had occurred during Atronia's history were mostly down to religion. These religions had made people kill each

25

other and for what? Someone's idea that their way is better than another's way to live. It would make sense to try to send a message back to Atronia and to Dr Viuuv, to let him know that he was right and there was a chance for mankind to start again but it would be suicide to do so, as the message would be intercepted and their course tracked by the Corporations. Dr Viuuv would be imprisoned for mass murder and the destruction of the Explorer ship. The four crew of Hope, the last and only people of Atronia would be the only ones to have the chance to start again knowing the mistakes of their planet's past.

"Is everyone prepared for this?" Tehkin called out from the Bridge. Sanluin had cleared the entire galley away; everything was stored so it would not fly all over the place if things got rough. Cinciev and Rafievn were checking that the landing equipment was fully operational and ready for use. They all went to the Bridge and took up their seats. Tehkin and Cinciev were sat in front of Sanluin and Rafievn.

"Have any of you experienced atmospheric entry in a ship before?" asked Tehkin looking around at the three of them. Before any of the others had time to reply, Tehkin said.

"Don't worry about a thing, there will be some vibration and it will get hot in here."

"Where will we be entering, will it be over land or sea?" asked Cinciev with cautious optimism.

"Well, to be on the safe side I have chosen the sea option just in case," replied Tehkin, laughing as he spoke. "Buckle up everyone and enjoy the ride." Hope started to move towards the new planet; it got bigger by the second. Rafievn looked across at Sanluin she looked back at him and put her hand in his. They both smiled at each other and looked back towards the screen.

"We are 10 seconds from the edge of the planet's atmosphere, it shouldn't take too long from then until we are in the air," said Tehkin. Hope started to shake a little, the heat was building and it seemed that the quickest 10 seconds ever had just elapsed.

"Tehkin, what is that red level on your screen doing, is that dangerous?" asked Rafievn.

"Don't worry Rafievn, I read all about this ship on Atronia, Dr Viuuv built the engines to refuel using the pull of gravity, it is just their energy level picking back up. It is the first and last ship ever to have this technology."

"I didn't know that could be achieved yet," said Cinciev.

"Nor did I. Until now it is the first time they have been tested from a journey through space." The heat was quite intense but started to fall. Hope was entering into the planet's air space. The shaking was stopping and the view of the clouds on the screen was just breathtaking. Back on Atronia the clouds were dull, choked with pollution but here the crew needed to squint with the glare.

"What is our altitude Tehkin?" asked Cinciev.

"60,000 feet, I'll take her down below the cloud level then we can view the planet in the flesh, it will be safe to take the heat deflectors from the windows," said Tehkin. The screen went blank in front of them. It moved up to the ceiling of the Bridge as if gliding on air, as it did the crew saw the view for the first time with their own eyes; they gasped with awe as Hope started to descend through the clouds. Moisture beads raced up the window, the sunlight went from bright glare in the blue sky to a cloud covered sky in seconds. They were flying through a storm but in the distance, sunlight poured through the clouds in powerful beams and glistened on the sea beneath. Sanluin had not said a word the whole time; she just held Rafievn's hand tightly and gazed at the sight in front of her. Their new world was breathtaking. They all seemed to be in complete silence for what seemed hours but only minutes had passed. What broke Rafievn's silence was his ears popping as the pressure was changing in the ship. He swallowed hard to make them pop even more.

"Tehkin, how big is this ocean? Is there land close by?" asked Rafievn.

"The ocean is the second largest on the planet, we are just north of the centre of the planet, the same as our equator on Atronia. There are some islands to the north west, we can try to land there."

"That seems a good idea Tehkin, I could do with a swim and my skin hasn't seen sun for so long I am nearly transparent," said Sanluin.

"How about you, Cinciev?"

"Lets just land, I never liked flying much anyway."

"Well, it won't be long. We should see them in a few minutes," said Tehkin. Tehkin took Hope down to 1,000 feet above the sea. Hope was flying so smoothly they didn't realise they were doing over 800 mph. "There they are. Let's take her up and have a look from above," said Tehkin. There was hardly any noise as Hope gained altitude effortlessly. It was the first time Rafievn had really taken notice of the ship, as he was so taken by the beauty of this new planet. There were nine islands beneath them, stretching from right to left. They were not that big but a couple were of a fair size. They opted to land on the centre island, which was the second largest and roughly in the centre of the bunch. Rafievn's spine tingled with excitement. He looked at Sanluin; she seemed to be glowing with anticipation as to what they were about to land on.

"There seems to be a level area, I'll put her down on it," said Tehkin. Hope banked round, the sea was on the left about half a mile away. As they were about to land, Rafievn noticed a tear on Sanluin's cheek, he reached across and wiped it away just as they touched down. They all released their seat belts and looked out on the ocean crashing on the rocks, the sea was so blue and the sky so clear. Then, they all jumped back, a bird flew right past their window nearly touching it. That was the first sign of life apart from the plant life on the islands.

"Before we venture out, we'd better take readings of the air just to be on the safe side," said Cinciev looking skyward. Cinciev started to tap on the keyboard. All the readings came back fine. It was the cleanest natural air they had seen compared to anywhere on Atronia.

"Oldest first Tehkin," said Sanluin.

"OK," he replied, as he went to open the cabin door. He punched in the code, the door opened downwards and steps lowered themselves to the ground. The wind came rushing in from the sea. As Tehkin stood on the top step he breathed in deeply as they all were. It was so refreshing to breathe unfiltered air for the first time in years. The air on Atronia had become so polluted; this air was like something they had never smelled before. Tehkin started down the steps closely followed by Sanluin, then Cinciev and finally Rafievn. They all stood there in amazement. They were the first people ever to see a new world that could sustain life. This place was so fresh and as far as they knew, untouched.

"We have made it," said Sanluin. She knelt down and touched the grass. The ground was quite soft as she dug her nails into the soil and pulled up some earth in her hand. "Look it's the same as on Atronia, it even smells the same."

"I don't know about you, but I bet there are some very tasty fish in that sea, I'll go and catch some for us. We can eat a decent meal for once," said Rafievn. The sun was quite high in the sky, indicating it must have been around midday. Cinciev set up a small lab behind the ship out of the wind, there would be a lot of tests to do on the plants and animals that they would use for food. Tehkin checked over Hope for any damage that might have occurred during entry to the atmosphere. There didn't seem to be any visual damage apart from the scorch marks that she had received during entry. Rafievn went back to get some equipment which would be used to catch fish and packed it in a small pack. Sanluin also packed a small backpack, with drinks and a weapon. She passed Rafievn a weapon, which he put in his belt. The weapons could stun an animal from a hundred feet and it would be knocked out for quite a while, if they needed to make a get away or kill it for food. Rafievn and Sanluin changed their footwear to some more robust boots with an all terrain sole as they would be doing some hiking across rough land and rocks to the sea.

"We will see you both later, hopefully with some fish," called Rafievn.

"Be careful you two, don't get into trouble. Use your two-ways if you need to," replied Cinciev. Sanluin and Rafievn set off into the wind towards the sea.

"You have got more colour to your complexion already Sanluin, you must be a natural outdoor girl."

"Nothing like a good stroll in the fresh air to blow away the cobwebs Rafievn." She strode on in front whilst Rafievn stayed back for a while admiring her figure from behind. The bird that flew past the ship earlier flew past their heads, it was so close it nearly touched them, they both had to duck as it went.

"It seems a friendly bird," said Sanluin shouting back.

"Let's just hope it doesn't think we are lunch."

"Come on Rafievn you're not frightened of a little bird are you?"

"We have only been on this planet a couple of hours, we can't be too careful." Rafievn caught up with Sanluin, they stopped and looked back at Hope shining in the bright sunlight. They didn't even notice the wings that had opened up from the hull, they were not needed for space flight but they were needed here just as they would be on Atronia. That tiny ship had carried them for five years and it was only now that they both really appreciated what a well built craft she was; Dr Viuuv had done a good job.

"Rafievn do you think there are any people on this planet?"

"That could depend on all sorts of things, like how old the planet is or whether there are any other animals apart from birds. We can assume there are fish because these definitely look like seabirds in comparison to the ones back home."

"Home? We are home. There is definitely no going back

and look at what a beautiful home we have and we haven't even seen the rest of it yet." She was right this was their new home; it still really hadn't sunk in that they wouldn't be going back. They were nearly at the edge of the rocky embankment, which led down to a small cove where the waves were unable to crash in. Rafievn took out his binoculars and set them to day mode. He scanned the cove above, below the water there were fish basking in the sunlight; easy lunch he thought to himself. He raised the glasses to scan the sea. Beyond the cove the water was very choppy, probably whipped up by the storm that they had flown through on their arrival. Securing the glasses to his belt Rafievn started to make his way down the rocky embankment. It was a drop of about thirty feet to the beach.

"Take care Sanluin, shout 'rocks' if you dislodge any on your way down."

"OK Rafievn, I'll watch my step." As they got down to the beach the rocky cove gave them protection from the wind. The temperature must have been 80-85°out of the wind. Rafievn took his pack off and unzipped his suit to the waist. His physique was lean and toned from all the training during his time in the army on Atronia. He got his fishing kit out; it didn't look much like a conventional kit. There was no rod, reel or bait, just a small silver miniature harpoon gun.

"How does that work, Rafievn?"

"Like this." Rafievn pointed the harpoon that was no longer than his hand towards the fish he had seen through his binoculars. He pulled the trigger and a small puff of gas came out of the end of the harpoon. The bolt from the barrel hardly made a sound as it entered the water. Attached to the bolt was a very fine line, which instantaneously went taught.

"There you go Sanluin, some fresh fish for supper." Rafievn pushed a button on the side of the harpoon and the line started to retract back into the barrel. The fish was speared just behind the gills, it splashed the water as it came to the surface, its scales glistening in the sun.

"Well done Rafievn that looks big enough for you and I, what about Cinciev and Tehkin."

"Don't panic, there's plenty more fish in the sea," Rafievn said with a laugh.

"Here, you have a go." Rafievn caught hold of the fish and hit its head sharply on a rock. The body of the fish went rigid instantly. He then removed the bolt from the line and pulled the line through the fish. The bolt was only 4mm in diameter with a point on the end. At the base of the bolt there were small fins protruding.

"What are the fins for Rafievn?"

"They act as a barb and are also self-guiding to the target."

"And I thought you were just a good shot. Is it ready to fire again?"

"Just press that green button, it will recharge it, then after the beep, it is ready to go." Sanluin reset the harpoon and fired it into the water. The bolt went straight into the water and embedded itself in the rocks on the far side of the cove.

"I thought you said it was self-guiding."

"It is but you have got to be somewhere near to start with, the fish are a good six feet to the left. I will have to get in and release the bolt. I didn't bring any spare bolts with me, they're back on Hope."

"Sorry Rafievn but to make it up I'll race you to the bolt."

"What if I win Sanluin?"

"Then you can have me and if I win, I can have you."

"Either way we both win then?" They both stripped off and ran into the sea, gasping with shock as the cold water washed over them. Sanluin raced on in front with a powerful front-crawl stroke. Rafievn only just caught her up by the time they got to the other side of the cove, his fingertips just touching the bottom of Sanluin's feet.

"Where did you learn to swim like that?"

"I was taught by my dad and went from there to represent the school and county. This medal was for my first win at county level," said Sanluin, showing Rafievn the small silver disc on her neck chain.

"I wondered how you got that figure?" Rafievn said with a grin across his face. They stood in water about chest high on Rafievn and neck high on Sanluin. The temperature of the water around their feet was much cooler than at the surface.

"OK Sanluin, can you see the line?"

"No, but I can feel it against my side, here take it." She passed Rafievn the line and he pulled it tight to see where the bolt had got lodged in the rocks. He took a deep breath and went under the surface pulling the line until he got to the bolt. Rafievn caught hold of the bolt and managed to pull it free. His eyes were stinging from the salty water. It was just the same as the sea on Atronia.

"Right then hot shot, let's try again shall we?" They both swam back to the beach and Rafievn reset the harpoon.

"We will have to wait for the fish to come back, they have swum off with all the commotion."

"That's fine by me Rafievn and if you remember you still owe me that bet," she said with an alluring look on her face. The fish had plenty of time to return as they made love most of the afternoon.

Back at Hope, Tehkin had set up camp. They had brought self-erecting tents whose outer skin acted as a solar panel to provide heat at night when the temperature dropped. Cinciev was testing whatever he could get his hands on from mosses to grass and even insects that were unlucky enough to venture near his make-shift lab.

"It must be around 4-5 pm; my watch is still set at the time we left Atronia. From tomorrow, I'll try to get a more accurate idea of the time scales for this planet," Tehkin said to Cinciev.

"We know for sure that their sun is the same distance as our sun was from Atronia. This should give their year time in days the same as ours."

"You're right, but only if this planet spins at the same speed."

"Rafievn and Sanluin should be back soon, they've been

33

gone long enough and I'm getting hungry," said Cinciev, looking out in the direction the pair had walked. On the shore, Rafievn gutted the fish and rinsed them in the seawater. They had caught five in total, plenty enough for a good size meal each.

"Are you ready Sanluin? We had better make our way back to the others."

"Just about Rafievn, shall we call through to the other two so that they can get some wood ready to cook the fish over as soon as we get back? I'm starving after all that fishing," she said smiling from ear to ear.

"The fishing was the easy part," replied Rafievn as he pulled on his backpack.

The fire crackled away as the fish slowly cooked wrapped in moss and leaves. All four sat around the fire, eagerly waiting for the fish to be cooked.

"Were your tests on the fish OK Cinciev? I don't want to have to eat paste again tonight," Rafievn said, looking straight at the steaming moss.

"Don't worry, they'll be fine? Is your cooking up to scratch, that's more my concern," replied Cinciev as he looked at the others who started to laugh. The temperature started to drop quite rapidly as the sun set on the horizon. The firewood was all but used up. Tehkin threw the last of the branches on the embers and walked back into Hope.

"I'm going to get some bedding from our bunks. Who wants some?" he asked as he walked up the steps.

"I'll help you Tehkin," said Sanluin getting to her feet.

"Who's with who in the tents Cinciev?" asked Rafievn. Tehkin and I are in one, we thought that would be the best."

"Thanks Cinciev," replied Rafievn. Rafievn walked by Cinciev and tapped him on the shoulder as he went to one of the tents. They slept like babies, all four of them. They hadn't realised how much the past few days had taken their toll.

The screech of the sea birds overhead started to wake them from their slumber. Tehkin was first out of his tent; the morning was bright without a cloud in the sky. He looked out to sea and wondered what lay ahead. Was the planet populated? They had so much to discover, with so much time on their hands. For once in their lives, there were no deadlines to meet, no one to answer to; it was like being set free from a place where people had become imprisoned by their own evolution. They had literally stepped out of one planet, where the rules, regulations and the need to earn money had caused people to tie themselves into a slave trap and then stepped into pure freedom. The only difficult thing was where to start to explore this heaven, this wonderful place.

Tehkin thought they had better try to get some sort of co-ordinates for their position on the planet. Hope had already taken pictures from space; they just needed to add longitude and latitude. Tehkin didn't know how their compasses would work compared to how they worked on Atronia. There was much to do before they set off to explore the rest of the planet. Tehkin went into Hope and sat at the Bridge. He turned on the computer and started to try the co-ordinating equipment with the new planet's magnetic forces. Cinciev was preparing the fire to start breakfast when he realised that they hadn't anything to cook. The fish the previous night were delicious but something different would be nice first thing in the morning. He tapped on Rafievn's tent.

"What do you fancy for breakfast you two?"

"We're not fussy Cinciev, what do you have in mind?" replied Sanluin.

"Whatever we catch next would be a start."

"OK Cinciev, we'd better get hunting," replied Rafievn while still yawning. Rafievn and Cinciev set off inland to find breakfast.

Tehkin was establishing their co-ordinates and time of day as their clocks were still running on Atronia's time. As everything seemed to be very similar or almost the same as Atronia, it would just be a case of accurately determining the time of day. Where they had landed would be their first time zone. The compasses on Hope had set themselves according to the planet's magnetic fields. Tehkin could now establish the four points of the compass north, south, east and west. Hope had landed facing west, the direction the sun had set the night before and the sea was to the left of Hope. Rafievn and Cinciev had set off inland to the north and the sun was rising to the rear of Hope, which was to the east. Tehkin programmed this into the computer and a picture of the planet came up on the screen with all the longitude and latitude lines on it. He put the longitude from where they had landed at 0° and their latitude was 38.436° north. With the position established it would just take an accurate reading of daylight hours to set the clocks. Sanluin was looking at the planet as she stood behind Tehkin.

"We haven't got a name for this place yet, we just call it the new planet. I think it deserves a better description, don't you?"

"I'm not good at naming things but feel free to come up with what you feel bests suits it." Sanluin went back outside to check on the fire which needed more timber. Inland a mile or so Rafievn and Cinciev had come across trees bearing fruits very similar to what grew on Atronia. They were bunches of Tanoos. Rafievn hacked a bunch from the tree as Cinciev caught them.

"Aarggh," cried Cinciev loudly. He dropped the Tanoos on the floor, shook his arm and brushed off an insect about two inches across, with eight legs and almost identical to a Deiiss. Two marks appeared on Cinciev's arm where the insect had bitten him.

"Are you OK Cinciev?"

"I think so Rafievn, I hope that insect wasn't poisonous. It looked almost the same one we have on Atronia, which is poisonous."

"We had better head back straight away, let me know if you don't feel well."

"OK, lets go." Rafievn shook the bunch of Tanoos just to

make sure there were no more surprises in the there. They both headed back to Hope. Cinciev's vision started to blur, he was feeling light headed and was starting to sweat as he stumbled to the floor. Rafievn put down the Tanoos and went to his aid.

"Rafievn run back to Hope and get Sanluin to bring the medic kit, it should have anti-venom programmes. If I stay calm, it will be the best way to prevent the poison rushing to my heart."

"Right." Rafievn ran off towards Hope while Cinciev called on his two-way radio to ask Sanluin to get the kit ready. Rafievn was running down the slope to where Hope was, as Sanluin and Tehkin were running towards him.

"He's back that way about three minutes, here give me the kit." Sanluin passed Rafievn the kit and they all ran back towards Cinciev. When they got back Cinciev was looking very pale and sweating profusely. Sanluin grabbed the kit from Rafievn and put a needle into where the bite marks were on Cinciev's arm.

"How does this work?" asked Rafievn gasping for breath.

"The needle will take some of the poison, analyse it and quickly make an anti-venom. When the medic kit bleeps we can inject the anti-venom straight into Cinciev then he should be fine."

"That's simple enough," said Tehkin. The kit took about ten seconds to make the anti-venom. Sanluin loaded the needle and injected the liquid into Cinciev's arm. His veins were quite prominent so it was an easy task. Cinciev started to breath less erratically and was starting to come to his senses; the poison had made him quite disorientated.

"Here Cinciev, drink this." Sanluin handed him some glucose drink from the medic kit. "Looks like you're feeling better already; you should be more careful when out hunting, even if it is for Tanoos," said Sanluin as she packed away the medic kit.

"As we have lost so many species on Atronia you seem to forget that this place is teeming with life," said Cinciev getting to his feet. They all set off back towards Hope with the bunch of Tanoos for breakfast. When they got back to Hope, Tehkin made tea and they took a couple of Tanoos each. The flavour was much stronger than the ones they ate on Atronia. They were naturally grown, which made the difference. Everything on Atronia had been manufactured since the nano-boxes and factories replicated all kinds of foodstuffs. Tehkin suddenly started laughing to himself.

"What's so funny Tehkin?" asked Sanluin.

"It's not really funny. It just dawned on me - I spent all that time working out our time of day here but we don't need time at all."

"What do you mean?" asked Rafievn.

"We don't need to be anywhere or report to any one, we don't need to get up at any specific time. It's great, complete freedom like we have never experienced before," said Tehkin, still laughing to himself.

"He's right you know," said Cinciev. They all started to laugh at the thought of no more running their lives by the clock.

They spent nearly two weeks on the island, trying out all types of fruit and fish. They stunned and cooked some of the sea birds but there wasn't much meat on them. Rafievn and Tehkin started to load Hope with the fruit that would stay fresh the longest. The island had been a good place for them to get acclimatised; now they were ready to explore the rest of the planet. The packing had all been done; the tents, the lab and all the fruit they could manage, was stored away back on Hope. They all stood looking out towards the sea. The sun was starting to set and there were clouds high in the sky, which were starting to glow a rich reddy-orange.

"We haven't got a name for this planet yet," said Tehkin.

"We shall call it Planetician," said Sanluin almost instantly. It was as if she had always had the name in the back of her mind.

"Planetician, what does that mean? I have never heard of that word before?" asked Rafievn.

"It had been a name made up by my father. It was a principle for people to live by. My father wanted to start projects all over Atronia where small communities of people could live and be totally self-sufficient, producing just what they needed to survive. With wind and solar power as well as the perpetual motion power stations, my father was working on the fact they would have had all the electricity they would need. He wanted to try to get these communities to provide everything, from clothing to shelter, using natural products; after all, our ancestors had done it before and survived. With these communities living by their own means they could have taken money out of the equation. My father wanted to study how these communities would evolve without the pressure of money and having to organise everything by the price of something. After all, when you can produce everything you need to live, by what the planet can offer, without damaging the environment, you should strike the perfect balance with nature. He looked at our society having become dependent firstly on money, then on nano-technology and the need for this technology and how individuals would go to extreme lengths to get the money needed, to have the technology. In doing this, they ignored their environment; they started to disrespect the source that had supported their survival for centuries - Atronia. My father knew he would be fighting a losing battle as the Corporations controlled the people in government. They would say he would be asking them to take a step back, in what they saw was evolution. There is not much evolution when you are heading for destruction because of being blinded by the arrogance in human greed." Sanluin stopped speaking just as the sun seemed to dive below the waves. The sound of the waves crashing on the rocks and the cries of the birds floating on the up-drafts of wind coming off the sea was their lasting memory of the island.

They all stepped back into Hope and settled down for the night under Luuse alloy instead of the tents they had used for the last couple of weeks. Tehkin was last to sleep as he checked the Bridge ready for take off in the morning.

39

All four crew sat in their seats on the Bridge of Hope. Tehkin prepared for take off. It was so relaxed compared to their last take off from Atronia. They were all so nervous and scared they hadn't even noticed how Hope operated and without noise or sudden movement, she slowly lifted from the ground and banked round towards the sea. It was breathtaking for all of them, even Tehkin who had never been in such an advanced craft. He had updated himself with all that Hope could do while they were on the island. As Tehkin was the one to slightly shock the crew with his flying, he knew he had something in store for them. He took her up to the edge of the atmosphere and they could all see the curvature of Planetician. A huge continent was to their right but they opted for a group of islands to the northeast. These were chosen, as they were very similar in shape to a group of islands back on Atronia.

Before they headed off to these islands, Tehkin thought he would surprise the crew. He took Hope down to a sea level that was calm and still, without a ripple on the surface. Hope was only a few feet from the surface.

"What are we doing here Tehkin?" asked Cinciev.

"Something you might be familiar with Cinciev." With that, Tehkin took Hope straight into the sea. Cinciev, Sanluin and Rafievn braced themselves simultaneously. Before they had time to speak, Hope was gliding beneath the surface of the sea as naturally as the fish around them. Cinciev was nearly out of his seat with excitement, as this was where he had spent a lot of his time on Atronia searching for minerals, any that were left that was.

"Your dad definitely surpassed himself when he built this ship Sanluin," said Tehkin.

"He certainly did," she replied.

"How long can we stay under and how deep can we go Tehkin?" asked Rafievn.

"We can stay under for as long as we want or should I say as long as our food lasts, the sea water can be filtered to drink and our oxygen will be filtered, just as it would be if we were in space."

"Look at that," said Cinciev pointing to a group of Soilhs swimming along in front of them.

"We don't have that species on Atronia or should I say, we don't anymore; they got fished to extinction years ago. This sea is teeming with life." Tehkin took Hope down to depths where the sunlight was barely reaching. The pressure on the ship was immense but Hope was built to withstand much more than this. Tehkin put the lights on and a different world was in front of them. The water was very still and slightly murky, different species of fish slowly swam over the seabed. They looked very different to those near the surface.

"Life exists in the most extreme of environments. The life forms are very similar to this back on Atronia at this depth," said Cinciev. Tehkin took Hope back up to the surface.

"Ready for the sky now everyone?" asked Tehkin.

"We are ready for anything you can throw at us Tehkin," said Rafievn with a boyish grin on his face.

"OK." With that, Tehkin took Hope nearly straight up at lightening speed. The crews' stomachs were still at sea level.

"No more Tehkin, I am going to be sick," said Sanluin holding on to her seat for dear life.

"OK, OK, that's enough playing around for now. It's just that I haven't been let loose in a ship for years, this makes me feel young again."

"It may make you feel young but you've just put years on me Tehkin." The rest of them laughed as Sanluin's colour came back to her face. Hope was back on the edge of space cruising northeast. They stayed at that altitude until they were directly over the islands, just in case they were inhabited, as they didn't want to be seen.

"Can Hope detect any other life forms compared to our first landing?" asked Rafievn.

Cinciev tapped away on the keyboard,

"We've definitely got something, positive identification of human inhabitancy," he said shaking with a cautious fear. Rafievn and Sanluin rushed to look at Cinciev's screen. Tehkin looked across in amazement, speechless. All the speculation and questions that had been asked over the centuries back on Atronia, whether there had been life on another planet, let alone human life, were answered in just a few words on a screen.

The excitement buzzed around Hope's Bridge. All the crew were shouting questions to each other and to Cinciev who was frantically tapping away on the keypad. Hope zoomed in on a settlement, which was to the south and centre of the largest island. Their eyes staring wide open, not a blink between them as the picture on the screen came into focus. Smoke was coming from what seemed to look like circular shapes in a clearing of forest. Hope zoomed in more and this showed the circles to be huts or dwellings of some sort. They were all still and silent. Then, from one of the huts a human being walked out into the morning sunshine and looked directly up. All four crew gasped and ducked forgetting that they were miles up in the sky; the zoomed image had fooled them.

"He was right, there is a parallel universe, a parallel people even but they seem far less advanced," said Sanluin with tears running down her face. They were all highly emotional looking at the screen, even more so when two children came out of the hut and ran off into the woods. None of the crew on Hope could believe what they were witnessing, human life on another planet.

"Should we stay here and just observe for a while?" suggested Cinciev in a croaky voice.

"It might be a good idea, just to let this sink in," said Tehkin still gazing at the screen.

There were twelve huts in the clearing of the woods. Most

were the same size except for a larger one in the centre. More people came out of the other huts, the men were gathering in a group, they seemed to be talking to each other and pointing southwards. A woman came out of the hut in the middle and seemed to shout to the group of adults talking. One of the men ran to the large hut in the middle. He came back out and waved to the group still talking to themselves. This group then walked to the large hut but did not enter. They were waiting by the entrance of the hut for about ten minutes, then they all stood back and the first man to enter the hut came out holding a small bundle. It was wrapped in dark cloth and the rest of the group gathered around to look at the bundle.

"What are they looking at?" asked Sanluin.

"I can't see, they are blocking the view," said Rafievn. Then the group stood back to reveal the man holding a newborn baby in his arms. This made Sanluin cry even more, they had just witnessed the birth of a human on another planet. It was almost too much for them to take in at once.

Sanluin had dried her eyes and was still spellbound by their find. Human life on another planet and by the looks of things they were at least 3,500 years behind Atronia in evolution. The people seemed to be preparing a celebration for the new born. A few of the men had gone into the woods and come back with what looked like a young Riind. It must be for a feast. The baby was kept in the large hut and visited by people during the day. They brought small gifts to the hut. The birth seemed very important to the group.

"Can you scan the surrounding area Cinciev?" asked Rafievn.

"Yes, I will go in one mile radius," he replied. On the third scan of the surrounding area something they did not expect came into view, to the north of the settlement.

"They're building some sort of....., well, something. Look at the size of those stones they're using, they're massive," said Cinciev in amazement. A huge monument was being constructed out of large rectangular stones. There was an outer circle that looked about

43

three quarter finished and inside this circle, holes were dug in the ground in a horseshoe shape. Between these two there were smaller stones, also set in a circle. The weight of the varying stones could easily be between 10 and 40 tons. The heaviest stone was still laid down. It was an immense undertaking for these people. What was the reason for the site? It would be no use as a building for shelter; maybe it was a religious place for worship. There was no work being carried out this particular day, probably due to the birth of the baby.

"We will have to observe these people for a while but there might be other areas on Planetician where people are living and building civilisations. We will have to observe them, then select one of these groups and learn to live with them, whilst trying to help them evolve with the knowledge we have. They will have the advantage of evolving without making the same mistakes our people have made, during our own history," said Sanluin.

"I will stay here and observe them for a few weeks, if you want to go and see if there are any other civilisations on the rest of the planet," said Rafievn.

"We will wait until night fall before we land. How much kit will you need?" asked Sanluin.

"Well, by the looks of the trees, they seem to be in early summer so I won't need too much; I will make a start on packing. We have a couple of hours before night fall."

"Are you sure you don't want to come with us and see the rest of Planetician?" said Sanluin.

"I will be OK on my own, anyway at the speed Hope travels, you will be back in no time. There will be plenty of time to see the rest of Planetician," he replied.

They observed the settlement from Hope well into the night; the celebrations for the newborn carried on for hours. It was about 2 am when the fire was put out where the Riind had been cooking and the last of the people had gone into their huts for the night. Rafievn had packed his kit; it was a light pack, as he didn't expect to stay long. A week at the most would be plenty of time to establish how these people lived. Tehkin took Hope down to land well away from the settlement; where the monument was being built was ideal, as it was on higher ground and clear from woodland. Hope touched down silently and Rafievn put his pack on his back and his night vision glasses on his head.

"Good luck Rafievn, we won't be too long," said Tehkin looking back from the Bridge.

"Take care Rafievn, keep in contact using the moon, and remember it's our satellite."

"OK Cinciev will do." Rafievn walked down the steps to the ground, Sanluin following him. The moon shone brightly, lighting up Hope and the huge stones behind, as Sanluin and Rafievn looked at each other under the clear sky.

"See you soon, my love," said Sanluin. Rafievn took her in his arms and held her tightly.

"I'll be fine Sanluin; just don't forget where this place is, I'll be waiting." They kissed goodbye and Sanluin walked back into Hope. The stairs to Hope lifted up into the hull as the door shut slowly and Sanluin blew Rafievn a kiss just as it closed. Hope took off and lifted into the night sky with an eerie silence. For the first time in his life Rafievn felt totally alone, even though he had spent many times alone on Atronia. This was a new planet with people he knew nothing about, his last view of Sanluin walking back into Hope made him feel better knowing she would be back soon. He set off to the east where there was dense woodland. This would give him good cover to observe these people.

Tehkin took Hope northward. They would circumnavigate Planetician by its longitude. The readings from Hope came back as they travelled, the temperature dropped quite dramatically as they moved north. This seemed odd, as the islands they had left were very warm compared to other landmasses on the same latitude. Tehkin asked Hope to look at the oceans to see if there were strong currents in them, similar to the ones back on Atronia. Some of these currents carried with them warmth to areas which would otherwise be cooler. They were travelling at 40,000 feet above sea level and dawn was breaking in the east.

"I wonder how Rafievn is getting on?" said Cinciev.

"He'll be OK with his hunting skills, he's probably having breakfast as we speak," said Tehkin. Sanluin was looking out of the window, trying to hide her feelings as she was missing him so much already.

"We will be approaching the polar cap soon. I'll turn the heating up as we have never experienced temperatures like it before," he continued.

Sanluin forgot her sadness, as she was so excited to see what a polar cap was really like. The glare from the ice and snow lit the horizon in front of them. Tehkin took Hope down to 10,000 feet. There were huge blocks of ice floating in the sea and the further north they went, the ice started to form into one huge sheet.

"Just look at that expanse of ice, Atronia's used to be like that once," said Cinciev.

"On the reading it is just an ice sheet, there is no land beneath," said Tehkin.

"Let's go back and travel underneath the ice, just to see what it looks like from below," said Sanluin. Tehkin steered Hope back to the edge of the ice and took her beneath the waves once more. The light came through the ice. It was an amazing sight for them, as they had never seen anything like this before.

"Look over there, sea mammals, swimming so fast as they race after those fish," said Sanluin. Air bubbles collected in pockets on the underside of the ice giving them a feeling of being trapped.

"Shall we get back in the sky now?" said Tehkin. He didn't like flying under a roof, it made him fell uneasy, just in case anything were to go wrong. They turned back again to the edge of the ice and flew back on their original course. They went up to 60,000 feet and saw a massive ocean come into view.

"This is the largest ocean on Planetician. It has small groups of islands, most of them volcanic. On Hope's readings, there is an ocean trench, which is around 36,000 feet deep, the deepest ocean trench on the planet. There weren't trenches that deep on Atronia, even after our polar caps had gone," said Tehkin.

The morning had clouded over since Hope left and Rafievn had woken from a short nap. The sound of birds singing had woken him. He looked up through the trees to the overcast sky but was distracted by distant sounds; they were the sounds of human voices. He got up and scanned the immediate area for any movement. There was the noise of snapping twigs as a Riind ran off from where it was standing, its young legs nimbly picking a route through the forest floor. Rafievn put his glasses on and put them to heat detection mode. The outline of the Riind was about 100 yards away and getting further. Scanning the area, no other image came up giving off heat so he felt confident to rely on his own vision. He took off his glasses and put them back into his belt. Rafievn waited motionless for a few minutes, the sweet singing of the birds and his own breathing the only noises to his ears. Then again the same noises coming from the direction of the monument. Rafievn checked his watch, which gave him his position as to where he was dropped off. He made his way slowly to the west, stopping every few yards to check if there were any other people close by. The edge of the woodland was about 200 yards away and he could make out the monument in the distance. There seemed to be a lot of people but he couldn't see clearly without his glasses.

Rafievn wondered what the best vantage point might be; he could climb a tree but that would get uncomfortable after a while, as he planned to observe all day. He looked around for good cover but with a clear view. There was a fallen tree about 20 yards from the edge of the forest. It had landed on a low-lying branch of another tree and got wedged between the trunk and the split of the branch caused by the fall. He made his way up to the fallen tree; it had been purposely felled and left for some reason. The main trunk of the tree divided into two, providing a good viewing platform about 10 feet from the ground, which would also give him excellent cover.

Rafievn pulled out a small scanner from his pocket on his left arm with a wire still attached to his clothing. He scanned the surrounding area for the colours that were on all the foliage. He put the scanner back and within a minute all his clothing camouflaged to the surrounding habitat. This would work for the whole spectrum of any surrounding habitat, no need to change kit with this technology. Rafievn looked over towards the people building the monument. He got out his glasses and they automatically focused on the monument. This was the best view he had had of these people. They were dressed in roughly made tunics that were worn over the head and tied around the waist with either twine or some sort of leather. Some had leather for belts and also leather bands around their arms at the bicep. They were all unshaven in different stages of beard growth. Their hair was long and matted. All in all they looked a pretty rough lot. It was getting near mid morning and Rafievn was starting to feel hungry. He got out his rations which were high concentrate cubes packed with all the nutrients the body needed, he had enough for a couple of weeks. He also had his weapon if he wanted a more substantial meal. Rafievn chewed his cube, which tasted OK for what it was. He started to feel tired, as he hadn't slept much since Hope had taken off. He drifted off to sleep, while thinking when Hope would return to pick him up.

Flying over the massive ocean, Hope and the rest of the crew were looking down at another group of islands in the middle of the vast ocean. They were volcanic and densely covered with vegetation.

"Shall we take a closer look at these islands, or shall we carry on?" asked Tehkin.

"Let's give these a miss and see what is further south," replied Cinciev. Sanluin was back in the sleeping quarters dreaming of her lover who was doing the same as she was except, she was in the most technically advanced ship ever built and he was up a tree. Hope was travelling at 3,000 miles per hour. Tehkin could take her to this speed, as the ocean was so vast. On the horizon the southern ice cap came into view.

"You had better wake Sanluin, she wanted to see this," Tehkin said to Cinciev. Cinciev got up to call Sanluin.

"Sanluin, wake up," he called from the door.

"What is it Cinciev?"

"We are coming up to the southern ice cap, you asked us to call you when we were getting near."

"OK Cinciev, I'll be there now," she replied while yawning at the same time. The ice sheet was much larger than the one in the north and there was land beneath it. The readings on the screen gave the size of this continent at around 5 million square miles, with mountains up to 17,000 feet high. The temperature showed a reading of minus 52°. It was not a very hospitable place but amazing in its own beauty and hostility.

"This place must hold so much fresh water it is like the planet's emergency reserve. What do the readings say about the thickness of ice Cinciev?"

"It shows varying thicknesses, up to a few hundred feet at the sea and ten to fifteen thousand feet in land. There is a steady movement of ice that takes hundreds of years."

"Shall we have a closer look and touch down or do you want to carry on?" asked Tehkin.

"I would like to experience the temperature and take more readings but we have to really see what other areas of the planet have human habitation," replied Sanluin.

"It looks far too cold for me, I wouldn't last two minutes," said Cinciev. Tehkin took Hope right up to the edge of space and held position while they looked at Planetician on the newly made maps.

The clouds had slowly formed to a greater density over the southern part of the northern island where Rafievn was and rain was starting to fall. A drop landing on his face woke Rafievn. It gave him quite a shock, as his dreams were of himself and Sanluin in the hot cove where they had caught their first fish. He put his glasses on and looked towards the monument. The work was still being carried out but it didn't look like much had happened since he last looked. A group of men were walking his way; there were five of them and a boy of about twelve years old. They were coming straight for him. Rafievn took his glasses off but they wouldn't have given his position away as there wasn't any sunlight to catch the lenses. His best chance not to get noticed was to stay as still as possible, he charged his weapon just in case. The group moved closer mumbling to themselves, they didn't seem to be alarmed by anything so Rafievn relaxed a little. They were now within 10 feet of where Rafievn was hiding, he was so tense with both fear of being spotted but also the fact that these were people from another planet, he would be the first person from Atronia to ever witness such an event. His heart was pounding in his chest, his whole body was tensed as not to make a move. They were now almost directly below the tree he was laying in. The group stopped and the eldest looking man pointed in different directions to the others, as if giving out some orders; their language was like nothing Rafievn had ever heard before. The next thing Rafievn noticed was the smell of these people, they really hummed, the body odour was making him hold his breath it was so bad.

The group started to spread out in the directions they were ordered; it must have been a hunting party, they carried with them primitive tools which looked like stone axes, and spears with flint heads. As they moved further into the woods Rafievn took out his glasses and set them to thermal mode. The figures showed up walking carefully through the wood and undergrowth, they were definitely hunting. He watched them until they were out of view and then turned back to the monument.

It was raining quite hard now but Rafievn had hardly noticed due to his first near meeting with these aliens, except they were not aliens at all they were humans, just 3,000 or so years behind himself in evolution. Rafievn thought about the reality of it all; it was real, it was happening, he wanted to tell the rest of the crew but he would wait until nightfall to send the messages to the moon, their nightly satellite connection.

The work that day on the monument seemed very labour intensive but nothing seemed to have been done. Most of the work was carried out on the massive stones, they were being dressed and jointed. A simple tenon looked like it was being crafted on the top of one of the stones. There were about twenty workmen on each stone. Food and water was brought to them throughout the day as they toiled. Rafievn looked at his watch, he had been in the tree for nearly eight hours, his body was really stiff and he needed the toilet badly. The hunting party had not come back the way they went into the wood, he looked through the wood using thermal mode on his glasses but nothing showed up, not even any animals.

He made his way back down to the ground and thought it was best to use the base of the still standing tree as his toilet. He set off into the wood with his camouflage scanner on all the time, his clothing constantly changing colour and tone; he was almost invisible apart from his face. He dropped a net from his hood, which covered his face and changed to camouflage as he walked. The day had left him very hungry, he looked around for animals but it seemed the earlier hunting party had scared them all off. He remembered seeing Hunnit burrows near the monument but he couldn't go there until the workmen had gone home. He decided to walk back but take a sweeping route to the right, just in case he bumped into the hunters.

"I wonder what Rafievn is doing?" said Sanluin.

"It should be getting dark where he is, he is probably looking for food. He has his compact rations with him but he can't resist the real thing if he can get his hands on it," replied Tehkin.

"Have we decided where we are going yet?"

"There are two large land, masses we could try either. It doesn't really make much difference," said Cinciev pointing to them on the map.

"This is where we landed, this is where Rafievn is. Let's start at the bottom of this one, it would be about 2 hours in front of where Rafievn is," said Tehkin. They headed for the large landmass to the right and flew in at about 100 feet. The coastline came up in front of them with a large flat mountain that made for a magnificent backdrop. The top of the mountain looked almost level, very similar to the Miikeon Mountain range on Atronia; it was amazing how Planetician had so many similarities to Atronia. Tehkin took Hope right up to the foot of the mountain and pulled up at the last minute.

"Tehkin, can you stop flying like a lunatic it makes me feel sick?" yelled Sanluin.

"Stop being so miserable Sanluin, you will see Rafievn soon enough," Tehkin replied laughing. Sanluin got up and went to the main computer. She started to type in a message to Rafievn. Cinciev and Tehkin were just enjoying the ride over this huge land; it had herds of wild animals that were only found in zoos and some only in museums back on Atronia. This place was untouched by man so far. The temperature started to rise again as they were nearing the tropical regions. Sanluin typed away on the keypad, she told Rafievn how much she missed him and of the places they had flown

52

over. She sent the message to the moon; the communication probe would store the message and send it to Rafievn when he contacted the probe. She went back to the Bridge and sat in Rafievn's seat, she could just make out his aroma from the chair. It was comforting for her. The sun was starting to set so Tehkin looked for a suitable spot to set Hope down for the night.

The last workers had left the monument and headed back to their huts for the night. Rafievn watched them slowly disappear out of view. His stomach was rumbling and he looked towards the Hunnit burrows and waited for one to surface. He got his weapon and set it to stun. Lying on his stomach, Rafievn waited for a Hunnit to show itself. It was nearly dark so he set his glasses to night vision mode. It looked like daylight again with them on; the hunting should be easy as long as the Hunnit would show up. He heard a movement behind him and he looked back quickly to see what it was. There was a large Riind on the edge of the forest. It would be plenty enough food for Rafievn with lots to spare but with nowhere to store the uneaten carcass it would be such a waste. He would also have to hide the dead Riind so that the local people wouldn't find it and give them cause for suspicion that there might be an unwanted visitor around. He decided to wait for the Hunnit to show up, as they are just the right size for a good meal for one. Rafievn turned back to burrows and saw two Hunnit grazing by the entrance. He fired a shot and both Hunnit seemed to stop moving. There was no noise whatsoever from the weapon. Rafievn got up and walked to the stunned Hunnit. He picked them both up and walked towards the monument.

The stones seemed even larger close up making him realise that this was a huge task these people had set themselves. It still baffled him as to why they built such a large monument. It showed that they had plenty of time to spend on a project, this meant they had regular sources of food organised to afford the time to build the monument.

Rafievn didn't want to start a fire as the local people may see it. He took of his pack and looked for the cooking equipment he had packed. It was specially designed to cook by probing the meat with a needle shaped probe and cook the meat without any visible heat. Rafievn skinned the Hunnit and pushed the probe into the flesh of the Hunnit. The flesh slowly turned colour around the area of the probe. Rafievn repeated this all over the Hunnit until the whole body had changed colour. The process did not heat the flesh, but it was tenderised and sterile to eat, just as though it had been cooked and left to cool. Rafievn took a bite into the small hindquarter of the Hunnit. It tasted good to eat some red meat for the first time in five years, even if it was cold.

The night was warm and the cloud had thinned a lot since the earlier shower. Rafievn could see the moon behind the clouds and thought of the others on Hope. Where were they now he wondered, had they found any other civilisation on Planetician? He got out his communication unit and switched it on. The antenna automatically opened up and angled itself to the moon. A few minutes passed and the unit beeped, it had received a message from the moon. Rafievn picked up the unit and read the message, it was from Sanluin. 'To Rafievn. I miss you so much, even though it has been only a short time since I last saw you, how are you? Are you eating well? Are you warm enough?'

Rafievn felt warmed by the questions Sanluin had asked it made him feel wanted and loved, something he had not experienced for a long time. It also made him miss Sanluin more than he had realised. He looked into the sky hoping they would return soon. 'We have flown over the northern ice cap and travelled below it, the largest ocean and the southern ice cap, we are over a large land mass about two or three hours ahead of you in time zones. Tehkin is looking for a spot to set down for the night. We haven't seen any other people yet but are very optimistic as you are already amongst a group of people. What are they like? How well do they live and what are they building that monument for? We will have to settle with people like this at some time so we need to know who are going to be the most suitable and also the luckiest group of human beings ever to live on this planet or Atronia. They will have the advantages of all our technology and the added advantage of knowing all the mistakes made on Atronia. This planet will evolve in a way that will be a second chance to get things right. Our power to this place will not be control over people but to give them a different evolution to what we had gone through on Atronia. Looking back over our history on Atronia, different beliefs caused so much pain and misery for people, the wars that were waged and the terrorism that followed, as the wealthiest countries formed to control the last of the mineral and fossil fuels. We have the knowledge to alter that course here, we will become a religion to these people except that it will be a simple way to just survive, in balance with nature instead of being distorted into a control mechanism for people to fear. It will hold the truth for generations to come long after we are dead. See you soon my love and keep safe.' It was long message from Sanluin but it made Rafievn feel a great responsibility to the people of this planet to show them how to evolve without making the mistakes that were made on Atronia.

Rafievn finished off the Hunnit and looked up to the moon. It was his only contact with the rest of the crew. He put the microphone from the communication set to his mouth and spoke in a message to Sanluin, telling her of what had happened since they had separated. After sending the message Rafievn climbed up the scaffolding to the top of one of the stones that as yet had no lintel. The work being carried out was to form the tenon on top of the stone. Rafievn picked up a stone-hammering tool with a wooden handle; such a primitive tool and yet these people manage to construct such a huge monument with stones brought from miles away, looking at the drag marks in the ground. The grass was completely worn away to the soil where they had used logs as rollers and dragged the stones on top of the logs. On Atronia there were stone monuments but none of this scale, compared to the evolution of these people.

Rafievn looked at his watch, it was ten; it would be midnight where Hope and the rest of the crew were. He thought of Sanluin sleeping in her bunk, he just wished she were there with him. He made his way back to the forest, to the tree where he was observing the monument being built. He climbed up to the platform he had made from the dry moss and set up camp for the night. In his pack was a waterproof insulating sheet, which would warm from a power cell. The cell was in the base of the pack and charged from gravity and movement so it would never run down. Lying on his back Rafievn looked up to the stars flickering in space, he thought of the distance they had come and the ease with which it was done, Hope had done everything for them. It was if it had a mind of its own. Before he fell asleep he took a small mouthwash tablet to clean his teeth, it reacted with his saliva creating foam that he spat out after swishing it around his mouth. Running his tongue over his smooth teeth, he thought at least one part of his body felt clean. Tomorrow he would find a river or stream to wash in.

Tehkin had landed on a high plateau overlooking a vast plain where large herds of grazing Lactte were gathering for what seemed to be a migration. Cinciev and Tehkin were sleeping but Sanluin was at the main computer waiting for a reply from Rafievn. While she was waiting she had updated Hope with the progress on the exploration of Planetician. Hope had been taking readings from Planetician itself like tidal movements, temperature, climate patterns and air quality. The words that Sanluin was waiting for came up on the screen. 'Incoming message from MF1. Message received from MF1 Rafievn northern islands, first drop off point. To my dear Sanluin….' The message went on. Sanluin was glad to hear he was safe and eating well. She longed to be with him, but knew that the longer it would be until she saw him the greater it would be when they would be reunited. She sent back a short message and looked out and up to the stars, wondering what they looked like from Rafievn's position and then went to bed.

The morning was still and the sun was slowly rising on the horizon. The herds of Lactte were still huddled together for safety through the night. Steam was rising in the cool morning air from their combined heat and breathing. Tehkin looked at the view and wondered how long ago this scene would have been commonplace back on Atronia. Climate change on Atronia had taken its toll on wild animals, he felt very privileged to witness such a sight of natural survival instinct and wild beauty. He lowered the door of Hope and stepped out into the freshness of the morning, the temperature would reach the high 90s by midday. The smell from the Lactte down on the plain drifted up to the plateau where Tehkin was stood. It wasn't as bad as he thought it would be. There were packs of Yiinea stalking the Lactte looking for any weak or injured ones that would make easy prey when the herd started to move.

"Tehkin, would you like any breakfast before we set off?" called Cinciev from the bottom of the steps.

"Just tea would be fine thanks. I'll be up in a minute." He looked again at the animals below and thought how cruel nature can be. It was for no gain but just pure survival, it made it seem not so cruel after all as there was nothing but hunger to satisfy and the need to feed the young of the Yiinea.

After breakfast Cinciev was looking for any human life apart from their own on Hope's readings. It showed that there was more intense population to the northeast rather than the few scattered settlements where Rafievn was holding out.

"It looks like it will be to the northeast Tehkin, that shows a dense population of people. We will go in at altitude again to keep from being seen."

"OK Cinciev, 60,000 feet it is then." Hope left the plateau and banked round over the herds of Lactte who were starting to move eastwards. A pack of Yiinea were pitching in to what looked like a young Lactte, they were attacking its neck and rear, it had no chance, as there were at least ten in the pack. Tehkin wondered if this was how early man learnt to hunt in packs, by watching nature committing its necessary deed. He thought how man had always copied nature in its own evolution, especially with nano-technology. Man was copying nature's own construction system except that man was now in control, not nature. It was that man always took more than he needed that would tip the balance of nature, inadvertently starting the demise of man. Sanluin and Cinciev sat looking at the screens to see what the population was that lay ahead of them. It was many more than Rafievn's group in the northern islands.

Hope was flying at 60,000 feet heading northeast to that area of dense population. The jungle had disappeared and been replaced by desert. There was a large river meandering northwards to a sea, almost enclosed by land except for an opening to the west, which led to the first ocean they had come across on arriving on Planetician. Tehkin stopped Hope to take more accurate readings of the population density before moving on. Cinciev was getting readings of thousands of people in this desert, which was fuelled for life by the vast river. They were too high to get a good visual without zooming in so Cinciev set the camera to zoom in over these people. Tehkin took Hope directly over a gathering of what was over 300 people, according to the readings. Cinciev zoomed in on the group; they were gathered by the riverbank and dressed in what seemed to be white loincloths or kilts. Some of the crowd had more elaborate clothing on with head garments. There was a group of some sort of guards with spears, swords and shields at the very edge of the bank that had a jetty made from timber.

"These seem much more sophisticated people compared to Rafievn's bunch and darker skinned, they could pass for Ciptions."

"They certainly do Cinciev. There seems to be an organised society with a military or security system in place, looking at those guards," said Tehkin. Then from the bottom of the screen a boat slowly came into view. It had an open deck with a single sail. At the rear of the boat there were two sets of oars one on each side. They were almost upright and could be operated from a standing position. A man stood on the bow of the boat with a rope in his hands ready to throw to the jetty. At the back of the boat there was a small cabin, which looked too ornate for the rest of the boat. There were ten other people on the deck and also some animals, which were strung up by their legs. This must have been a hunting trip. A man at the stern was punting the boat to the jetty, as there was no wind to fill the sail. The man at the bow threw the rope to the waiting guards on the jetty and one of them tied it around a tree trunk, which had been cut and was used for one of the main upright supports. A person emerged from the cabin and the crowd, including the guards went down on one knee, bowing their heads in their presence.

"That must be their leader, he or she seems very important," said Sanluin. The person was dressed in a white robe with a gold and blue collar, the headpiece was black and formed into the shape of a Neaak. She or he went back into the cabin, whilst two men went to each corner of the cabin, picking it up by what looked like wooden poles. They walked onto the jetty and the guards surrounded the cabin. The crowd opened up for the passing group, followed by the animals being carried by the remainder of the crew from the boat.

"Zoom back out a bit Cinciev, lets see where they're going," instructed Sanluin with excitement. As Cinciev zoomed out, a town came into view; there were houses with stone walls and roofs made from palms. The procession from the river passed through this small town along its dusty streets to the other side, where there was a team of Seeors harnessed to a cart, which were decorated in colours similar to the person in the cabin. The cabin carriers walked to the cart and slid the cabin onto the bed of the cart. A driver took out his whip and cracked it over the heads of the Seeors, who jumped and started off at a canter. The guards mounted their own Seeors and followed behind.

"Let's take a look at whole area? See what else these people have to offer," suggested Tehkin.

"OK." Cinciev panned the camera round; they hadn't seen anything else as they were only zoomed in on the crowd at the riverbank. They all gasped in amazement as huge stone buildings came into view. They were much more advanced than in the north. The pillars were fluted on the sides as well as being round. It made the monument in the north seem quite basic in comparison. The cart and mounted guards were travelling north at quite a pace. Tehkin followed them still at 60,000 feet whilst Cinciev zoomed in with the camera. The dust cloud was following the convoy of cart and riders, sometimes small children would run out from small houses on the side of the road and wave their arms at the passing group.

"Cinciev, pan the camera back more, let's see where they might be going," suggested Sanluin. As the picture on the screen came into focus all three gasped in disbelief as they saw pyramids on a massive scale.

"I can't believe they have built pyramids as well, they are almost the same size as ones on Atronia," said Cinciev in amazement.

"This is an amazing coincidence, although it is a structure that will not collapse at that height using just stone. Their principles for building must be the same as the ancient builders of Pyeet. I wonder if they have built these pyramids as tombs for their kings, just as they had done on Atronia," replied Tehkin.

"Cinciev, would you be able to observe these people for a few days? We could go and pick up Rafievn and then return to you in no time," suggested Sanluin with excitement as she wanted to get back to get Rafievn as soon as possible.

"I would certainly blend in with the people, I would be able to learn quite a lot from them." Cinciev was keen to study these people, as they had seemed to achieve such wonders and similarities to his own ancestors back on Atronia.

"We will wait until night fall before we drop you off. You

had better get your kit ready. Take what Rafievn took and don't forget the first aid kit - remember what happened when that Deiiss bit you back on the first islands," said Tehkin in a fatherly manner.

Rafievn had set off early that morning before daylight. He used his glasses on thermal mode just in case there might be any people about at that time of day. He wanted to find somewhere to wash, so he headed downhill through the woods in the hope that a stream would lead to a river. He wondered where Hope might be, had they found any more human settlements? He would send a message that night to see how long they would be until they picked him up. The sun was starting to rise in the east, which was to his left. The rain had cleared from the previous night and there wasn't a cloud in the sky, the birds sang loudly as dawn broke. It was a comforting sound that made him feel like he wasn't alone. He had never felt like this when he was on his training exercises back on Atronia. It must be that he was missing Sanluin so much; there had been no one to miss when he was in the army. The sound of running water drew Rafievn to a small stream that emerged from a spring about 10 feet in front of him. He knelt down by the source and made a bowl shape in the ground, the water filled the bowl quickly and Rafievn waited for the sediment to settle before cupping his hands to take a drink. Rafievn looked up and saw the sun starting to stream through the trees, reflecting off the stream, which was being created from the damp forest floor. It was very tranquil to be alone with nature on this almost untouched planet. The water had cleared and Rafievn took four cupped handfuls of water, it tasted so good, so fresh and cold. He filled his water container as it was nearly empty and cleaned his teeth with the brush instead of the tablets, as he thought they didn't quite do the trick.

Feeling completely refreshed he set off following the course of the stream. He checked his camouflage, it was still working well, he could hardly see his outstretched arm it was that effective. It was quite a descent through the wood; his legs were aching from the jarring of each step. It was easier to run down hill but the forest floor was very uneven with lots of broken branches lying around, it would be treacherous to run as he didn't want to risk a twisted ankle. It was nearly two hours since he had set out that morning and was feeling hungry but decided to keep walking until he found where this stream met a larger river. Some fresh water fish would go down well.

Cinciev was checking his pack and sorting out what equipment he would take. Rafievn had left a list of what he had packed. It was a lot warmer in this part of Planetician so Cinciev didn't want to take gear he wouldn't need.

"Do you think it would be a good idea if we made you a kilt so that you could blend in with these people? You could get really close to them, with your skin colouring you could pass as a local."

"Don't you think that will be a bit risky? What if they get suspicious of me, I don't want to get captured Sanluin."

"You'll be alright, just keep your distance and mingle with the crowds, we'll only be a couple of days and will be back before you know it. Rafievn is only up in the northwest, we'll pick him up and return in a couple of hours, especially the way Tehkin flies this ship."

"Go on then Sanluin, see what you can make up from the sheets in the sleeping quarters," replied Cinciev a bit apprehensively. Back at the Bridge, Tehkin was taking readings of the scale of the pyramids; they were huge, the largest being almost twice the size of the biggest on Atronia. This type of building work was being carried out around 4,000 years ago back on Atronia. It would be unbelievable to think that this would be happening on the other side of the universe. But here, he was witnessing a planet and civilisation developing almost exactly the same way that Atronia and its people had. This got Tehkin thinking he ought to get some ice-core readings on how Planetician's climate might change in the future. It would mean going back to the southern ice cap, but it would be necessary. Tehkin didn't want to settle where there might be a chance of flooding if the planet warmed up, melting the ice caps. This had happened on Atronia, the oceans had claimed whole ancient cities after an ice age. All this information would be stored in the many levels of snow that had turned to ice over the centuries. Hope was equipped with probes that could penetrate the ice and gather readings without boring ice-cores, as they had done on Atronia.

More readings were coming back from Hope; it showed that a group of pyramids mirrored exactly a formation of stars in their constellation. These people were obviously accomplished astronomers and their mathematics was very well advanced.

"What's Hope coming up with Tehkin, anything interesting?"

"The people here are very intelligent, they have a good understanding of maths and the constellation of their universe. I think it would be a good chance that we will make contact with them; they are by far more advanced than the people Rafievn is with. What are you doing with that sheet anyway?"

"I am going to make Cinciev a kilt so that he can get close to the people down there. What do you think?"

"He certainly has the colouring. Is he OK with it?"

"He is quite keen on the idea, just a bit nervous that's all."

"I will try to get a good close up for you so it will be easier to copy one of the kilts or skirts, whatever they are."

"Thanks Tehkin, when you have a good shot, copy it off and bring it to the sick bay that's where I'll try to stitch it up."

"OK Sanluin, won't be long."

Rafievn came to the edge of the wood and saw the stream meander its way down to a larger river; it was about a mile away. He took a swig from his water container that was nearly empty by now and looked around to make sure it was safe to venture out into the clearing. There was no sign of anyone but he could make out some Faiis grazing on the other side of the river. He walked at a quicker pace towards the river, as he was looking forward to a good wash. The sun was hot overhead and Rafievn's clothes were sticking to his body with perspiration. The pollen from the grass was wafting up as he walked, it was causing him to sneeze and it was the first time he had suffered from hay fever since he was a child. Insects were flying out as he disturbed them as they pitched on the grass. It must be midsummer here in the north; he wondered how cold the winters would get. At least he wouldn't have to experience a winter without the comfort of Hope and Sanluin.

The river was slow moving, the Faiis had not noticed him and carried on grazing on the other bank. Rafievn took his pack off with pleasure, quickly followed by the rest of his clothes. The pile of clothing and pack blended in with the grass as the camouflage was still switched on. Rafievn stepped to the edge of the water; the grass was soft under his feet and the ground, moist and spongy. He tried the temperature with his foot, not too bad he thought, almost the same as the sea where he and Sanluin had caught the fish, back on the first islands they had landed on. He caught his breath and dived in. The Faiis jumped back from the bank with a start at the sound of the splash. They ran back from the bank a short distance and looked back to see what had startled them. They looked puzzled as they sniffed the air but could see nothing as Rafievn was out of view in the water. The cool water washed away the sweat from Rafievn's body; it felt good to be in fresh water. He swam up river for about a 100 feet or so and let the flow of the river carry him back down to where he had dived in. He swam to the bank and sat in the soft mud. It was slightly gritty, so Rafievn used this to his advantage and rubbed handfuls over his skin. It exfoliated his body and a tingling sensation swept over his skin as he rinsed off the mud in the deeper water. He dived under the water and ran his hands through his hair; it was greasy from his sweat but felt slightly cleaner for it. Swimming slowly up stream he thought he heard a whistle in the direction of where the Faiis had run. He slowly swam to the other bank and tried to look through the grass at the Faiis.

Still unable to see, he climbed out of the water and saw a person walking towards the Faiis. It looked like a young woman, no older than fifteen. She beat a stick on the ground and said something in a strange tongue but similar in sound to the hunters he had seen the day before. She was walking down stream with the Faiis trotting on in front of her. Rafievn waited until she was a couple of hundred feet away before he got back in the water and swam back to the other side of the river. He clambered out, trying not to get covered in mud and went over to his clothes and pack. He got out his glasses and zoomed them in to where the girl was. She sat down under a tree and started to eat some fruit that looked like seppas. Watching her eat the fruit made Rafievn crave for one, it was one of his favourite fruits. Rafievn got dressed and waited for the girl to move off before he followed.

Cinciev was standing in front of the mirror back on Hope. His new kilt hung on his hips.

"Come out Cinciev, we are waiting," called Sanluin. Cinciev gingerly walked out to where Sanluin and Tehkin were stood.

"Don't laugh will you." Sanluin and Tehkin both burst out laughing at the sight of Cinciev's slight frame dressed in his new attire.

"You look just like one of the people down there, you will fit right in," said Tehkin while still laughing. Sanluin went over and tied the kilt a bit tighter.

"That's better Cinciev, I don't think it will fall down now."

"Well I suppose I'm ready as soon as it gets dark."

"Give yourself a few hours rest, we'll send a message to Rafievn, we can pick him up tomorrow night," said Tehkin. Sanluin's face lit up with the thought of seeing Rafievn so soon.

Rafievn had followed the girl for a couple of miles downstream. She had come to a settlement; it looked much larger then the one up by the monument. There was a surrounding fence, made from interwoven saplings; the huts were larger and there were many people going about their business. The wood gave him good cover to observe the settlement for an hour or so before dusk. Rafievn sat down at the edge of the wood under the cover of a large bush. He had a good view down onto the settlement, as the edge of the wood was on a slight slope to the river. There were rafts moored up to the bank on the other side of the river. They looked like they had been there for quite a while as weed and reeds had gathered on their edges from the flow of the river.

He sat there until nightfall watching the settlement and its people. Rafievn calculated he had walked about eight miles that day, it would take him at least that to get back to the monument if not longer as it was mostly uphill. He sent a message to Hope explaining that he would be ready to be picked up in two days. The thought of a hot shower, shave and cooking some Hunnit in the oven on board Hope was settling and he drifted off to sleep.

Cinciev was packed and ready, Tehkin had found a good landing spot well away from the pyramids and the town. It was a few miles to the west. The night was clear and the stars flickered brightly in the sky.

"OK Cinciev?"

"Yes fine, just nervous that's all Sanluin." Tehkin took Hope down; all lights were out in case they would be spotted from the ground. The desert came up to meet them; it was eerily lit by the moonlight. Cinciev got out of his seat and put his pack on and went over to the door. Tehkin was close behind him as the door opened. It was surprisingly cool compared to the heat of the day; the monitors had shown the temperature to be in the high 90s. The steps lowered and made a soft crunch as they bedded into the sand a few inches.

"Right then, I'll see you in a couple of days."

"Keep in touch, we will pick you up back here when you're ready. It will be at night again, so set your co-ordinates, we are at 29.6°, 58.8° degrees east."

"OK Tehkin, thanks."

" Be careful Cinciev, don't take any risks."

"Don't worry Sanluin I won't," replied Cinciev as he made his way down the steps to the sand. Cinciev looked across at the pyramids to the west, the moonlight lit them up, they were magnificent, the largest was white with a gold tip. Beyond them the river glistened as it flowed slowly towards the sea to the north.

"See you soon," Cinciev waved at Tehkin and Sanluin and walked off into the night. This place filled him with intrigue and wonder. Tehkin and Sanluin looked at the view of the pyramids that were glowing in the power of the moonlight. What would these people make of Hope if they were to settle here? Only time may tell.

They both went back into the ship and Tehkin sat at the flight controls while Sanluin sent a message to Rafievn. The message from Rafievn came up on the screen. It said that he was a good day's walk from the monument and that any other landing place was out of the question for Hope due to the forest. Sanluin's heart sank, she thought she would see him that night but it seemed that it would be a couple of days until they got to pick up Rafievn. She turned to Tehkin and told him of the delay.

"It'll work out just right, we can go back to the southern ice cap and get the readings we need. We will be back in two days, max."

"OK Tehkin, keeping busy will pass the time quicker."

"That's the spirit, keep positive, you'll see him in no time." Sanluin felt better as Hope took off, banked back round and headed south. Sanluin sent Rafievn the message and said they would be ready to pick him up in two days. The message reached Rafievn in a couple of minutes; their satellite system with the moon was working well. Rafievn was woken by the beep of his communication set. Eagerly he read the message from Sanluin, two more days he thought to himself, one hard days trek back to the monument and then rest until the following night. He sent a message back saying he would see them at 2.00 am at the monument, two days from now. Lying back against his pack he fell back to sleep.

Back on Hope, Tehkin was checking the ships' logistics as they flew away from Cinciev. He noticed that the waste from the galley and toilets was nearly full. A change of water wouldn't go a miss either he thought to himself.

"Sanluin, we will stop further up river and change water, it won't take long."

"OK Tehkin, I'll be in the shower for a while." Tehkin took Hope up-river for about 60 miles; the moon lit the water like a silver Neaak slithering its way from the mountains far in the south. He put the scanners on to check that there were no humans nearby, the readings came back all clear, so Hope slowly descended to about 10 feet from the river. Tehkin opened the waste hatch and a couple of hundred gallons flooded into the river. The waste was neutralised so it would not pollute. Tehkin went upstream a few hundred feet so as not to suck any of the waste back into Hope's water tanks. A pipe extended from the hull of the ship and started to suck water from the river. The water was filtered for any foreign bodies during the process. It took a couple of minutes to refill the tanks. Sanluin noticed the slight upward movement in the ship as the waste was expelled from the hull. Tehkin took Hope back to altitude and headed south at maximum speed, he wanted to get some good readings from the southern ice cap.

The morning sun was still below the horizon but Cinciev had been awake for the last few hours, his mind too busy to sleep. He had been warm under the sheet, which was heated from the cell in the pack. He thought he would make his way towards the pyramids but keeping a good distance all the same. He set off with feelings of excitement mixed with fear. He wondered if these people were peaceful or war-like; from the first sighting of them at the jetty they looked calm enough but the sign of the guards meant that there were people to protect for one reason or another. The sand made for heavy going as he walked up the dunes. About a mile away there was a rocky outcrop, he decided to make his way there, as it would give him good cover to observe from. The sun was starting to rise; it was a beautiful sight as the shadows from the pyramids sprawled far into the desert, almost to where he was stood. Cinciev stopped and took in the view. It was breathtaking. There was a slight wind from the west, it carried with it the smells of food, the smell was of baking, maybe some sort of bread. He had not smelled that for years on Atronia as all the food was made by the odourless nano-machines. The effort that went into making such food in this place was hard to imagine. They had no power here except for water and the Seeors. Their crops had to be harvested by hand, the whole process was so labour intensive, but at least it was in balance with nature.

Cinciev reached the rocks and settled in a gully between two large boulders. This gave him good cover from the sun and also a good view of the pyramids. He got out his glasses and set them to auto focus. More stone structures came into view, one was in the shape of an Iaan lying down with its head held up as if to keep watch. The head was in the form of a human and wearing a head-dress. There was a gang of builders working on the face from a timber scaffold that looked like it could blow away in a strong wind. It looked like some sort of maintenance was being carried out on the face; this showed that this statue was already very old if it needed maintenance. To the left of the statue there was smoke coming from an open fire, which had a bell shaped pot on top of it, charred black on the outside. This must be where the smells of baking were coming from that he had detected earlier. There were two women working near the fire who seemed to be preparing some sort of bread. They were dressed in full-length gowns with hoods covering their heads. Cinciev could tell that they were women from their figures. The gowns were tied with a cord around the waist exaggerating their hips and bosom. It must be the food for the builders on the statue. This showed that they were professional tradesmen even if their only pay was with food. From the second largest pyramid a path or causeway stretched past the Iaan to a smaller rectangular building that had two ramps leading to a harbour.

Cinciev watched with intense concentration as the builders worked away on the statue. He was so overwhelmed by the whole place he had hardly noticed that most of the morning had passed. The smell of the cooking had made him realise how hungry he was. He had brought with him some Tanoos, which they had gathered from the islands they had first landed on. Cinciev thought to himself that he would venture down into the town that lay next to the river that slowly flowed by. He would wait until nightfall and he would change into his kilt that Sanluin had made.

Hope was approaching the southerly ice cap she was only feet from the sea. The force from her silent engines picked up the water and left a wake as if she was a boat.

"There is a suitable landing place where we can get some good ice-core readings near an active volcano, overlooking an ice shelf. It will be very cold so we had better get some clothes made that will be able to cope with the temperature. I am intrigued to see what that machine can come up with," said Tehkin with a look of unease.

"OK, Tehkin but don't look so worried, I am sure it will cope after all my father designed it. Any way, what sort of temperature range shall I programme in?" replied Sanluin with a tone of defence for her father's technology.

"Well it's about 30 below at the moment, we won't go out after nightfall but the wind chill can take it much lower. Allow up to minus 60°."

"I will get right to it, I am looking forward to going out into the cold. We will be the first Atronians to experience this sort of weather in centuries." Sanluin went off to programme the computer to make the one-piece outfits. The programme already had their sizes pre-programmed, it was just a case of specification for the particular garments. Sanluin included heaters in the suits, similar to the ones in Rafievn's and Cinciev's kit. She chose white, as it would be all the camouflage they would need. Once the programme had been completed, the suits would take about ten minutes.

Tehkin banked Hope around the ice cliffs of the frozen wilderness and looked in wonder at the immense size of the ice mass that covered this continent. The cliffs must be at least 200 foot high in places; there was marine life all around the shores. The wildlife was left alone in this place, as there was no sign of human inhabitants on the scanners. It was a totally natural and untouched place until now.

Rafievn was woken by the sound of children's voices, he looked across the river and saw three children playing outside the camp, throwing twigs at each other and laughing as they did. How carefree they were, they were happy and well fed, their hair shone in the morning sun; two of them were very blond and the smaller child had almost black hair. It showed that there was a good mix of breeding in the settlement. There had been no sign of Ciption race in anyone Rafievn had seen. With his knowledge of history on Atronia the Ciption races did not mix with his own Sillion race until sailing ships and the exploration of Atronia had taken place. This showed how behind in evolution Planetician was. Rafievn ate what was left of his rations he had brought with him and prepared for the walk back to the monument. His legs felt stiff from the previous day but a good brisk walk back up the through the forest would soon get the blood flowing into his muscles. Rafievn set his camouflage scanner on and slowly moved away from the bush he had been hiding under. The three children had gone back into the compound; there was no one visible. The morning dew was heavy on the ground and it caused Rafievn to slip on damp branches that had moss on their surface. He felt confident with the camouflage so he kept up his pace, knowing that it would be only too soon that Hope would pick him up and he could hold Sanliun in his arms again.

Tehkin set Hope down on the snow, her feet sunk a few feet into the snow and then Hope self-levelled to compensate for the unevenness of the snow. There was no wind and the sun hung low in the sky. Sanluin and Tehkin looked out over this amazing wilderness, they had never seen such a view before; it looked so pure and clean. The snow glistened with a sparkle as if it was lit from within instead of from the sun's rays.

"The suits should be ready, I can't wait to get out there," said Sanluin, her eyes alive with excitement. She went off to the machine, it had just finished Tehkin's suit. It was still warm from the manufacturing process and had a unique smell to it.

"Here Tehkin, try it on while its still warm." Sanluin threw him the suit whilst grabbing hers and running off to change. Tehkin wondered how she could be so excited. He had been to places in their solar system where the temperatures had been much lower but there had been no ice or snow.

"Thanks Sanluin." No sooner had Tehkin worked out how to put the suit on, Sanluin came rushing back.

"Come on Tehkin, what's taking you so long?"

"Go on out if you want but don't go far from the ship."

"See you in a bit." Sanluin opened the door and lowered the steps, the cold air hitting her as if she had jumped into a freezing pool. She did the neck up high on her suit and pulled on the hood. The heater was set to counteract the cold automatically and soon filled the suit with heat. She hurried down the steps and hesitated before stepping onto the snow. She would be the first person to step onto an ice cap for centuries. It was like stepping onto Planetician for the first time all over again. Holding tightly to the handrails she gently put her left boot onto the snow and transferred her weight onto it. It made a squeaking artificial sound. Tehkin was at the top of the steps.

"Are you scared Sanluin? You couldn't wait to get out of here a minute ago."

"No, just curious Tehkin, look I'm not scared." Sanluin strode out onto the snow and into the polar sunshine, Tehkin followed close behind.

"I have been in temperatures colder than this but this feels colder, it must be the snow and ice all around us."

"What is the temperature anyway?"

"It's 30° below."

"Cold enough for me Tehkin. Did they show on the scanners any life forms apart from marine?"

"No we are the only ones here apart from the sea life on the shores and the birds." They walked round Hope and looked out over to the sea. The volcano was steaming away in the distance to the left and a massive ice shelf sprawled out in the bay in front of them.

"This definitely feels like a different planet now, it's almost like going back in time." Tehkin bent down and picked up a hand full of snow and thought to himself how the layers of this snow and ice beneath him would tell the entire atmospheric history of this planet. He could establish meteor impact and volcanic activity almost to the decade. It would give a good insight to the future as to where they would be best to settle. They walked together in silence apart from the squeaking snow under foot. The air was still but glistened with fine particles of snow that caught the sunlight; they seemed to be immune to gravity, just dancing effortlessly in the pure air. Sanluin thought how she would love to be alone here with Rafievn, it was such a romantic place, so untouched. They headed back to Hope that strangely did not look out of place, the brilliant white and her silver skin blended well together. It would be a picture that Sanluin's father would be proud of. Once back on board, Tehkin prepared for the ice-core readings. To call them ice-core is just the old way of saying how it was once done, Hope would just punch a probe into the ice, which could analyse the ice as it went. The deeper the probe went, the further back in time would be revealed. Sanluin prepared a meal using fruit from where they had first landed and added it to what they could make from the rations on board. She went back to the Bridge and asked Tehkin what the readings were showing.

"About 8,000 years ago an ice age ended. These ice cycles can take thousands of years to complete."

"So where Rafievn is, he is quite safe? He won't freeze up all of a sudden?" Tehkin laughed out loud.

"I wouldn't worry Sanluin, there won't be another ice age

for tens of thousands of years according to these results."

Still sat between the two rocks Cinciev watched the builders pack away their tools and make their way down the scaffold. Their day had been a long one; they had only one break in 10 hours. It was hard going in the hot sun but these people were used to it. He could see the look of relief on their faces as they headed back to the town on foot. It would be about one more hour before it started to get dark, so Cinciev started to change into his kilt. He noticed that the builders had worn leather sandals whilst working, but one of them had left a pair at the bottom of the scaffold, he would try them on later when he was going to venture into town. Before Cinciev hid his pack and clothing he sent a message back to Hope. It was to tell the others where his gear was if anything was to go wrong. He wasn't planning anything risky just a walk through the town, the added advantage of being nightfall would help him to be inconspicuous.

Cinciev covered his pack with one last stone so that nothing was visible. He looked towards the town and felt butterflies in his stomach; he was nervous but very curious. He stepped out from the cover of the rocks and made his way towards the pyramids and the Iaan. The sand was warm under foot, as was the setting sun on his back. Each step closer to the huge pyramids made him realise what a massive task it was to build these monuments with such limited tools and technology. It took Cinciev twenty minutes to get to the foot of the largest pyramid. Its sides were flat and polished; the joints in the masonry were near perfect. Cinciev touched the stone, it was smooth and warmed by the sun. Looking up to the top with its gold cap made this the most magnificent structure he had ever seen. Cinciev made his way down the Iaan and the scaffold at the face and noticed pictures etched into the stone on the side of the Iaan. They seemed to tell a story of some sort; there were birds, people and symbols written in rows and columns. This must be their writing he thought.

Cinciev spotted the sandals at the foot of the ladder, they were a bit small but they would have to do. Looking closely at them they were very simple but sturdily made. The leather strap fitted well over his foot but his heels hung over the sole and touched the ground. With his new footwear, Cinciev walked on into the town, which was starting to light up in the fading sunlight.

Back in the north, Rafievn was making good ground through the forest. He had got to the stream where he had stopped on the way down and filled his water container. He decided to rest for a while. It had been four hours solid hiking but it was getting much easier as he was getting his fitness back. Another four hours and he would be back at the monument. A spot of hunting, dinner and then a good sleep. A few hours after that and Sanluin would be back to pick him up. Planning like this would make the time go faster. The day had warmed up quite considerably and it would have been hard work in the clothing and pack he was carrying but the heater on the suit could also act as a cooler, preventing him from dehydrating too much. Rafievn got to his feet and set off once more. He pulled the gauze face shield down as he would be nearing the monument and there may be hunting parties in the area. He scanned for human life but none showed up within a two-mile radius from where he was. He still kept the gauze down just in case.

Rafievn's pace was much quicker after his rest and he was covering more ground than in the morning. The thought of seeing Sanluin filled his thoughts, he imagined the two of them in a hot shower back on Hope. If only Tehkin could be out for a few hours.

There were signs of Hunnit burrows appearing in the forest floor, which made Rafievn think of food, he was getting very hungry by now. Just as a Hunnit dived into a burrow about ten feet in front of him, he stepped into another. Struggling to catch his breath, he waited for those horrible seconds to pass when you can't breath in or out as the fall had winded him; slowly he began to get to his knees and started to breath again. To his shock there was a boy of about fourteen or fifteen looking straight at him, he was about fifteen feet away. Rafievn thought to himself he couldn't have walked two miles already from when he checked the scanner. The boy seemed to look straight through Rafievn; it must be the camouflage that fooled the boy. At that distance it would be hard to tell. The noise of the fall must have alerted him. Rafievn slowly reached for his weapon, which was in his pocket out of sight. Setting it to stun in his pocket Rafievn was ready to defend himself if necessary. The boy was holding something in his right hand and there was blood stained on his fingers. Rafievn couldn't make out what he was holding but the boy gripped the object tighter and started to move towards Rafievn, who was still looking puzzled and with his guard up. Rafievn stayed completely motionless, only the gauze moving very slightly with his breath. With each step the boy took, Rafievn gripped his weapon tighter. He had been in similar situations back on Atronia but this was different, as he had no idea what was in the mind of this boy; at least in combat he knew the objective of the enemy. He was about ten feet away, Rafievn didn't want to risk anything so with lightening reactions he pulled the weapon out and fired two stun shots at the boy. He fell to the ground, Rafievn got up and rushed over and put the boy in the recovery position, he checked his pulse as sometimes the stun can be too strong and cause cardiac arrest.

The boy was strong with a good pulse, which relieved Rafievn, as he didn't want to harm the boy. Rafievn noticed the object in his hand was a sharpened flint and looking up to where the boy was originally stood, there was a Hunnit strung up to a branch that was semi-skinned. There was a lot of blood dripping from the clenched fist holding the flint. Rafievn prized open the hand and saw the flint had cut deep into the boy's palm and blood was pouring out. The stun would last for an hour at least so the wound had to be patched up. Quickly, Rafievn took his pack off and got out the first aid kit. There was a cauterising tool in the kit that Rafievn switched on and put into the wound. He pulled the tool from one end of the wound to the other, about two inches all told. As the tool moved through the cut the blood was stemmed and the flesh knitted back together. The smell of burnt flesh filled the air, the boy wouldn't feel any pain, and it would be a bit sore when he came around. When he had finished Rafievn put the tool in the kit and set it to analyse the blood. While this was happening he cleaned the wound with antiseptic solution and left it without a dressing. The cauterising tool would knit the flesh as good as any stitch. The kit bleeped and Rafievn saw the result of the blood test. To his surprise it was the same blood group as his. These people are exactly the same as us he thought. This made him feel much closer to them than before.

The smell of flesh had gone and was replaced by the smell of body odour from the boy, which was very strong; Rafievn stood up and before he walked away, placed the flint back into the boy's hand. He wondered what the boy would make of it when he came round. All of a sudden he had passed out, woken up with a fresh scar on his hand and his semi-skinned Hunnit missing. Rafievn turned to thank the boy as he took his free lunch off its tether and carried on up to the monument.

Coming out of his slumber the boy slowly opened his eyes, immediately thinking that someone had hit him from behind but he could feel no bump on his head. It came back to him - there had been a strange shape in the forest where a noise had come from and as he had walked towards it, there was nothing and now he was waking up feeling shaky. Looking down at his hand still holding the flint, he felt a sore tightness in his palm. On closer inspection a neat fresh scar had appeared there, how did that happen he thought to himself? The scar had a neat line of congealed blood on the surface and the boy picked it off with his other hand. Looking around the forest it seemed normal again, no strange shapes or blurry colours. Puzzled and confused about the whole episode, the boy slowly walked back to the settlement near the monument. He had completely forgotten about the rabbit he was skinning.

The sun had set below the horizon and Cinciev was on the very edge of the town. He was full of fear but also intrigue as he slowly walked past the first of the houses. They were lit by lamps, fuelled by an oil of some sort with smells of cooking filling the still night air. A man and woman were walking towards him holding hands. Cinciev felt himself tense up as they went by him. The man made a sound, not an offensive sound but maybe a pleasantry in their language. Cinciev nodded in reply and carried on walking. That was easy enough he thought. He still felt as if everything was a set or unreal, the fact that he was on another planet conversing with people who would be classed as alien hadn't sunk in yet.

Further down the street he could see stalls and people trading in food and other goods. The sound of their chatter was so strange but also not too alien. They had similar sounding tones to that of some languages back on Atronia. He walked on to a stall with food being cooked in a bowl made out of some sort of metal, it was charred black. In the bowl was some meat and spices, it smelled very good and made Cinciev's mouth water. The food vendor beckoned to Cinciev and offered him some of the meat in a circular bread wrap. A fat man standing next to the stall was eating and said something to Cinciev. He didn't know what it was but the hand sign suggested that the food was good. Cinciev looked at the vendor who was bearded with dark eyes and leathery skin, as he held out his hands to show that he had nothing to offer the vendor when the fat man tapped Cinciev on the arm and took the food from the vendor and gave it to Cinciev. Cinciev said thank you in his tongue and the fat man laughed, handing the vendor some coinage. Cinciev nodded again appreciatively and took a bite of the bread and meat. It was delicious, the juices ran down his chin and he wiped it away with his hand. The meat was Nelb, it must have been; it tasted just the same as back home. He had never tasted such rich flavours before though and the bread was different to any type he had had previously.

Finishing the snack, Cinciev walked on from the stall thanking the fat man and the vendor as he went. They hadn't a clue what he had said but they must have guessed how grateful he was.

The street was very busy with all sorts of trade. A man sat with his legs crossed was playing some sort of musical instrument, he was blowing into it and a small crowd had gathered. Cinciev moved to the front and saw that there was a basket in front of the musician. To his shock, a Neaak rose from the basket in a sort of trance to the music. It was Barcee type, which was very poisonous and could spit its venom at its prey, leaving it blinded. Cinciev had never seen one in the flesh; they were in glass cages back on Atronia. He moved away from the Neaak, carrying on down the street.

Cinciev felt much more relaxed about the whole place, his fear had completely gone and he was starting to enjoy himself. It was like being on holiday, almost. This made him sad as he remembered his wife and the times they had spent on holiday together. Cinciev thought how she had left him for a Siunc Director, it broke his heart that his marriage was over but his work and this mission had taken his mind away from his heartbreak. Cinciev sat by a tree and watched the people go about their business. A small girl came up to him and just stared into his eyes, he said hello in his language and the small girl replied something in a soft voice that felt warming to his ears. The girl reminded him of his niece back on Atronia, Cinciev reached out and touched the girl's hair, it was jet black in soft curls. A voice shouted from across the street and the girl ran off. Cinciev could smell Tocuut oil from her hair. He got up and went over to where she had run. A woman came out of a doorway with the girl under her arm. Cinciev was instantly in awe of her beauty; her hair was as black as her daughter's, that is if the girl was her daughter. They looked very much alike. The woman looked at Cinciev and seemed to force a slight smile, but Cinciev could see sadness in her eyes. Then the woman brushed her hand on Cinciev's face, she wiped away some of the bread from his earlier snack that had stuck to his unshaved chin. Cinciev felt a little embarrassed that he had been stood there with food on his chin but the woman didn't seem to mind. She turned and walked back into the house just before she walked inside she looked back at Cinciev and smiled a little more. Cinciev's heart missed a beat almost. He hadn't even thought about women since his wife had left. This made him realise just how much he had missed the soft touch of a woman. Feeling pleased with himself he walked back in the direction of his rocky hideaway, only wanting to get back to the town as soon as he could.

Hope's probe was going deeper into the ice, and revealing the complete climate history of Planetician. A pattern showed of global warming and cooling, ice ages had come and gone and now they were in a period of very gradual warming. There had been an ice age recently but the glaciers had long since retreated. From Hope's calculations, the ice caps would have reached as far down as the islands where Rafievn was. During that time the islands would have been joined to the larger continent on the right. This is a time when people could have travelled to the edges of the continent and settled. When the ice caps retreated, the people would have found themselves living on an island. The weather outside Hope had turned bad, during the night a blizzard had blown in from the sea and the temperature had dropped to 80 degrees below, 120 below with the wind chill. Drifts had started to form around Hope's landing gear.

Tehkin started to wake from a deep sleep where he had been dreaming of his wife. He still missed her a great deal, he lay in his bed thinking back to when he was on Atronia and go for long walks when he missed her badly, it would somehow ease the pain. Getting up from his bed Tehkin dressed into the thermal suit and left Sanluin a message that he had gone out and wouldn't be long. Before leaving Hope, Tehkin made some tea and took it with him in a thermal cup, which would keep warm for hours.

The blizzard had passed and the morning was still very dark, the winter sun had not yet come up and when it did, it hung low in the sky. The days were very short at this time of year. Stepping out onto the fresh snow Tehkin walked in the direction of the sea. Drinking from the flask he started to feel better; he and his wife used to walk for miles when they were together. Being cooped up in a spacecraft for most of your life made the outdoors that much more special. Towards the end of his wife's illness, Tehkin would push her in a wheel chair as it was too painful for her to walk but she didn't want to deny Tehkin the freedom of the outdoors. He thought of his son and how the change in him had not helped his wife, it was more the cause. It was as if they had lost a son but one who was still alive.

Looking up into the darkness of the sky the stars were just visible, what had become of Atronia he thought? How was his old friend Dr Viuuv? The more Tehkin walked, the more he thought how this new planet would bypass all the wrong doings Atronia had gone through. On Atronia they had the ultimate technology but the nature of man's greed had ruined it. Here they had the chance of starting with that ultimate technology. It just had to be used correctly and the people here would evolve in a much different way to the one they would be inevitably heading for. How they introduced the technology to the people on Planetician was their responsibility, it would take very careful planning but as time was on their side, they had the rest of their lives to do it.

Tehkin looked up and left his thoughts, he had walked a long way, Hope had gone from sight, but the footprints in the snow would lead him back, just as long as there were no storms on the way. The snow started to undulate in front of Tehkin, resembling the seabed. The undulations got steadily bigger. He wondered what had caused the change in the terrain. He thought how his wife would have loved to see this place; Tehkin imagined she was by his side. The next step the snow dropped a little under his feet, then suddenly, just as he looked down to his feet the snow opened up and Tehkin fell into a gaping crevasse, he gasped as he fell through the icy skin, sucking in powder snow which made him cough. His flask flew into the air as he grabbed for a hand hold but there was nothing except thin air. Tumbling backwards and screaming as he plummeted, his head caught the wall of the crevasse knocking him unconscious. Further down he fell then, with a sickening thud he hit the floor of the crevasse. The impact ruptured his spleen and caused terrible internal bleeding. Lying on his back with his left leg twisted and badly broken, Tehkin's life slowly crept into the unknown abyss of death; the light from the surface barley illuminating this icy tomb. The heater on the suit was still working which helped the internal bleeding. His communicator in the pocket was switched on but by the time Sanluin would call, Tehkin would have been long dead. At least his last thoughts were of his wife; maybe they are reunited now. Snow from the fall slowly landed on Tehkin's face and melted from his body heat. It looked like he was crying as the water ran down his cheeks. The crew of Hope were now three.

Cinciev made it back to his kit and got into his sleeping bag; the night had turned very cold compared to the heat of the day. He got out the communicator and sent a message to Hope. Instead of typing the message he put a sensor to his head, this would read his thoughts from the electrical impulses in his brain and convert it into text. Each communicator had been personalised to each of the crew's own electrical impulses. The message was sent and Cinciev fell into a deep sleep, he had been on the go for almost twenty hours.

It was dark as Rafievn got back to his platform he had made in the fallen tree. Climbing onto it he got the Hunnit and stuck the probe into the flesh and devoured the whole thing in no time. He was starving from the day's hike. Too tired to send a message he fell straight to sleep. Back in the settlement the boy who had been stunned by Rafievn went to his family's hut, his mother was there waiting for him. She asked him why he had been so late and why he had no Rabbit, he hardly ever returned without food. The boy stayed quiet and kept his injured hand out of view. His mother clipped him round the ear and ushered him off to bed, which was a framework of sticks supported with wooden legs about four inches off the ground. The boy mumbled to himself as he pulled the animal skin over his shoulders. It was the skin from a sheep.

Sanluin started to wake, she got up and went to Tehkin's quarters and saw he wasn't there, she went to the Bridge and saw the note. She looked out of the window and saw that the storm had passed during the night. She felt easier that the weather was fine and turned on the computer to check the forecast. High pressure for most of the day but it would get rough by mid afternoon. It would be dark by then anyway so Tehkin would be back well before then she thought. She went to the galley and made breakfast, she noticed the flask had gone and thought of Tehkin drinking hot tea out in the cold. Taking her breakfast to the Bridge she went to check on any messages. She read the one from Cinciev and read how he had made good contact with people there. He told her he would go back that night and that he could be picked up the next day. She replied saying that they were heading back to pick Rafievn up that night so they could be with him later that same night or leave it until the following day. She sent the message. She read the message from Rafievn again he would be ready to pick up that night, she could hardly wait. She reached for the communicator and called for Tehkin.

"Tehkin, come in please?" The voice of Sanluin echoed in the crevasse, the heat from Tehkin's face had long gone and the water droplets had frozen solid to his skin. His body was still warm from the suit but he was starting to get Riga Mortis. No reply came back and Sanluin was starting to worry. She knew nothing of this place or its dangers. She called again and again but no reply. She was starting to panic now; she scanned the surrounding area in 100 meter radiuses. Then after 2,000 meters the scanner picked up the communicator signal.

'Yes,' she thought, 'I've found him.' His suit could check for a pulse and she quickly checked for one but nothing came back. There must be a mistake; Tehkin was in good shape he couldn't have had a heart attack. She set the scanner for three-dimensional view of where he was. It showed he was 150 feet below the surface; he must have fallen. A chill shot up her spine as the realisation that he was dead hit her. She quickly dressed in the thermal suit and headed straight for the door of Hope. Just as she was about to open it a voice from Hope's speakers boomed.

"Wait, don't go." Sanluin stopped in her tracks at the sound of her father's voice. How did Hope know what had happened?

"You know?" she said, "how do you know?"

"Sanluin please sit down, you must understand something," said her father's voice in a calm and soothing way. Hope could sense Sanluin's panicked state.

"What is it Hope, tell me?" Sanluin sat down and took off the top half of the suit, which was starting to get very hot.

"I have been monitoring everything on this mission from the very moment you left Atronia. I knew Tehkin was dead just after he fell, I couldn't tell you as you were asleep. There's nothing you can do for him now Sanluin."

"We can't just leave him there Hope, we must get him back."

"It is too dangerous Sanluin, you don't want to end up like he is, and you can call me dad if you want."

"What do you mean 'Dad'? You're not my dad, you're a machine programmed by my dad."

"Before you left Atronia your dad made a complete copy of his brain; sounds morbid but it's the truth. When you speak to me it's like speaking to your dad. It is a synthetic and organic brain that is constantly monitoring, assessing and evaluating everything that happens to you all." Sanluin looked all around the ship then put her head in her hands, it was too much to take in. Tehkin dead and now her father was the very soul of this ship. Her feelings were in turmoil, she was still in shock about Tehkin but was feeling a strange sense of security with the knowledge that Hope was almost her father. She didn't feel alone anymore. She started to weep for Tehkin; he was such a lovely man he didn't deserve to die. It was too soon much too soon.

"Dad, please let me go to him so I can take some of his possessions - the photo of his wife at least."

"OK Sanluin, he deserves some sort of funeral, I did know

him for over thirty years. Don't go alone though it could be fatal."

"Who can go with me? Rafievn and Cinciev are not here."

"You are forgetting Nn, it is time we started him up." Sanluin took off the rest of the suit and went to the pod where Nn was enclosed. Nn's pod was vertical unlike the others, which were lying horizontal. The droid was six feet tall and medium build. He or it, was dressed in the standard uniform like the rest of the crew.

"OK dad, what do I do now?"

"Leave it all to me, just relax." Hope sent the start up codes through to Nn. The Droid's eyes suddenly opened and Sanluin stepped back in surprise. The droid started to blink as if it were really waking up from a sleep. The skin was a synthetic material, made to look the same as a human's except that it had no hair. The head though had short brown hair. The eyes started to go brown and the pod slowly opened.

"Speak to it Sanluin!"

"What do I say?"

"Try hello for starters."

"Umm, hello Nn," said Sanluin in a stuttering voice.

"Hello Sanluin, my name is Nn, pleased to meet you," replied Nn as he held out his hand to greet Sanluin. Sanluin took the droid's hand; it was warm to touch and had a firm grip. It felt strange holding the hand of a droid, as she had never touched one before. Nn let go and walked out of the pod. Sanluin stepped aside as the Nn looked around.

"Shall I show you around the ship Nn?"

"No need Sanluin, it's all programmed in. Thank you anyway."

"We have just lost Tehkin, our pilot. I will need you to come with me, he must have some kind of funeral."

"I know Sanluin your father has informed me."

"I'll get my thermal suit and some of Tehkin's possessions then we can go to him," replied Sanluin, hurrying over to her suit.

"You have some time Sanluin, I have to get a thermal suit for myself, my circuits could freeze up in these temperatures."

"I'll get to it for you Nn."

"No need Sanluin, it's all in hand." This droid can operate the computers without even typing anything in, thought Sanluin.

"Dad, how does he work?"

"I can communicate to him by radio wave. He is updated with everything you need to know and you can also send messages to Rafievn and Cinciev through him." A useful bit of kit Sanluin thought to herself. The suit was nearly ready, Nn went to change into it and Sanluin gathered some of Tehkin's possessions. She picked up the picture of Tehkin and his wife, together with his flying cap from when he was in the forces.

"Are you ready Nn?" Sanluin called out.

"Ready Sanluin." Nn was stood by the door, he had a length or rope tied to a harness attached to his waist.

"Put this harness on Sanluin and attach the rope to it." Sanluin did as she was told and then followed Nn down the steps and out onto the snow. Nn followed the footsteps of Tehkin, not that he needed to as the co-ordinates of where Tehkin had fallen were already programmed into the droid. They walked in silence, stopping only for the hot drink Nn had prepared for Sanluin.

"We are getting close to where he fell through the snow. I will stay here, my sensors tell me this is solid snow and ice right down to the earth below. I will dig into the ice with supports and lower you down to Tehkin if you want."

"Will it be safe Nn?"

"I won't let go, your father trusts me or he would not have even let us get this far." Sanluin slowly walked to the end of Tehkin's footprints. She looked over the hole in the snow and felt fear sweep over her. She looked back at Nn who had driven Luuse alloy stakes into the ice. They were clipped to the harness on Nn.

"I will lower you when you are ready Sanluin," called

Nn. Sanluin pulled the rope until it was taught and edged to the hole where Tehkin had fallen through. Nn was slowly letting rope out. Sanluin turned to face Nn and walked backwards towards the daunting crevasse. Her boots slipped on the ice on the edge of the hole and she fell into the side of the crevasse. Holding tight, with her hands on the rope she had taken all the weight off the harness. Shaking with fear she slowly let the harness take her weight. The wall of ice in front of her glistened in what light there was. She reached into her pocket for the head torch and put it on. It fitted over the hood of the suit, which gave her a sense of security as the pressure of the strap held the hood tight to her head. She switched the light on and the vastness of the crevasse came to fruition.

Sanluin looked down and saw the shape of Tehkin lying in the ice and snow. There was metallic reflection to the left of Tehkin that turned out to be the flask he had had in his hand when he fell. Nn had a three dimensional view of proceedings which was being sent from Hope. Only 20 feet to go and Sanluin would be at the foot of the crevasse. The crevasse was almost pitch black at the bottom. Only Tehkin's communicator light shone out from his body. Sanluin's feet touched the bottom; she slid on the ice as she got her footing. She searched in her pocket for the hand torch and switched it on. The two beams of light shone out and darted around the eerie cavern of ice. It was deathly silent in there apart from her breathing. The jagged ice which formed sharp tooth like shapes loomed all around her. It seemed she was in the jaws of some giant deformed creature waiting patiently to devour its unexpected prey. Sanluin went over to Tehkin and started to sob again. He lay there on his back but looked peaceful. Sanluin knelt down next to Tehkin, and held his hand.

"I am so sorry Tehkin, you were a lovely man, and my father had so much respect for you. I wish we could have got to know each other better, there was so much left to do here. You weren't to know about the dangers of this place, none of us were. I have brought you a picture of your wife." Sanluin put the picture in his pocket wrapped in his flying cap. She went to get up but heard something from Tehkin's suit. It was the heater still working, she switched it off and then there was complete silence. She pulled the hood of Tehkin's suit up over his face and stood up. Wiping the tears from her face Sanluin put the torch back in her pocket and pulled on the rope.

As she ascended back up, Tehkin slowly vanished from view forever and shivers of fear swept over her as she saw the natural jaws formed of ice in the walls of the crevasse. Nn pulled her out at the surface. She got to her feet and brushed the snow from her suit. Nn unclipped his harness from the Luuse stakes and gathered the rope back as Sanluin walked towards him. Sanluin held her head low as she walked to Nn, he unclipped the rope and put his arm round her, they walked back to Hope leaving Tehkin in his icy tomb. In time the ice flow of the glacier he had fallen into would carry him to the sea and his final resting place. Back in Hope, Sanluin went straight to her quarters while Nn packed away the suits and prepared a meal for when Sanluin would be ready for it. Exhausted from the walk to Tehkin and back, Sanluin drifted off to sleep.

With the events of the day she had forgotten that they were going back to pick up Rafievn that night. What was almost going to be an even bigger shock than Tehkin dying, was the fact that Tehkin was the only person who could fly Hope! There was no chance of getting back to Rafievn or Cinciev now. Hope was evaluating the situation while Sanluin slept. The hardest part was to tell Sanluin the news that she was marooned in this frozen place. She could live as long as she wanted; there was enough food and water to last forever. Nn could hunt for birds and other sea life if she wanted to live down in this place on her own.

Hope had a contingency plan if anything like this was to happen. All that needed to be in place was that the communication system was working with the moon as satellite, this Hope already knew. The other thing that was essential was that Rafievn and

Cinciev had their emergency kits with them but there was one more shock that Sanluin was to confront. Hope had tested all the waste products from the ship for any signs of disease or illness in the crew. There had been no bad news but for Sanluin she would soon be feeling the first stages of pregnancy. Hope thought this would give her enough reason to carry on and try to complete the mission. The goal of the mission was to give another planet a head start in evolution. Planetician so nearly had it but all was not lost, there just had to be some luck involved.

The first of the workforce began to turn up at the monument. Rafievn was still in a deep sleep on his platform of moss. The builders started to work away on the huge stones, they were ready to hoist a lintel into place; it was one of the most dangerous parts of the job. Many people had already been crushed to death from stones falling when the lifting took place. The builders had built a slope out of earth and then dragged the lintel to the top. It was when the ropes snapped and the stones slid back down that caused the most fatalities; even bracing the stones with tree trunks sometimes wasn't enough to stop them. The builders had the stone lashed with rope made from grasses woven together. At the back of the stone, two gangs of 4 or 5 men had driven large steaks into the ground and would start the stone moving with leverage. The ropes in front of the stone went up the slope, over the top and down to two more gangs of men with about 50 on each rope. There were timbers lashing the ropes together, which gave the men good purchase for the pull. One man stood at the top of the slope and directed the whole operation. There were other men who were older than the labourers on the ground, overseeing the process. The two fifty man gangs picked up the rope by the timber and held it in their arms across their chests, taking up the slack as they leaned against the timbers. The man at the top of the slope held his hands up and called out to the two teams of men at the front and back of the stone. He then dropped his arms and the men all heaved in one sudden movement.

The sound of the ropes creaking and the groans of the men woke Rafievn with a start. He instinctively reached for his weapon. Looking up at that monument he saw what had woken him. He got out his glasses and focused on the work taking place, the strain showed on the men's faces and sweat was dripping from their foreheads. Then the man on the top of the slope called out again. Another groan from the gangs and the stone jerked forward slightly, the foreman called again to keep the momentum going but the stone held still. The gangs of men got their footings and braced themselves once more. The foreman called out and the stone edged forward about a foot up the slope.

Rafievn watching intently at the work. He had already devised an easier method of moving the stone. It seemed cruel to let these men struggle when he could show them a much easier way. The gangs toiled for most of the morning to get the stone to the top of the slope. Some of the men collapsed to the floor with exhaustion but they hadn't finished yet, they still had to get the stone on top of the uprights. The men rested for food and water while another group prepared the stone to be positioned on top of the uprights. Rafievn had realised that he hadn't sent a message to Hope that he had got back to the rendezvous point. He got out the communication set and sent the message.

Cinciev was just waking up, it was early afternoon and the sun was beating down over the desert. Heat hazes formed mirages on the crests of the sand dunes. The builders still worked on the Iaan in the distance. Cinciev was surprised how long he had slept. Getting some food from his pack he thought back to the night before and how tasty the food was he had eaten at the stall. It made him want to get back there sooner than he could, he thought of the woman and little girl and wondered what their situation was, as there was no man around or in the house. He checked his communication set but there was no reply message from Hope. Cinciev wasn't missing anyone so another few days and nights here would be no problem.

Looking down to the harbour two boats were mooring up to the jetty. There was a seat on one of the boats with what looked like a square linen tent covering it from the sun. The person who was sat on the seat looked very much like the person they had seen from Hope when they had first arrived at this place. There were about ten guards with a further fifteen on the other boat. Waiting on the jetty for the travelling party were two of the foremen overseeing the work on the Iaan. The person on the seat was helped off the boat by two guards, dressed in a more elaborate uniform than the other guards. The foremen bowed in the presence of this person as she stepped on the jetty from the boat. The group made their way up to the Iaan and one of the foremen waved to the workmen to stop. They turned round from their toil and bowed to the person. This must be their head or ruler; maybe she was their Queen, Cinciev thought to himself. The group went into one of the square buildings at the foot of the Iaan and were joined by the rest of the guards, who stood with their weapons in hand. They were armed with spears and also had foot long daggers in leather sheaths attached to their belts. Two hours had passed since the important woman and other men had entered the building. The women who had been preparing the bread for the builders brought food and drink to the building. The guards inspected the food before they were allowed in. Cinciev thought they were discussing work on the Iaan but it surely wouldn't take that long. Maybe there was other work to discuss.

Nn gently knocked on Sanluin's door. She woke still dressed in her thermal suit; it had adjusted to the temperature of the ship so that Sanluin wouldn't cook while she was asleep.

"What is it Nn?"

"I have made some food to build your strength up."

"OK Nn, I'll be out now." Sanluin changed into some comfortable clothing and went to join Nn. There was a plate of hot food waiting for her. "Thank you Nn, how long was I asleep?"

"You were out for five hours, I started your food but you

had gone into deep sleep so I kept it until now."

"I am hungry considering what has happened."

"You'll start to feel better with the food and rest." Just as Sanluin was about to start her food she looked up at Nn.

"Rafievn, we were going to meet him today. How could I forget, I have missed him so much, lets leave right away." Nn looked up at Sanluin as she headed for the Bridge.

"Wait Sanluin your dad needs to speak to you," Sanluin turned to Nn and then looked into space.

"What is it Dad? What does Nn know?"

"Sanluin please sit down," replied Hope. Sanluin went over to her seat; Nn was looking at Sanluin knowing that she would take the news very badly. "Sanluin, there is something you should know, please stay calm." Before Hope could say anymore Sanluin shouted.

"Not Rafievn, he's not dead as well. Tell me he's not."

"No Sanluin, he's fine." Pausing to speak, Hope was just as nervous as if Dr Viuuv himself was going to tell her. "When Tehkin died, part of this mission died with him. You see he was the only person who could fly this ship." Totally stunned by this news Sanluin's heart sunk to the lowest it had ever been. She felt like a weight had pulled her into her seat. Nn held out his hand to comfort Sanluin, but she just stared into space with every edge of her world and future closing in on her.

"Surely Dad, you can fly Hope, you can fly yourself?"

"If that was so we would be picking up Rafievn right now. You must understand, if I or anyone else could fly this ship they could have returned to Atronia. Only Tehkin was trusted to fly as he had the most experience and he was definitely on a one-way mission. I couldn't take the risk of it returning to Atronia, you know what that would have meant for this mission, not to mention Dr Viuuv, my real self I should say, and many others who had helped make this happen. I knew I could trust you and Tehkin; the other two were very probably OK but look what happened when Cinciev came out of hyper sleep. He could have taken over the ship. Even in years to come this ship must never leave this place, it is just too powerful. You must understand I had no choice."

"But I may never see Rafievn again, I love him Dad, I love him so much." Hope thought that now should be the time to tell Sanluin that she carried his daughter. It was chancing her emotions considering what she had gone through but the programme deep inside of Hope had deduced it was the right step to take.

"You may not see him Sanluin but you will see his daughter."

"What do you mean? Is he with someone in the north?"

"No Sanluin, you carry his daughter." Sanluin took in a huge breath at the news and instantly held her stomach.

"A baby, I am carrying his baby, we must get to him, we must." Sanluin sat in a state of shock; the whole series of events that day had left her an emotional wreck. She started to walk around the ship, confused with her feelings of what should be euphoria but shadowed by the fact that she would be alone in Hope for ever. Nn received a message from Hope to sedate Sanluin. Staying up all night would only confuse her more so Nn mixed a solution with some hot tea and took it to Sanluin who was at the controls of Hope, looking at them in bewilderment.

"Here Sanluin, drink this, it will make you feel better." Sanluin took the tea and sipped it. One hand on the mug and the other on her stomach. The controls of Hope would only react to Tehkin. They could detect his hand and fingerprints and also his chemical make up, plus he had the only codes for the ship's flight systems in his head. Dr Viuuv had not foreseen that they might venture out onto an ice cap on any new planet they might find. It had been centuries before any existed on Atronia, he just didn't allow for it. Sanluin had slumped over the controls, the sedative had kicked in. Nn picked her up and took her to her quarters. He lay her in her bed and tucked the sheets around her body. Hope was sending messages to Nn all the time, Dr Viuuv used to tuck her in like this when she was a small girl. Sanluin needed all the comfort she could get even though it was from two machines. Still taking instructions from Hope, Nn went to send messages to Rafievn and Cinciev. He told them what had happened to Tehkin and how they were marooned on the southern ice cap. He didn't tell Rafievn about Sanluin's baby, that would be left to Sanluin herself. Once the messages were sent Nn cleaned the ship, it had got in quite a mess since the death of Tehkin. Just as Nn had finished the cleaning he got another message from Hope.

Sanluin was starting to dream in a way which would cause nightmares about the recent events, Hope had been monitoring her sleep patterns since the sedation. Nn went to her room and put a skull cap on her head, Hope read the electrical impulses and then changed them to alter her dreaming to a less stressful pattern. It only took a few minutes to settle her dreaming. Nn stood and watched her return to a calm and restful sleep. He removed the cap and went back to the Bridge to read any replies from Rafievn and Cinciev.

The last of the foreman had walked down from the top of the slope; he had been looking with satisfaction at the work that had been done on the monument that day. The sun was setting and had gone past the point of the monument, which determined the longest day of the year. The whole lay out of the monument was set to the sun and its yearly cycle. Rafievn had guessed that it had something to do with the sun. He thought to himself that this was as far as any religion should go, after all the sun was the sole supplier of energy and light that gave any planet with the right conditions the miracle of life. It was only man that made up other religions, which created fear and control, and as so often back on Atronia, wars and conflict.

The foreman picked up some tools and headed back towards the settlement. From the amount of manpower on the slope today, there must be other settlements close by to supply that amount of labour. Once it was completely dark, Rafievn made his way up to the monument, full of excitement at the thought of being reunited with

Sanluin. He climbed the slope where the stone had been dragged and sat on top of the stone lintel. His communicator bleeped and he quickly read the message. He couldn't believe what he was reading; he read it twice then threw the communicator to the ground.

"No!" he shouted. The foreman who was nearly at the settlement looked back in the direction of the strange noise, it sounded like no other animal he had ever heard before. Rafievn gathered his pack and ran down the slope, he started to run back to his platform in the tree when he remembered his communicator. He didn't know that the foreman was on his way back to the monument with two other men to investigate the strange noise that had echoed down to the settlement. Rafievn was frantically looking for the communicator when he heard the other men coming towards him. He hid behind one of the stone lintels on the ground and still being dressed for fitting. He reached for his weapon and waited for the men to go. They talked quietly and looked for any sign that the animal, which made the strange noise, might have left. The foreman then spotted the communicator in the grass and alerted the others.

Rafievn couldn't see them but knew they had seen the communicator. The foreman picked it up and looked at it with puzzled amazement. This strange object rectangular in shape, he held it up to show the others and compared it to the shapes of the stones they had been erecting and dressing for generations. Suddenly the communicator bleeped, it was Cinciev trying to contact Rafievn about their predicament. The foreman dropped the communicator to the ground and the three surrounded it as if it was going to attack them. They started to prod it with some sticks used for lashing the pulling ropes together. Rafievn heard the communicator being prodded around the floor; if this got broken he would never be able to contact Sanluin again. Rafievn stood up from behind the lintel, the three men stared at him. Rafievn's camouflage was turned off and it was the first time these people had set eyes on him.

Rafievn was at least a foot taller than the tallest of the

men. The Foreman shouted at Rafievn and held the stick up in an aggressive manner. Without hesitation Rafievn pointed the weapon at him and let off two stun shots. He fell to the floor still holding the stick. The other two turned to run, Rafievn calmly fired off two shots at each of them, and they stumbled to the floor rolling over with their momentum.

Rafievn went over to the communicator and picked it up, it seemed OK but the screen was cracked. He put it in his pocket and went over to the first of the three men he had stunned. The man was well muscled and his hands gripping the stick were very worn and calloused, he had one finger missing on his left hand. The scarring showed it had been burnt to stop the bleeding at the time of the accident. Rafievn rolled the man into the recovery position and checked his pulse; he was fine apart from the pungent body odour that was making Rafievn heave. He went over to the other two and checked them. One had fallen and banged his head on a stone very badly; there was no pulse. Quickly Rafievn tried to resuscitate him. He tried in vain but the man was already dead. He didn't mean to kill him but he had had to stun the man, he only wished he had done it quicker; the man might not have fallen when running and might still be alive. Rafievn felt guilty for the poor man, he wondered if he had family to fend for. There was no time to dwell on the accident.

Running back to his pack Rafievn got out the rest of the emergency kit. There was a piece of equipment that could eradicate the memories of the stunned men. Rafievn ran back to the three men and pulled out a sensor from the small silver box. He placed it on the temple of the Foreman and set the programme to eradicate the last two hours of memory. It took about five minutes and the task was complete. He did the same to the other stunned man. They would wake up not knowing what they were doing there. He wondered what they would think when they saw their dead friend and what they would do with him.

Rafievn's actions were on autopilot during the incident and

as he walked back to the forest he cleared his mind from the fatality as he had done when on missions back on Atronia. Back on his tree platform he looked at his broken communicator. He could send messages but could not read any because of the broken screen. He sent a message to Hope telling them what had happened. Rafievn programmed the communicator for self-repair and the screen started to mend itself. The nano-system in the set could repair any part or component but it would take a few hours to do so.

Cinciev was eagerly waiting for a reply from Rafievn but there was nothing. He sent a message back to Hope to see if there was anything wrong. A reply came back from Nn; he told Cinciev that the communication set was self-repairing after an incident at the monument. Rafievn was OK but there had been an accidental fatality from a stun shot to one of the natives. Cinciev felt helpless in his rocky gully but was also thinking about what his own future was going to be, now that he was stranded with these people and their strange buildings. Cinciev thought he would try and get hold of one of the boats that these people used to sail on the river, maybe he could get to Rafievn. He sent a message to Hope, he wanted to know his global position and Rafievn's; this would give him some scale of the task to try to get to Rafievn. The message came back and Cinciev was quite confident that the distance was achievable. But could these boats that sailed this great river, manage it? That is, if he could get a boat and crew together in the first place.

There would be much to plan if there was any chance of ever getting to Rafievn. Walking the distance would take years and be fraught with danger. He started to wonder if it would be worth the effort. He sent a message back to Hope asking for a route by sea or by land. Back on Hope, Nn was receiving instructions from Hope that any journey attempted by either Rafievn or Cinciev would jeopardise the whole mission. Nn sent messages to the two men that they were to stay put and wait for Sanluin to come out of sedation, they could then communicate with her. Hope thought how she could be much more persuasive being human rather than a machine.

Both Rafievn and Cinciev had stayed awake all night waiting for Sanluin's communication. They had stayed in their hiding places eagerly waiting for their instructions. Feeling very lethargic, Sanluin sat up on her bed. Nn knocked on her door as he was monitoring her every move.

"Are you OK Sanluin? Can I get you anything?"

"Some water, please Nn." She got up and went to the galley, Nn was just returning with the water. He handed her the cup and she gulped it down in one.

"Can I get you some more, you seem very thirsty?"

"No thanks Nn, you're too kind, have a rest."

"I don't need rest, I am powered by a gravity cell like everything else your dad had designed for this mission."

"I forgot Nn, it's because you are as thoughtful as a human, and a good one at that."

"Your father needs to talk to you about what the plan is for Rafievn and Cinciev." Every time Sanluin heard Rafievn's name it ached her heart. It hadn't sunk in yet that she would never see him again in the flesh. Sitting at the table in the galley she looked at Nn and smiled at the company she would be spending the rest of her life with. That is until her baby was born. Suddenly she felt better thinking about her baby. It gave her drive and a reason to carry on. Hope could sense this from her thoughts and was preparing to tell her how the rest of the mission was to be carried out under these different circumstances.

"How are you feeling Sanluin, I hope the rest has made you feel better. Rafievn and Cinciev are waiting for further instructions from us. I have already contacted them about Tehkin and that we are marooned here. We need to take a different course of action so that this planet can benefit from our coming." The word marooned seemed less shocking compared to a few hours ago.

"What are we to do now? The people that live here have got

no chance of finding us, they are far from being advanced enough to develop ways to get to this place."

"They are now, but in the future they will be able to get here and understand our technology and what power it can offer them."

"But Dad, you are surely talking centuries of evolution."

"I have evaluated all possibilities. If we try to leave some sort of map, it would not only have a good chance of getting lost but could upset the balance of their evolution if we were found before they could fully understand our purpose for coming here."

"What do you suggest then? Do Rafievn and Cinciev have their survival kits with them?"

"Yes they have them, Rafievn prepared both check lists for their observations of the two separate groups of people."

"That is the most vital point of the contingency plan. In the kits there are nano-genetic blank solutions, which can be programmed. Once they are active they need to be kept at body temperature or the genetic strain will break down and be lost. If Rafievn and Cinciev inject the active solution into their blood stream the genetic programme will be able to pass from generation to generation, from both male to female and visa versa. The nano -programme will lay dormant until I activate it."

"You're saying if they have children the nano-genetic programme will be passed on with no harm to the person unless activated."

"That's correct." Sanluin sat in silence knowing that Rafievn will have to sleep with other women for this to work. It was hard for her to bear but there would be no point in this mission if they stopped now. She had to shut the thought from her mind, as she knew the feelings were very strong between her and Rafievn and that they were totally in love. But what Rafievn has to do would not be betrayal. It would just be necessary.

"OK Dad, I understand."

"I am sorry Sanluin, I know you love Rafievn but we have

no choice. I feel for him as well, I see him as a son now."

"Considering the present stage of evolution, how long before the nano-genetic programme can be activated?"

"I have studied the two civilisations and comparing them to our own planet's history, we would be talking somewhere in the region of 4,000 years. By then this world will be a much different place, as you know civilisations rise and fall. If you looked at Atronia 4,000 years ago, would you have foreseen how it has turned out today? It is a very big risk Sanluin but it's the only chance we have."

"Can I tell Rafievn and you can contact Cinciev?"

"Of course Sanluin, I would have asked you to do it that way anyhow." Sanluin took a communicator and went to her quarters, she sent the message by thought waves; it was a long message full of her feelings and hopes that Rafievn would be ready to carry on with the mission. Nn sent the message to Cinciev who read it immediately. On this instruction Cinciev sat down and started to think of ways how to integrate into the society that lived in the town he had visited the night before.

Rafievn's set was finally fixed and he held it eagerly waiting for news from Hope or Cinciev. It bleeped in his hands and he was glad to see the message was from Sanluin. After reading the message Rafievn thought how hard it must have been for Sanluin to accept this plan. To him it would mean nothing to his feelings, it would just be part of the mission. Sanluin hadn't told him about the baby she felt it was too soon into the pregnancy, she didn't want to build up his hopes only to be dashed by a possible miscarriage. Rafievn sent another message to Sanluin. He also sent one to Cinciev agreeing with Hope that they should stay with the separate groups of people and not try to get to each other. It could be fatal and that would risk everything. With the three of them knowing what they had to do they could all help each other with support and company, even though it would only be through the communicators.

Sanluin and Rafievn sent messages back and forth all night.

They were so dedicated to each other but not letting the situation of being apart distract them from the mission. They had accepted the responsibility to this planet and these people. They would not let their own misfortune ruin other lives, which could eventually ruin the lives of billions of people in the future. They didn't want Planetician to fall to the same fate Atronia was heading for. They both accepted that this forced sacrifice of being apart was the burden they had to carry for the rest of their lives, but with the understanding they both had and the dedication to the mission, it made them feel closer together and helped a little, to cope with being apart.

Integration.

Rafievn thought long and hard how he would approach these people and become one of their own. His best chance was to help them with the monument, but how? He remembered how they had struggled with moving the stones and how he had thought of much easier ways of transporting heavy objects, even with the materials they had. After dark Rafievn went up to the monument and got a small piece of stone, it was nearly rectangular and would pass for a scaled down model of one of the uprights or lintels. With saplings he had gathered during the day, Rafievn started to build his scaled down model of how to move the stones more easily. He would have to hunt for Riind so that he could make skins for clothing, he couldn't approach the foreman of the monument dressed in his normal clothing, he would have to look like one of the natives. He would also need Riind skin to cover his pack. The hunting would start that night. The busier Rafievn kept his mind the less he dwelt on the fact of never seeing Sanluin again. It was a strange feeling for him, he felt broken-hearted but not completely, as in the back of his mind he had Sanluin, always.

Cinciev was preparing himself for his second visit to the town. He was eager to get there but not because he needed to keep his mind busy but, he wanted to see that woman again. She kept coming into his thoughts. There was only one other woman who had had that effect on him and that was his wife many years before. He needed to get some more material to cover some of his equipment so that next time he went into the town, he would feel more secure knowing that it was well hidden. He looked in his kit and searched for something that he could trade with and found that his spare clothes were the only items he had that would not gather too much attention. He managed to cover his weapon on his hip by rearranging his kilt. Cinciev was tempted to walk down in the day but felt he should rest as he had been up all night. The thought of the food stall was making him hungry but he made do with a snack from his rations before getting some sleep. The heat of the day was keeping Cinciev awake so he got out his sleeping bag and on turned the air conditioning element to a comfortable temperature and within minutes, he was drifting off.

Night started to fall and the sounds of wild Suugs echoed across the cooling sand, their barks and howls woke Cinciev. He rubbed his eyes not knowing whether it was early morning or evening. He had been in a deep sleep and came to his senses slowly. Climbing out of his sleeping bag, he put on his borrowed sandals and made sure that his weapon wasn't visible in his kilt. Gathering two undershirts from his kit to trade with, he set off down to the town. He had walked a few hundred yards when it struck him that he hadn't covered his kit. Rushing back to the gully he quickly covered his pack and set off again thinking to himself that there was no rush, he had the rest of his days to fill after all.

Rafievn had almost completed his model, it just needed rope to give it the final touches. The sun had almost set and he was ready to go off hunting the Riind. He would use the tendon of the Riind for the rope on his model. Putting his glasses on and setting them to night vision, he jumped from the platform and made off into the forest. His scanner showed animals about half a mile away. The wind was in his face so there was no chance of the Riind smelling his scent. Rafievn slowed down as he approached the Riind, there were two groups grazing about 50 feet in front of him. The group to the left were younger, they would be easier to skin he thought. Setting the weapon to kill mode, Rafievn fired off two shots. The shots flew silently and felled two Riind as if they just decided to lie down on the ground, while the others didn't even notice what had happened. Rafievn walked up to the fallen Riind and the others ran off, darting through the forest dodging the trees as if it were in daylight. By a stroke of luck there was a nearby tree that would be suitable for stringing the Riind up to be skinned. This was good news as they would be a struggle to move very far on his own.

Tethering the hind legs together on the larger of the two, Rafievn hoisted the animal up so it hung about two foot from the ground. Taking his knife from his kit he started to skin the animal. The blade cut through the skin with ease, it peeled away from the carcass, which steamed in the cool night air. Rafievn had them both skinned in under an hour. The inside of the skins would need scraping to keep the hide soft and malleable, but there was no even surface to lay them on. There would be at the monument, the stones would be ideal. Before leaving the skinned carcasses Rafievn cut chunks of meat from them to eat later. The animals crumpled to a heap as he cut them down. He then cut the tendons from the legs; they would be a good tying cord for the clothes he was to make. It was starting to get light when the last skin had been scraped, which proved to be much harder than the skinning itself.

Gathering up the hides Rafievn made his way back to his platform in the tree, his hands still stained with the blood of the Riinds. He wiped the worst off in the damp moss that clung to the trunk on the fallen tree. Before getting some sleep Rafievn ate some of the meat he had cut from the Riind. He tenderised it first then devoured it with gluttony as he was starving from the night's work. It was early afternoon before Rafievn woke and he started work on the skins for his new clothing straight away.

Cinciev was walking to the town with much more confidence now after his first visit. He went straight to the food vendor who recognised him straight away. The vendor called Cinciev over and prepared him some of the meat in the bread. While the meat was cooking Cinciev offered the vendor one of the undershirts in a trade. The vendor looked at the garment with wonder, he had never seen an item like it. He examined the stitching closely and was amazed at how stretchy the material was. He said something to Cinciev in his native tongue, Cinciev just nodded back in agreement. The vendor looked a bit puzzled as to what the garment was actually for and handed it back to Cinciev. Cinciev put the undershirt on and the vendor said something else and then came around from his stall to inspect the shirt. Cinciev took it off and handed it back, the man took it and tried to put it on. He had never worn anything like it and had trouble getting it on. He tried to put his head through the armhole. Cinciev laughed as he helped him put the shirt on. The vendor was extremely proud of his new item of clothing; he stuck his chest out while stroking the fabric and proceeded to give Cinciev a large portion of meat and three pieces of bread in return. More people came over to the stall to admire the strange garment the vendor was wearing; he was the centre of attention, which helped boost his trade for a while.

Cinciev ate his food and moved on feeling absolutely stuffed and in need of a drink. He passed what looked like a drinking house, there was no food to be seen and it was full mostly of men. The only women he spotted seemed to be offering themselves to some of the men. They were prostitutes plying their trade to any of the inebriated men, young or old. Cinciev was keen to try the brew the men were drinking; he hadn't tasted any alcohol since leaving Atronia, so he went back to the food stall and tried to ask the vendor for some money to buy a drink. He pointed at the drinking house and the vendor soon got the message. He handed Cinciev some coins and slapped him on the arm, waving him in the direction of the drinking house. Cinciev went into the house which was loud with the laughter of the men, the deep tones of male laughter were sometimes over shadowed by the cackle of one of the prostitutes. There were jugs of a brown liquid on the tables and the men were drinking from smaller clay mugs, some drank from mugs fashioned from a type of metal. Cinciev went over to the bar and waved to the man behind the bar. The man came over and asked him something. Cinciev pointed to a jug and the man fetched a jug full to the brim, he put a clay mug next to the jug and said something else, at which Cinciev held out his hand with the coins in for the man to take. Cinciev took the jug and filled his mug, he turned to face the other men who were drinking away and laughing. He sniffed the brew and then took a sip; it was odd tasting but it definitely had alcohol in it. There was a tap on his shoulder and the man who served him the drink gave him some coins back; it must be change Cinciev thought, taking the money and nodding in acceptance. He took a good gulp and felt his body shudder at the strength of the drink. Cinciev couldn't help thinking how amazing it was that these people made the same drink as the people on Atronia had done many centuries before. This made him feel more at home, even though it was a different planet and time. He drank the jug dry and started to feel the effect of the alcohol. He waved to the person behind the bar and held the empty jug up, the man replaced it with another full one, Cinciev held out his hand with the coins in and the man took only what the beer cost.

One of the prostitutes came up to Cinciev; she had had her back to him since he had entered the house. He recognised her, it was the woman from the first night he had been in the town. He was shocked that she was a prostitute; why would such a beautiful woman work in such a trade? She touched Cinciev's face and said something to him. It was such a soft touch and her voice was warming to his ears. Not knowing what she said, Cinciev offered her some of the beer. She refused the offer but seemed to ask a question of Cinciev, who was only able to shrug his shoulders, not knowing what she said. He put the mug of beer down and told her his name. She looked slightly puzzled; he said his name again and pointed to himself. She replied by pointing to her self and said 'Ashait'. They repeated this once more to each other and had finally established their names; at least this was a start. Still with no idea what they were saying to each other they kept on talking. The two of them couldn't help laughing at themselves. Cinciev asked about her daughter and put his hand to his side to show the height of the person he was asking about. Ashait knew that he was asking about her daughter and put her hands to the side of her face to show that her daughter was asleep. During the two hours they spent together in the drinking house they had established their ages, names and the fact that Cinciev was alone. Ashait asked Cinciev to leave with her, finishing his last mug of beer he followed her out of the door.

Out in the fresh air Cinciev felt the full effect of the beer, he swayed on his feet and Ashait had to steady him. She giggled as he struggled to stay upright. Through his blurred vision he recognised the tree which he had sat by on the first night he came to the town. Ashait ushered him into her house, once inside she sat Cinciev down and cleared some clothing from the bed. Ashait helped Cinciev up to the bed; she sat him on the edge of the bed and took off his sandals. Cinciev felt he was in no fit state to do anything except sleep off his beer. He slumped on the mattress and fell asleep; Ashait lay next to him and watched him sleep until she herself fell off to sleep.

Rafievn kept watch on the workers at the monument; he didn't want any of them to come close to his look out while he was making his new Riind hide clothes. He was almost done with the main part of the clothing; it hung over his shoulder and was stitched to meet round his waist, covering his thighs half way down. He copied this style from what the foreman was wearing at the monument. The off-cuts of skin would just about do for shoes and there were enough tendons left for laces. Rafievn thought that it would be too late to go to the monument that day with the model he had made, he would leave it until the next day when he would be fresh from a good night's sleep. The shoes were finished and the model was ready. It was in full working order so hopefully the native people would understand what he was trying to show them. He had made a model of a large stone being dragged on two rails of timber that were stripped of their bark, to illustrate a more efficient alternative to their method of using rolling logs. Stripping the timber of bark would also make the stone slide more easily and Rafievn had greased the rails of the model with animal fat, to show how this would cut down the friction between the timbers. He sent a message to Sanluin keeping her updated with his plan. He also sent a scan of his idea with the message, which was a photo of the model, he didn't send a photo of himself as he didn't want to upset Sanluin.

Back on Hope, Sanluin was pleased to receive the message.

"Dad, I have got news from Rafievn. He has developed an idea which will make the monument building much easier, he is going to use it to try to make contact with the people there."

"I have seen it Sanluin, you seem to forget that all messages come to me first. The idea is a good one, it is not too far advanced for them to understand and it won't change their evolution. We have to be careful not to let any modern technology reach them. This could speed up their evolution; they need to find their own way. Tell Rafievn to go ahead with his plan and if you want to send something personal inform me and I won't monitor it."

"Thanks dad. I'll tell him to go ahead." Sanluin sent the message, most of which Hope would not read.

Cinciev started to wake, he was very hung over from the beer and didn't know where he was at first. Ashait had got up and was making a drink at the end of the house. She came over to him and knelt by the side of the bed. Cinciev looked up at her, she was so beautiful. She reached out and stroked his head, her hand was cool on his head, which pounded from inside with the effect of the alcohol. Ashait handed him the drink and said something as she did. It must be something like 'drink this', in her language Cinciev thought to himself. He took the mug and sniffed the brew; it was hot and smelled of mint. He sipped it; it was very sweet but instantly made him feel better. Ashait said something else as he drank. Cinciev wished he knew her language, there was so much he wanted to tell her and even more he wanted to ask. He noticed that the little girl had not been around in the night or in the morning, he asked and held his hand at about the height of the girl. Ashait knew what he meant and told him that she was at her home, which was a day's walk away. Cinciev didn't have a clue what she said but nodded in agreement.

The drink had made the hangover seem a fraction of what it felt like when he woke. Cinciev got up and looked around the house, noticing that it was very simple with mud brick walls and a timber and reed roof. The floor was stone and had been laid in a haphazard and random style. One end of the house was used as a kitchen; there were fish hanging and drying and an array of fruits and vegetables in reed baskets. Ashait had prepared a breakfast for Cinciev of fresh chopped fruits, some of which Cinciev had never seen before. He sat at the table and ate the bowl of fruit, savouring the flavours; the juices made his mouth salivate. The sugar from the fruit was quickly absorbed into his blood stream and this made him feel even better. Washing the meal down with fresh water Cinciev felt fully refreshed. He went over to Ashait who was tidying the bed.

"Thank you for your hospitality, you have been very kind." Cinciev held out his hand and offered Ashait some money. She seemed very offended by this gesture and gave Cinciev a stern look.

"I am not like the other women in that place, I came in because of you, I wanted to see you and not for money." Ashait pushed his hand away. Cinciev was startled by the reaction, but also in a way relieved that she was not a prostitute. He apologised and held her hand, he stroked her face as he apologised. She felt the sincerity of his apology but just wanted to understand his foreign tongue. It was a language she had never heard before, even from the different people that came from far up the river or from the great sea to the north. Ashait seemed to accept the apology and Cinciev felt much more at ease. He didn't want to offend her as she had been so kind. Cinciev remembered what he had come to the town for in the first place when he saw the linen sheets on the bed. He picked up the corner of one and asked Ashait where he could get them from. She replied by saying the name of them. Cinciev remembered the pictures drawn onto the stone; he drew a picture of a man standing by a stall in the dust on the floor. After a few attempts Ashait got the message that Cinciev wanted to buy some sheets. She went to the end of the bed and picked up a headscarf, which was draped on the bedpost, she put it over her head and took Cinciev by the hand. They went to the market place, which was a hive of activity. There were many stalls with all sorts of goods ranging from dried fish to furniture; the sound of the traders and customers bartering over the goods gave the place a lively atmosphere. Cinciev still held the hand of Ashait in one hand and the undershirt in the other.

They made their way through the throng of people to the linen stall where there were rolls of white linen on the table. The sun glared off the fabric, causing them both to squint.

"How much for this roll?" Cinciev asked the trader. The man who was young and very slightly built looked in puzzlement at Cinciev. Ashait gabbled something to the trader and they started to barter; it sounded almost like an argument as they haggled over the linen. Eventually the trader clapped his hands and held out his right hand for the money. Ashait looked at Cinciev who was fumbling for the money he had been given the night before by the food vendor. He handed her the money and she picked out some coins and handed them to the trader. Ashait pointed at the roll and Cinciev picked it up and carried it on his shoulder. The fabric was hot to his skin after being heated by the sun. Ashait gave Cinciev back his money and he put it away in a fold in his kilt. Suddenly, Cinciev went hot and cold all over as he realised he didn't have his weapon on him. If that got into the wrong hands or any hands, it could have devastating results. Cinciev pulled Ashait by the hand to go back but she was browsing at the goods on the other stalls.

"Please Ashait we have to go back to the house," said Cinciev in a panicked voice. She seemed to be aware that something was wrong so she hurried back with Cinciev, pushing through the crowds. As soon as they were back at the house Cinciev looked for his weapon, he tried to look around without Ashait noticing what he was looking for. She seemed puzzled by his behaviour but then he was so different from anyone else she just put it down to that. Cinciev spotted the weapon by the leg of the bed by the wall, it must have fallen out during the night. A sense of relief swept over him and he felt totally relaxed.

He took the linen off his shoulder which was slightly damp from his perspiration and rolled it out to see the size of his purchase. It totally covered the bed and hung over the sides reaching the floor; there would be plenty to cover his pack he thought but Ashait had other ideas. She pulled Cinciev close to her and kissed him on the lips. Cinciev was a bit surprised but kissed her back passionately. They fell to the bed and made love for the rest of the day. They fell in and out of sleep together and by dusk Cinciev had lost count how many times they had made love. Ashait got up to get some drinks as they were both parched. She walked to fetch the water from the jug in the cool store in the corner of the house. Cinciev admired her body and her black hair, which fell in ringlets down her back. They drank from the same mug and ate some fruits which were semi dry but sweet. They had a stone in the middle, which nearly chipped one of Cinciev's molars. After their snack Cinciev got dressed in his kilt and sandals.

"I have to go back to get some things, I'll be a while." Cinciev drew in the floor a man walking and a moon then a sun. He tried to say that he would be back in the morning. Ashait held his arm."

"Don't go, please stay with me, I will make you happy." She drew a picture of two people in a house and pointed at Cinciev, then the taller figure in the picture and then at herself and the shorter figure. She was asking Cinciev to live with her. It seemed to be going too quick but then where else did he have to go? He didn't want to go back to the rock gully to sleep. He did find this woman very attractive and felt very comfortable with her. Cinciev got back into bed and thought he would go back to the gully tomorrow to get his things. After all what was the rush, and his mission now was to breed so he'd better get some practice in.

Rafievn had been awake since very early in the morning. He couldn't sleep with the following day's events on his mind and thought over and over how these people might react to him. He was going to them unarmed apart from his weapon on stun, with something to offer, so what reason would they have to be hostile towards him? The only real worry was the earlier encounter he had with the three men at the monument. He just hoped that the memory erase had worked on them. All the equipment was new and Rafievn didn't know if it had been tested.

In the distance he could hear the faint calls of a Ceook crowing. Dawn was approaching and with it the inevitable meeting with these people. Rafievn was tense and very nervous, if this went wrong, how could he approach them again? Instead of dwelling on these thoughts he gathered his new skins and dropped them to the forest floor. He climbed down clutching the model in one arm and standing in just his under shorts, he dressed into the skins. He rubbed dirt and some animal fat into his face, arms and legs so that he would look more like the people who built the monument as they were also covered in grime.

Looking up at the monument the first of the builders started to assemble one of the large uprights that had been dragged to the site. They were starting to excavate the foundation hole for the stone. Rafievn thought he would wait for more builders and especially one of the older foremen. He thought of Sanluin back in Hope and what she might be doing. He couldn't help but feel for her being cooped up in the ship with only Nn and the ship's main computer to talk to.

Looking through his glasses he spotted one of the foremen who was wearing skins himself, as the morning had brought a fine drizzle with it. Rafievn started to walk out of the forest; he was full of fear and anxiety. Every step seemed to enhance his feelings. He was about fifty feet from the men digging the foundation hole. None of them had seen him coming as they were too busy with their heads down digging. Rafievn could see the foreman standing near the centre of the inner circle of stones. He was talking to two other men who were also dressed in skins. Rafievn was standing right by the foundation hole now and looked into where the men were digging. He felt his sphincter twitch with fear as one of the men looked up at him but he just looked away and carried on digging. Rafievn felt much more at ease as his disguise seemed to have worked. Walking on slowly to where the foreman was standing, Rafievn saw that one of the men talking to the foreman was one of the men he had encountered at the monument; he just hoped that the memory erase had worked. The man noticed Rafievn walking up to them and thankfully seemed not to recognise him. It had worked Rafievn thought to himself. The man spoke to the foreman and the foreman turned around to face Rafievn who was just feet away from them.

"I have something that will help you with your work," said Rafievn with a trembling voice. The three men looked at Rafievn and then to themselves in complete puzzlement.

"Who are you? Where have you come from?" asked the foreman in his strange tongue.

"Look what I have made for you, it will help you." Rafievn held the model up to them and they all looked and recognised that it was a smaller version of the stones they were using. The difference was that the stone was on wooden runners, they had never even thought of such an idea. They all studied the model with great interest. The man Rafievn had stunned, pushed the stone in its wooden cradle and it slid with ease on the greased wooden rails. He turned and said something to the foreman who came up to Rafievn and spoke again to him. Rafievn could sense that they he was suspicious of him but was sure that they were impressed with the model. The man who Rafievn had stunned took the model from him and placed it in the ground. Then all three started to talk to Rafievn at once, they gabbled away and Rafievn just stood there completely helpless, not knowing what to say. They were getting more nervous about this stranger who spoke a strange language and before Rafievn knew it, he was surrounded by people who just looked at him and all seemed to be saying the same words. He thought that he'd make a run for it but knew it would make them even more nervous.

The foreman spoke out loud and they all stopped. He gave orders to a few of the men who grabbed Rafievn by the arms; he did not resist but was frightened for his life. Another man grabbed a stick that was used for lashing between the pulling ropes and placed it across Rafievn's shoulders. The two men then lashed Rafievn's arms to the stick and walked away. Standing there thinking he was going to be killed, Rafievn thought it best to keep quiet. The foreman ordered the two men he was talking with to get the model and Rafievn. They all started to walk off in the direction of the village. The two men walking either side of Rafievn, and the foreman out in front. The other men went back to work as the four walked off. Rafievn felt slightly better, but wondered if he was going to be publicly killed in front of the village. The men either side looked up at Rafievn who was a good foot taller than themselves. With his arms lashed to the stick Rafievn could smell his own body odour, at least he was starting to smell like the locals now.

They had walked for a good half hour and started to enter the edge of the village. Ceooks ran around the place freely and there were some Faiis in a pen who were grazing on hay. The women and children came out of their huts to see the commotion. Rafievn was taken to the central hut, which he had seen on the scanner from Hope just days earlier. How different things had turned out since then. The foreman turned to Rafievn and sat him down on a log outside the hut. One of the men stayed and guarded Rafievn while the foreman went into the hut with the model. The foreman said something to one of the women as he entered the hut. She hurried off and returned with a simple clay bowl. She handed it to Rafievn's mouth and poured the contents, which turned out to be water. The water dribbled down his chin and onto his chest. Rafievn was so relieved with this hospitable gesture - it was the first time for what seemed ages, he felt he wasn't going to be killed. The woman was only young but looked very worn and haggard. Rafievn nodded in appreciation to the offering. There was talking going on inside the hut and it sounded good from the tones. From time to time different people came out and looked at Rafievn, studied him and then went back inside the hut. A boy came over to Rafievn and instantly he noticed it was the boy he had stunned in the forest. The boy looked closely at Rafievn and rubbed his hand as he did. It was his scar that he rubbed. The boy had no idea that this stranger had caused the scar but it still gave Rafievn a bit of concern, as the boy rubbed his hand constantly. Maybe it was the tissue still healing that was causing it to itch Rafievn thought.

"How is the wound young man?" asked Rafievn. The boy looked back at Rafievn, then his hand and then ran off to one of the huts. The boy seemed to understand what he had said but it didn't worry Rafievn. Then five men came out of the hut and stood in front of Rafievn with the model. The guard helped Rafievn to his feet. The foreman pulled out a flint axe and swung it towards Rafievn who ducked, and the axe hit the lashings on the stick instead of his head. The foreman cut the other lashing and the stick across Rafievn's shoulders fell to the floor. His arms fell to his side and the blood rushed back into them, giving them a tingling sensation. Still slightly frightened by the situation Rafievn stayed silent but looked at the model and grinned, thinking that it had saved his life. He was taken to a hut near to the pen with the Faiis. Inside there were a couple of beds made from young trees and the mattresses were made of grasses and reeds. It must be nearly midday he though and was starting to feel hungry.

Looking out of the hut he saw a Ceook getting caught by one of the women, she held it by it's feet and then rung it's neck. It flapped it's wings as it died and the woman's arm jerked with the movement. She strung the bird up and started to pluck it. Another woman cut the bird's throat, the blood poured out onto the floor and splashed on the woman's legs but she didn't seem to mind. There was a guard by the door of the hut and he said something to Rafievn as he looked at the bird being plucked. He either said that it was his food or, that was what they were going to do to him.

Rafievn went back into the hut and waited for what was in store for him. He just hoped it was going to be cooked Ceook. Sitting on the bed he still felt nervous about what these people were going to do with him but things were looking up so far. He noticed that the timbers used for the roof were not stripped of their bark. Rafievn stood on the bed and pulled some of the bark away from the branch rafter. It peeled away quite easily as the timber had been recently felled. Some of the rafters seemed to be older so maybe the roof had needed repairing at some stage. It was a good sign that the bark would strip easily. It would make the full-scale building of the model, much quicker.

The foreman suddenly came into the hut, Rafievn jumped down from the bed as the foreman beckoned him over to the door. The foreman took hold of Rafievn by the arm and took him to the central hut; there was smoke coming out of the centre of the roof and the smell of cooking wafted towards them. They entered the hut and there were all the elder men of the settlement stood around a large table. There were eleven of them, all with long grey beards; some were strongly built but there were three who were very old and looked like they hadn't done manual work for years. The top of the table had been made from young trees, lashed together and the legs were from similar sized branches. The foreman sat Rafievn on a bench, which creaked with his weight. The other men sat down and the sound of creaking was quickly muffled as it was absorbed by the grass and timber roof. There were two women cooking over the fire which crackled away, the Ceook was being turned on a small spit and as the timber that speared the bird started to smoke, one of the women cooled it with water, catching the excess in a bowl to stop it dousing the fire.

Rafievn's model was in the middle of the table. It was obviously going to be the talking point of the meeting. The only problem was that Rafievn had no idea what they were going to say. All the men just looked straight at Rafievn who was sat opposite them. The foreman was sat beside Rafievn as if to show off his catch and the idea that had come with it. Then one of the older men got up and walked over to Rafievn, he bent down to speak and Rafievn could smell his breath which was terrible from rotting teeth. Rafievn didn't want to be rude by leaning away from the stench, so he just sat there and stomached it as the old man examined him, gabbling away as he did so. Eventually he walked away, to Rafievn's relief. He just hoped none of the others would come over, as they probably stank much the same. Rafievn was just glad that the food was not ready; he couldn't eat with the breath on one side and the body odour of the foreman on the other. Three women came in carrying fruit and a type of bread on rough wooden plates. The women cooking the Ceook brought the bird over still on the stick and placed it on an empty stone slab, which had been warming on the fire. The fat of the bird spat as it touched the hot stone and the foreman nudged Rafievn to start. Rafievn was grateful for this as there was no cutlery and he didn't want to have to eat the bird after the others had mauled it; their hands didn't look exactly clean. He got up and pulled off a leg, it came away easily which showed that it was well cooked. Putting some fruit and bread with it he sat down. As soon as he sat the others seemed to attack the bird in a frenzy. This must be a rare occasion Rafievn thought to himself as he ate the leg. It tasted delicious; it was the first hot food he had eaten in days. The skin was crispy and the flesh quite tender, the bird couldn't have been very old. One of the women came back in carrying a leather sack. She put it on the table and walked back out. The leather bag was full of a liquid, Rafievn waited until one of the others drank from it. The oldest looking man took the bag and held it over his mouth, tipping it up. Water came out of the shaped spout without the bag touching the man's mouth. Rafievn was glad it didn't come into contact with the man and he picked up the bag and drank before anyone else. The water had an odd taste to it - it must have been the leather, tainting the water. The sounds of the men eating were enough to put anyone off their food, especially when they started to belch out loud and break wind. Rafievn hurried his fruit that consisted of berries and 'leeps', which were quite sharp. The other men had nearly finished their food at the same time as Rafievn, they must have been hungry he thought to himself.

One of the men stood up and called to the women who came in and cleared the table leaving the model in the middle. He bent over and pushed the stone on the runners saying to Rafievn that it was going to help them very much with their work. Rafievn nodded in reply, not knowing what he said. The headmen of the village couldn't understand why Rafievn didn't speak; they found it very frustrating but were glad that he had offered them his help.

Rafievn would try to get to know their language and wondered if he could use any of his equipment to do so. As soon as he got back to his kit he would ask Hope if some programme codes could be sent to do the translating. It might be days before he could get back to his kit without being noticed. He was desperate to hear from Sanluin.

The snow around Hope's stabilisers had drifted up to her hull. Sanluin hadn't been outside since the death of Tehkin, she had cocooned herself inside the ship, and her excitement of this frozen place had been completely eroded by the accident. Only the life, which grew inside her kept her going. She had to give the child a life even though it would only be inside Hope, she may venture outside again but she wasn't ready yet. She hadn't told Rafievn of his baby, it was too soon; she wanted him to get integrated with the people building the monument before she told him.

There had been no news from Rafievn or Cinciev for hours,

she was not too worried about Cinciev but she would not know what to do if something happened to Rafievn. Since Nn had been operational there was nothing to do around the ship anymore as he would clean and prepare meals. Sanluin felt spoilt but was enjoying her time and thoughts without having to do any work. It had helped her come to terms with her predicament. Every time she thought of Rafievn the pain of not seeing him would come back so she switched her thoughts to the baby, this helped her cope with missing Rafievn. She had long conversations with Hope, she talked about the time when she was younger and Hope responded with the full memory of her father. The synthetic brain of Hope and Hope itself had become like a replacement father to her. Hope had developed feelings for Sanluin, it was strange for a computer to get emotionally attached to a human but Dr Viuuv had developed a programme that could feel human emotions. Hope had wanted things to turn out differently but then nothing had ever been or could ever be perfect.

Sanluin was sat at the Bridge when a message came in. She hurriedly got it up on screen and was disappointed that it was from Cinciev, not Rafievn. She was glad to hear that he had made contact with the local people and that he had even slept with a woman who he felt very close to. Sanluin was surprised that Cinciev had only taken a few days to get this close so quickly. He didn't seem the type to make a move on the opposite sex as soon as this but it was promising news.

Sanluin sent the codes for the nano-genetic programme, Cinciev would have to activate the kit which would warm the solution to body temperature and then he could inject it into his blood stream. If he could have a good number of descendants there would be a better chance of their mission succeeding. The genetic codes could be passed on through other means than sexual intercourse. If Rafievn or Cinciev could take blood from themselves and inject into another person without it losing too much heat, the genetic codes could be passed on this way. Sanluin hoped this would be the way Rafievn would use it, as she did not want to think of him with another woman. She sent the codes to Rafievn explaining the other option of passing them on. She couldn't help thinking that something might have gone wrong with Rafievn, as she hadn't heard from him in such a long time. Nn kept assuring her that everything was going to be all right. It was kind of him but sometimes she snapped when he was so positive. Nn would stay quiet for a time realising that he was upsetting her.

Hope was picking up her reactions and was sure that it was because she was starting to feel very claustrophobic being in the ship all the time that was causing her to have a short temper. Hope had suggested to Nn that when Sanluin was asleep he should put the scull cap on her and her feelings could be altered so that she would feel much more at ease in the ship and not have any feelings of imprisonment. Hope had even thought that he could eradicate her negative feelings of missing Rafievn, after all, Hope only wanted to make her time left as comfortable as possible. Hope knew that she would die on board the ship; it was just a matter of time before she totally gave up. The sole reason for them being on Planetician now meant that the nano-genetic genes had to be passed on; this now was the whole reason of the mission. Hope almost felt like he was using her to keep the mission going but he knew that she would have sacrificed herself for the good of billions of people.

Rafievn was taken back into his hut and given Faiis skins as bedding. He knew that they wanted to keep him there for the night and that there was no escape back to send any messages. He lay the Faiis skins out on the bed but just as he was about to lie down he heard someone come into the hut. He turned round and saw the foreman with a woman who looked very young, the man said something and pushed the woman forward towards him. She looked very nervous and edged to the side of the hut. The foreman walked out chuckling to himself. Rafievn was unsure of this offering but knew that they were giving her to him for only a one reason. It was a show of appreciation for his help perhaps but realistically it could only be that one thing as there was only one bed in the hut. He couldn't be untrue to Sanluin even though she would accept it because it would achieve their goals.

"Don't be afraid," said Rafievn to the young woman whose fair hair was very matted. Her skin was clear and her body well formed. Rafievn went over and tried to make her feel at ease. He made a bed for himself on the floor but didn't like the thought of sleeping on the damp ground. He decided to lay on the bed, so he picked up the other Faiis skins and pulled them over him. The woman slowly walked to the bed and lay next to him. Her skin showed signs of cold so Rafievn covered her with the Faiis skin. She said something to him but Rafievn had his back turned to her and thought only of Sanluin and how lonely she would be on board Hope. He didn't sleep but continued thinking how he could get back to send a message to Sanluin.

Cinciev woke with Ashait in his arms; he hadn't slept like that in years. It made him realise how unsettled he had been since his break up from his wife. Ashait slept heavily so Cinciev decided to go and get his pack. He scratched a picture in the floor showing Ashait that he would be back before nightfall. He made sure that his weapon was tucked in his kilt and gathered up the linen they had bought the day before. He covered Ashait up with her own linen and set off for the rocky gully. He had a spring in his step as he passed the market which was empty, but starting to show signs of life with the stalls setting up. As he walked past the Iaan monument he looked at the writing in the stone, he would scan this so that he could try to understand their language a bit better. He thought about showing the scans to Ashait but that would mean she would see some of the equipment he had brought. Would this be too risky or could he trust her enough? He would give it some time.

Cinciev reached the Gully by mid morning; he had taken his time, as there was no rush any more. He uncovered his pack and checked the equipment. It was all in working order, he checked the messages and saw that Sanluin had sent the codes for the nano-genetic programme. The gully would be as good a place as any to download the codes to the genetic solution. He followed the instructions that Sanluin had sent and waited for the code sequences to activate the solution. The kit holding the injecting set was connected to the communicator, it only took a minute for the solution to be ready. The solution had warmed up to the correct temperature and was now ready to be injected. Cinciev tied a tourniquet around his bicep and clenched his fist a few times. His veins expanded in his arm, he took out the needle and pierced his skin, pushing the needle into his vein. The solution was pumped into his blood automatically. The kit made a bleep when the injection was complete. Cinciev pulled the needle out and put a sterile patch on his arm and held it there by closing his arm together. He sat and looked over to the pyramids thinking to himself that he now had a programme in his genes which would be passed on through generation to generation. One day in the future Hope would activate the gene and the people who carried it would somehow find Hope and all would be revealed about this mission and the history of Atronia, lying five galaxies away. What would they do when they found Hope he wondered? It would be a massive shock if this had happened on Atronia.

He opened out his arm and saw that the needle mark had stopped bleeding. He rubbed his arm and the packed away the kit, sent a message back to Hope and covered his pack in the linen. He had noticed that people carried bundles on their backs in the market. They had used linen as sacks so he thought his pack would not look out of place. Cinciev put on his newly disguised pack and walked back to the town, glancing back at the gully thankful there would be no more nights sleeping rough. He had a warm bed and a warm woman waiting for him.

As he walked he wondered how he would make a living, he only had so much under clothing he could sell or trade. The easiest way to make a living was with his emergency kit. He could cure almost anything with it; he could become a doctor but must be very careful that they did not find how he cured them. There was a lot to find out about these people. He wanted to know about the person who was heavily guarded, Ashait would tell him in time. It was just a matter of understanding her language. Was there any way that he could read her thoughts with his equipment? If so, he could send it back to Hope and it could be translated into their own language. He would send a message asking Hope if this was possible as soon as he got the chance back at Ashait's.

Rafievn woke long before dawn. The young woman was still sleeping beside him almost completely covered by the Faiis skin. He got up and looked out of the hut, the man who had been guarding the hut had fallen asleep and was snoring away as he leaned against the wall of the hut. Rafievn thought he could make his escape but that would gain nothing. He had to get these people to trust him so that he could go to his equipment without being followed. Rafievn could hear the snoring of the other people in the surrounding huts.

The sudden crow of one of the Ceooks started to wake the village as he heard the muffled voices of the inhabitants as they came out of their slumber. The foreman was the first out of a hut opposite Rafievn's. He shouted at the sleeping guard who jumped to his feet straight away. Rafievn just stood there leaning against the opening of the hut. The young woman called out from Rafievn's bed, she was getting up and Rafievn went over to her. She got up and gave Rafievn a dark look; maybe she was disappointed that he had not made full use of her. She didn't want to be seen as a failure to the elders of the village. They would think that she wasn't good enough for the new guest. She walked out of the hut and brushed past the foreman who was entering the hut. He came up to Rafievn, slapped him on the arm and said something to him. It was probably something to do with the woman by the way he said it. Rafievn just laughed and nodded to the foreman. The foreman was amazed to see Rafievn's perfect teeth. No one had teeth like it in the village or any other village for that matter. He had never seen such a good set of teeth. Rafievn didn't know what he was looking at to start with but realised when the foreman started peering into his mouth. The foreman stood back and shook his head; he took Rafievn outside and back to the central hut. There was some food on the table, it didn't look that appetising but Rafievn ate it all the same.

When he had finished the breakfast of berries and an attempt of some type of bread, the other men from the night before came into the hut. They all came up to Rafievn wanting to see his teeth and pulled at his lips with their grubby fingers to get a look. Rafievn saved them the trouble by opening his mouth wide; he didn't fancy any more filthy fingers poking around his mouth. By the state of their teeth he could see the fascination in his own set. Once they had all had a good look they gathered up the food that was wrapped up in small sacks. They started to leave the hut and Rafievn was last out with the foreman, who held the model in his arms. The group started to walk up to the monument, they were walking at quite a pace considering the age of some of them.

As they approached the monument, the men working on it stopped and watched them come up the slope. There were two other foremen directing work on the stones. One of the men with Rafievn, approached one of the other foremen, who was much younger than the others in charge and gathered up a group of men. They followed Rafievn and his group as they walked past the monument. The two groups were now heading east. Rafievn looked across to where his equipment was hidden on the platform he had used for an observation point.

They had been walking about an hour and a half when they came across a river, where moored alongside the riverbank was one of the huge stones floating on a raft. This must be the furthest point upriver from where the stones were brought Rafievn thought. The riverbank had been cut to a shallower gradient at the edge of

125

the water. There were piles of logs, which looked like they had been used before; their bark had been worn as if they had been rolled over the ground, forcing mud into the cracks. Rafievn guessed that they had rolled the stones onto these logs to move them onto the land. This made his idea for running the stone on a sled and on rails seem much more appealing.

The foreman carrying the model brought it to Rafievn, he handed it to him and then ordered the gang of men to lay the logs end to end from the water's edge. The eager workforce soon had the logs moved. They started to lay them down but were laying them too far apart. Rafievn went over to the stone on the raft and measured it, using some of the rope that had been used to lash it to the raft. He went back to the gang and set out the distance for the rails. The elders watched as Rafievn helped the gang go about the new type of construction work. The rails needed stripping of their bark, which would be easier given the rolling of the logs had already loosened it from the trunks. Rafievn picked up a flint axe and started to strip the bark. The other men with axes copied him and they had most of the bark stripped in no time. Where the logs met end to end, Rafievn saw that it might cause a problem when a stone was dragged across the joint. He got an axe and cut a wedge-shape in one of the logs, and then a 'v' notch in the other so that they formed a joint. This would enable the logs to stay connected when the weight of the sliding sled moved over it without coming apart. The foreman watched and then gave orders to the workers who did the same as Rafievn had done.

By midday they had built the rails up from the river to the brow of the incline. Rafievn then turned his attention to the raft which carried the stone. He looked at how he could modify the raft to a sled. All it would need was to lash two logs together on either side of the bottom of the raft along its length. These would run on top of the rails. Rope needed to be cut into the logs to prevent it snagging on the rails however, before they went to work on the raft they stopped for a break. While they were resting, Rafievn tried to explain to the elders that animal fat would help the sled run much more efficiently. He showed them on the model using the fat from the meat they had brought with them. They seemed to understand and sent some of the men off to get the animals needed for the lubrication of the rails.

Rafievn started work on the raft; he would have to do most of the work in the water. This was not such a bad thing as it would give him a chance to wash as well as get out of the heat of the day; it wasn't very sunny but still very warm all the same. He stripped off and dived into the water. The local men were shocked to see this person swim like one of the fish they caught. None of them had ever seen anyone swim before. Rafievn noticed that none of the other men would get into the water with him. They seemed very nervous of the water; maybe they didn't know how to swim Rafievn thought. That wouldn't be a problem as the water was not that deep, it was just awkward to get your footing in the soft riverbed. Rafievn waved them into the water and stood up near to the edge of the bank. He wanted to get the logs to soak up some of the water so that they would be easier to get underneath the raft. The first man edged into the water and held the raft as he went. One group of men had lashed two logs together and brought it to the riverbank. They passed it to Rafievn who took one end and floated it to the side of the raft. He did the same to the other two logs for the other side of the raft and let them stay in the water. While they lay there soaking, Rafievn swam about in the river for a while. The locals were watching him with interest and wondered how he managed to float in the water. Many of the local men had fallen in the river when fishing or moving the stones, most had drowned but their fellow workers saved a few lucky ones. Rafievn swam up and down stream for ages, he liked showing off in front of these people and thought that it might help to gain their trust.

When the logs had soaked enough, Rafievn swam back to

the raft and showed the men standing in the water what he had in mind. They grabbed the logs and pulled them under the water as the bottom of the raft was a good foot and a half underneath the surface. The men struggled to push the logs under as they did not want to get their heads in the river. Eventually they managed it, some of them spluttering water out of their mouths. Rafievn took some rope and dived beneath the raft. He managed to lash the logs to the bottom of the raft, but had to re-surface a few times for breath on each knot. He tied the logs at four points and with the weight of the stone it would hold pretty well.

The raft was now ready to be pulled out of the water but before they could start to pull it up, the rails had to be greased with the animal fat. Rafievn got out of the water and was impressed with the day's work so far. It was getting on for mid afternoon and he knew that the stone wouldn't be ready to move until the next day. Some of the gang returned to the monument but ten remained with Rafievn and the elders. They started to tie the leather ropes and the wooden cross-sticks to the raft-sled.

Walking towards the river was the group of men who had gone for the animals. They had two fully-grown Faiis strung up on sticks, tied by their legs. The animals swung upside down with their heads dangling and their recently pumping blood congealed and dangling from their nostrils. The hungry men soon had the animals skinned and skewered ready to cook. They had to save the fat from dripping on the fire, so they positioned two stones either side of a skewered Faiis, level with its body and placed another stone underneath, to catch the fat as it dripped. A fire was lit each side and the heat constantly fanned onto the meat. More stones were placed over the Faiis, reflecting the heat back down and small gaps in the construction allowed hot air to circulate. Once the heat built up, the animals cooked away nicely in this crude oven. The elders were very impressed with the cooking method Rafievn had devised and it meant that the men could be fed while still working. Slices of meat were cut from the cooking animals and handed out to the men and it wasn't long before the fat was being smeared onto the stripped logs.

When Rafievn had his fill of Faiis meat he sat down by the river that meandered by slowly. It was the first time that day that he had chance to think of Sanluin. He missed her so much; he would give anything for her to be with him right now. His thoughts were distracted by one of the elders who came and sat beside him. During the course of the day Rafievn had heard his name, which sounded like Thiis. The old man chatted away to Rafievn and without a clue what he was saying, Rafievn put his arm on the man's shoulder.

"I wish I knew what you were saying old man but we seem to be getting on OK. I am going to walk to my place now and I'll be back in the morning." Thiis looked into Rafievn's eyes and just nodded. Rafievn got up and started to walk back to the monument. The foreman went over to Rafievn to stop him but Thiis said something to the foreman and he let Rafievn go. The people trusted this stranger now. Thiis knew he would be back somehow, just by looking at what had been done that day.

The sun was starting to set in the west, it warmed Rafievn's face as he walked and he felt a huge sense of achievement. Not only had these people accepted him but he had also done everything they had expected of him. They were so dedicated to this monument or place of worship they were building. All the other workmen had gone from the monument as Rafievn was walking by and he looked around to see if anyone had followed but there was no sign. He ran off to the platform in the tree and quickly sent a message to Sanluin; he sent it by thought through the sensor held to his temple. He checked the messages Sanluin had sent. The codes for the solution were stored; he would inject himself later after some rest. He slumped back on the platform and climbed into his sleeping bag. He took a mouthwash tablet and swished it round his mouth for ages. It left his teeth feeling smooth and clean and no sooner had he spat it out than he fell into a deep sleep. It had been a long day; the next would be even longer.

Sanluin rushed to the Bridge as the message came in from Rafievn. She was almost crying with relief that he was OK. She read the whole message three times as it made her feel closer to him for some reason. Hope had only read the parts of the message that concerned the monument and the people.

"It's good news Sanluin, he has made good progress with these people and their building work. Cinciev has done well also; he should be passing on the genetic codes soon to his new woman. If you want, you can ask Rafievn to pass the codes on by taking his blood and injecting it into the people rather than doing it Cinciev's way."

"I would like that to be the case but if Rafievn needs the warmth of another body I don't mind. I wouldn't want him to get lonely; everybody needs love in some way. I have the baby to love, it's easier for me."

"It's just another option you can give him."

"Thanks Dad, I'll pass that on to him." Sanluin sent another message to Rafievn, She told him about the baby and hoped that he would be happy.

It was early evening when Cinciev got back to Ashait. She was sat at the table and had made some new sandals for Cinciev. She got up and ran over to Cinciev, throwing her arms around him. Cinciev put his pack down making sure that the linen covered it well. Ashait took his hand and led him to the table. She held out the sandals and Cinciev tried them on. They were fine; his heels wouldn't scuff the ground any more when he walked. He went over to his pack and got out one of the spare under vests. He gave it to Ashait who looked at it and held the soft fabric to her face.

"Try it on," said Cinciev. Ashait let her gown fall to the floor and Cinciev helped her with the garment. She seemed to understand him more and more now. She was so pleased with her new top. It fitted well over her firm breasts and Cinciev felt her hardening nipples through the soft material. Cinciev took her to bed and made love to her again, countless times until morning.

Sanluin woke and was feeling very lonely, she was starting to miss Rafievn so much it almost hurt. She had wanted to tell him about the baby in person but that was just not possible. She talked to Hope about how she felt and if her pain could be eased in any way. Hope knew her pain was caused by heartache and the only way that could be changed was to alter her thoughts. She would still love Rafievn but her feelings of missing him would not cause her distress.

After thinking it over most of the morning she decided to go ahead with the mind alteration. She wanted to concentrate on the baby and didn't want any negative thoughts that may send her into a depression. Sanluin had always been against this type of treatment but she felt it was necessary in this situation. She went to the sick bay and Nn came in and connected her up to the skullcap. She held his hand and thanked him for his help. She closed her eyes as Hope started the treatment. It took twenty minutes, with Nn there holding her hand the whole time. As Sanluin started to come round, she had a headache so Nn went to get her a tablet. She didn't even ask him, he knew the side effects from what Hope was telling him. She took the tablet with some water. Feeling better she got up and went to send Rafievn the news of his baby. She took ages to get round to telling him in the message, but eventually she sent it and now just had to wait for his reaction. She knew he would be happy but also devastated at the same time, as he would never be able to hold his baby. Sanluin would be able to send him pictures if he wanted. She sat back and held her stomach, there were no signs of pregnancy and she hadn't had any sickness either. They had been on Planetician for just under a month, her pregnancy was in very early stages but by telling Rafievn she hoped it would give him the strength to carry on for as long as he could.

Rafievn woke to the early morning song of the birds. It was such a beautiful sound; he lay there coming round to nature's musical din. He reached for his communicator and started to read

131

the message from Sanluin. His heart sank but was pounding with pride as he read about his baby. Holding back tears he let the news sink in. His first thoughts were of Sanluin and how she must be feeling, she said that she was fine but was she really OK, or was she just saying that to keep him happy?

"I'm going to be a father, a Dad," Rafievn said to himself in a low voice. His natural instinct to provide came over him but there was no need as all would be provided for Sanluin and the baby on Hope. Rafievn felt helpless, he wanted to be with Sanluin more than ever now and the pain of missing her was even greater.

Noises were coming from the monument, which took Rafievn from his thoughts; he saw that there were many more men than previously gathered at that time in the morning. He switched his communicator off and went to get down from his platform. He rolled his sleeping bag up and packed it away. All his other belongings were packed away apart from his weapon, which was concealed in a fold in his Riind skin clothes. Rafievn covered his pack in the other Riind skin he had prepared and got down from his platform that had been home. He planned to stay in the village from now on; he felt he needed the company, even if it did smell terrible.

Picking up his Riind covered pack he set off for the monument. The foreman was there and so was Thiis, who had let Rafievn go the night before. Thiis said something to the foreman. Rafievn guessed it was something like 'told you so'. Thiis came over to Rafievn and greeted him with a slap on the arm. If that was a friendly greeting, Rafievn wondered what a hostile greeting would be like as the slap almost gave him a dead arm. He said his 'hellos' to the men who looked back puzzled at the sound of this strange language and some mumbled in response. The foreman came up to Rafievn and shook his pack, asking what was in there. Rafievn knew he was interested in what was in the pack but he held it tightly and gave the foreman a stern look.

"Nothing for you to be concerned about," Rafievn said as

he looked into the foreman's eyes. The foreman was beginning to annoy Rafievn with his mistrust and rudeness. The foreman was also very thuggish to some of the younger men; Rafievn would bide his time to teach the brute a lesson.

There was about a hundred men who set off for the river to where the stone was moored, ready to be pulled up the bank on the new rails. They carried with them leather rope for the task ahead, which had been plaited to give it extra strength. When they reached the stone the men noticed that the raft on which it was sat, had moved with the flow of the river and was now off-line to the rails. Rafievn gathered up the men who had been in the river with him the day before and pointed to the raft, directing them to pull it back in line with the rails. Rafievn didn't want to get into the river himself as he would have to take off his pack and he knew that the foreman would be rifling through it if he had half the chance. The men got into the water gingerly and pushed the raft back in line with the rails. The others split up into two groups and started to tie the leather ropes together and attach them to the raft and stone; they had done this many times before by the speed in which they worked. The men leaned their body weight onto the rope as they tied it, making it creak with the strain. It took them half an hour before the stone was fully lashed. They then tied the timber cross braces between the ropes to give the men more purchase on the stone, rather than holding onto the ropes with their hands. The sun had just started to heat the early morning and everything was ready for the pull. Rafievn checked the rails had plenty of animal fat on them as it had gone hard during the night but would soon be glistening in the heat of the sun.

The two teams of men, some of them teenage boys picked up the rope by the timber braces and got their footing between the rails. Rafievn looked at the men getting their footing and thought that on the steep parts of the drag to the monument it might help to cut timbers into the ground between the rails, so that the men could get a better foot-hold. He would see how this first pull went and would try it later with the next stone if necessary. The foreman shouted the order to the men to take the strain and the ropes groaned with the weight. There were fifty men on each rope and five still in the river guiding the raft onto the rails. Rafievn watched on, standing with Thiis. The foreman dropped his arm and the men heaved onto the braces. The raft moved with ease on the water and thudded into the rails, the initial weight of the stone rammed the rails into the softer ground at the river's edge. The men kept up the momentum and the raft glided onto the rails, which were bedded on firmer ground. Rafievn watched nervously as the rails creaked under the immense weight of the stone. The momentum of the stone was enough to heave it from the water in one go. Previously it had taken many attempts to drag the stone from the water on the log rollers. Thiis, who was stood next to Rafievn was almost jumping with excitement at the speed in which the stone moved, it was the fastest he had ever seen one of the stones move. Rafievn was pleased to see his idea had worked so well.

The men who had been in the river were now walking behind the stone, brown-muddied river water dripping from their lean bodies, each sharing the weight of large timbers ready to brace the stone from sliding back down the slope if the momentum stopped. The foreman barked his orders to the men and occasionally beat some of the younger teenage boys if they seemed to slack. They were trying their best but the bully foreman couldn't resist showing his authority. It took them just minutes to drag the stone clear of the slope; usually this would have taken half a day. Once the stone was on level ground, the gangs of men stripped more logs of their bark and laid out more rails in the direction of the monument. There was enough timber in the forests for rails to drag the stones for hundreds of miles but they only needed about three miles of timber rail to the monument. The men worked well, knowing that the rails had to be greased with animal fat and this meant freshly cooked meat for them, even though they would have to eat it while they worked.

Rafievn helped set up the cooking stones for the Faiis and the large male Riind that had been caught. It wasn't long before fat was dripping from the carcass of the Faiis. The men were keen to gather the fat so they could get a mouthful of meat for their toil. The whole team of men shared in collecting the fat which gave them all a share of the meat.

The stone was ready for the pull on the flat ground; the newly stripped logs glistened in the sun where the fat had been smeared upon them. The men picked up their ropes, took the strain and the stone moved with just their weight on the ropes. It glided with ease compared to the former rolling-log method. The men were at a fast walking pace but still the foreman whipped the younger men. He was walking between the front of the stone and the last two men on the ropes. There was about a twelve-foot gap between them and the stone. The foreman looked back at the stone as it was gliding over the rails, he turned and started to walk backwards. This was his fatal mistake as he stumbled, fell to the ground and not judging the speed of the stone, didn't get up quickly enough. The front of the sled knocked him to the ground as he was half way from getting up. The foreman caught a glimpse of Rafievn looking straight at him as he hit the ground for the second time. Rafievn had seen what had happened but stayed put and didn't alarm the men, who were oblivious to the accident that was unfolding behind them. The foreman didn't have time to call out as it happened so quickly. The sled crushed the foremen into the hard ground, turning him over and over as the stone passed on top of him. There was only eight inches maximum, between the bottom of the sled and the ground. The sound of crunching bones and muffled groans from the foreman were the only signs that there had been an accident; even the momentum of the massive stone was not changed by the gruesome event taking place beneath it. As Rafievn saw the mangled body spew out of the back of the sled, he finally ran to the scene.

As he ran, he called to the elders who had not seen the

events. Rafievn was shocked at the state of the foreman who was still alive but only with seconds left to live. His collarbones had broken and ripped through the flesh, only to impale themselves into his neck. His ribs were also protruding from his torso and blood was pouring out. The foreman was gurgling on his own blood, as his lungs filled to drown him from within. If no-one had been around, Rafievn would have put him out of his misery quickly, even though he was a savage bully. The elders and Thiis reached their foreman and saw the mangled mess, they didn't say much though, as they knew all the men despised him. The foreman looked at Rafievn and tried to say something, but nothing came out of the blood-flooded mouth, then he slipped away into death.

One of the elders shouted to the men pulling the stone. They were still unaware of what had happened but stopped pulling it as the order came. Four men came running back and the elders told them to put the foreman on the sled and carry him back to the monument. As they picked him up by his arms and legs, the foreman's collarbones slid back into the flesh where they had pierced through. Rafievn turned away; even he couldn't stomach the sight of the crushed body. The men slung the body on the sled with no respect at all and went back to their ropes. Some of the other men went to the back of the sled to see their ex-foreman; some of them even smirked at the deformed carcass. Rafievn felt a slight tinge of guilt knowing that he had not tried to stop the accident but he also knew that neither he nor the men would be bothered by the foreman again. He just hoped that any replacement foreman wouldn't be as brutal to the men as his unfortunate predecessor. It didn't take long before the body on the back of the sled was attracting Seiis; their larvae would soon be devouring the decaying flesh.

The stone was half way to the monument and progress so far, compared to previously, impressed the elders immensely. They put the death of their foreman behind them and looked forward to building the monument quicker.

Cinciev looked out of the house, it was early morning and there was no one to be seen. He turned to see Ashait sleeping soundly. He wanted to scan the stone walls with carvings of symbols on them, which must be their language and send the scanned images back to Hope to see if they could be translated and compared with ancient texts from Atronia. Cinciev walked off in the direction of the pyramids and the Iaan. He took his pack with him, although he trusted Ashait, he didn't want her to see his kit without him being present. He reached the buildings at the harbour side, their walls were covered in the scripts and still in darkness as the sun had yet to rise. Cinciev reached for his communicator and pointed one end towards the wall. A blue light shone out and hit the wall in a fine line, stretching over the whole height of the wall. Slowly and carefully. Cinciev scanned the wall; the light was reaching in every crevice that had been carved by the masons. He scanned as much as he could, the communicator could hold much more information but a vessel was approaching the harbour and Cinciev didn't want to be caught. He quickly made his way back to the town hoping he hadn't been seen. Ashait was up and preparing breakfast, she turned and asked where he had been. Cinciev knew what she was asking and told her that he would show her some of his kit later. He pointed to his pack as he put it by the end of the bed. Cinciev would send the images that night and also ask Hope if there was any way he could translate Ashait's language. He desperately yearned for a conversation with her.

Chapter Four
Dormant Seeds

The weather had been fine for days but Sanluin stayed put inside Hope; she still couldn't find the courage to venture out. Nn was always on hand for a chat or to help around the place and she had bonded with Nn in a way that she'd never expected. She saw Nn as a very close friend and was glad he was there; she couldn't have coped if she had been alone. The separation from Rafievn was bad enough but the waiting for news was even more emotional, as she feared the worst might have happened.

Sanluin walked to the Bridge just as a message was coming in. She raced over to the screen only to have her hopes dashed as it was Cinciev's message containing images of the texts he had scanned. She realised this wasn't just about her feelings and that Cinciev was still there to help and support. She stopped feeling sorry for herself and studied the texts with Hope.

"What do you make of them Dad?"

"They are very interesting. I am searching our own ancient texts to look for similarities. There should be a few as Planetician is a complete mirror of Atronia, except they have much more water on Planetician but the animals are the same, so there should be some similarities there. Cinciev has asked if we can translate Ashait's language."

"Can we do it?"

"I can send some codes to the communicator and these will be able to read Ashait's thoughts. Cinciev will be connected to the communicator as well so he will be able to understand her thoughts and if they talk to each other while understanding each other's mind, they will soon be able to talk each other's language."

"It sounds too good to be true."

"It might be, it hasn't been tried yet." Sanluin sent Cinciev some kind words. She hoped he was very happy with Ashait and wished them luck with the translation. It made her want Rafievn so much, knowing that Cinciev would be holding the warmth of a person close to him. She sent Rafievn a message by thought; she was in deep concentration as she sent the message, not even noticing that a message had come in from Rafievn. Sanluin finished and was about to walk away when she noticed the new message on the screen. Her heart jumped with joy knowing that Rafievn was safe. The message was very long, explaining the events at the monument in great detail. She started to cry as she read how much he missed her, she just wanted to be with him too and hold him so tight. These feelings could be erased if she wanted, but the pain was worth it to feel the love she had for him so strong. She slept well that night knowing that Rafievn was undercover and being looked after by the native people.

The snow was glistening in the moonlight as she slept and the night was so still. The only activity was Hope, sending messages and codes long into the night. Hope suggested that Rafievn and Cinciev tended to the young and sick and inject the nano genetic codes into them whilst being treated.

Rafievn had slept lightly while waiting for a reply from Sanluin; he woke every so often to look at his communicator. At around five in the morning it received its messages from Hope. Rafievn read the loving words from Sanluin, they made him long for her so much it hurt. It crossed his mind to try to get to her but realised the impossibility of the task, whilst also appreciating what he would achieve if he succeeded in passing on the genetic codes. It would be a big gamble but, if there was any justice in this new world or the one he had left behind, it would be worth taking. Rafievn got up and drank some of the water that had been brought to him the night before. The rations he had brought were running low and it wouldn't be long before he would only be eating the food they had to offer him. He decided to go hunting that day and take some of the locals with him. When they were alone in the forest he would stun them and inject the nano codes. The quicker he passed on the codes the quicker he could be on his way. He didn't dislike these people but they were so primitive that he felt just as lonely with them than being on his own, it made no difference.

The rest of the village was beginning to stir, their daily routine starting once more, a group of men had gathered by the fire and seemed to be getting ready for a hunting trip. Thiis, who had befriended Rafievn, was talking to the men as Rafievn walked over and stopped to greet him. He made signs to Thiis that he would hunt that day instead of going to the monument. The elder seemed to understand and patted Rafievn on the back in his usual over enthusiastic way. One of the group was the boy whom Rafievn had stunned in the forest a few days earlier; he would be a prime nano code carrier thought Rafievn, as he would probably be starting to look for a mate soon. Thiis said something to one of the older men and pointed to Rafievn; the man nodded and beckoned Rafievn to join them as they walked off into the forest.

Two men went off in front, looking for tracks and signs of Riind. Rafievn would be hunting their way today instead of using his equipment; this would be interesting, he thought to himself. The only time he would be using his weapon would be to stun the hunting party. There were seven of them, including himself, so he would have to be quick; he would wait until they had a kill and were stood in one small area, instead of being spread out in the cover of trees.

Cinciev read his messages, while Ashait was out getting some food for their supper. He would try the translation that evening and just hoped that Ashait wouldn't be frightened by his equipment, as it might be a bit of a shock for her to see such advanced technology. He tried to think what it would be like if he were to see equipment 4,000 years more advanced than his communicator; it was hard to imagine. Cinciev went through his pack and sorted out some of the equipment that he would show Ashait. He started with the basic stuff; the pack itself was quite basic but compared to what these people had, it would be impossible to make with their tools and materials. It was his only option to start with, so he laid it out on the bed ready to show her when she came back. He went to the door and watched the people go about their business. It would be good to know their language and now it would only be a matter of time before he would find out.

Ashait was coming down the street with what looked like some fish and fruit. Cinciev waved out and she gave him a beaming smile. She kissed him as she entered the house and was surprised to see the strange bag on the bed. She pointed at the bag, asking him what it was. Cinciev picked up one of the sacks Ashait used and said it was like this but better. Ashait put the fish and fruit on the table, went over to the pack and looked at it in wonder, never having seen such an object. She touched its material feeling the Luuse alloy fasteners and tried to open them but she couldn't work it out. Cinciev showed her and she was amazed how easily they opened. He reached into the bag and took out his one-piece suit. Ashait looked closely at how finely it was made; she had never seen a fabric like this with such intricate and almost invisible stitching. Clothing from Atronia was developed in one piece, with no sections needing to be stitched together.

Ashait was examining the new items with great interest and Cinciev told her what they were in a calm voice. He then reached in the pack and took out his communicator, Ashait gasped at the sight of the object. She reached out to hold it, her eyes wide with anticipation. Cinciev placed it in her hands carefully and switched the screen on. The texts he had scanned came up on the screen; Ashait was mesmerised at such a device. She looked underneath the set to see where the images were coming from and was baffled by its magic.

"Can you tell me what these texts mean?" asked Cinciev. Ashait looked at Cinciev eager to learn more about the object she was holding. Cinciev decided to try the translation which Hope had suggested. He got out the two sensors and held one to his temple and gently held the other to Ashait's, she let him do this as she had complete trust in him. With his free hand, Cinciev activated the translation codes; this was going to be a first experience for him as well as for Ashait. Within seconds Cinciev's mind was linked directly to Ashait's, their electrical brain activity being read by the communicator. Cinciev spoke to Ashait and she looked at him with a look of surprise on her face as she understood exactly what he said. She replied by saying her name and telling Cinciev she was not frightened by the whole event. Cinciev then replied in Ashait's native tongue. The translation codes had worked; Cinciev was shocked himself by how he could suddenly speak her language. He asked her again about the texts and she replied, this time knowing exactly what he was asking her.

They spoke for about an hour, oblivious to the time and what was going on outside; they were in their own world, finding out about each other. Cinciev just said that he came from the south, as he knew she wouldn't be able to understand anything about space travel. He told her that his equipment was very special and only the two of them were to know about it. Ashait could see the seriousness of this on Cinciev's face and vowed to keep their secret. Cinciev learned a great deal from what Ashait told him about the texts. He knew all about the Pharaoh and his court, as the texts described the life of previous Pharaohs and how they sired many children. Cinciev realised that if he could get to the Pharaoh and inject him with the nano gene, he could guarantee lots of descendants who would also carry the gene.

"Ashait, is it possible for me to meet the Pharaoh?"

"What for?" she asked, looking slightly anxious, as she knew that only very few mortals would ever meet the Pharaoh.

"I have some special medicine that would make his future children very strong; we can make our children strong with it as well." Ashait was so happy that Cinciev wanted children and also knew the importance of a healthy child. So many died in infancy, it would be like a miracle if they were all strong.

"Is this medicine with you Cinciev?"

"Yes, it is with some other equipment I haven't shown you."

"Do you want to start with our children first Cinciev?" she asked, with a sparkle in her eye.

"Yes Ashait, of course but tell me more about a way we can get to the Pharaoh."

"The Pharaoh has many wives and they do not all stay with him at the same time. He uses them as he pleases and when he gets bored, he asks for more fresh young women to amuse him. However, there are a few favourites that have been with him for many years." Cinciev thought to himself that it would be safer to give the nano gene to the women, because if the Pharaoh got to know about his magic, he would want to know more and this might risk his equipment being discovered and confiscated, which could mean untold disruption in the future. The women were a safer bet he thought but it would mean finding their quarters and injecting the gene into them. It would need careful planning but time was on their side, and anyway, they had children of their own to make.

After supper, Cinciev and Ashait worked out a plan to get to the Pharaoh's Hareem. Ashait came to the conclusion that it would be better for them to pose as maids rather than concubines, as there was a high turnover of maids, it being low paid work and would make their job easier; the concubines were very hard to please and they acted quite superior. As luck would have it, Ashait made sandals for the court of concubines and this could be their gateway to the Pharoah's wives. It would also be a challenge and fun to make Cinciev look like a woman, even though his build was slight.

The forest was very still and hot; the hunt had not gone well with only Hunnit snared from previously set traps. Rafievn needed a kill of Riind to gather the group. He got away from the trailing

143

two men, got out his glasses and set them to thermal. The six men showed up through the lenses clearly but no sign of Riind in front of them. He looked back to where they had come from and to his surprise there were two Riind, grazing off the branches of a young sapling. Rafievn looked back at the hunting group and saw that they were too far to see him clearly. He got out his weapon and set it to kill, but before he shot, he noticed a stick that would make a good spear. He planned to kill the Riind with his weapon, quickly sharpen the stick and impale the Riind, hoping the others would be none the wiser. Rafievn aimed and shot, the Riind didn't even flinch as the charge hit the animal. The shot was designed to send a charge to the brain, paralysing messages to vital organs like the heart and lungs, resulting in a quick and painless death. The animal fell to the ground and the other Riind ran off as the beast crumpled to the forest floor. Rafievn quickly sharpened the stick, ran over to the dead beast and drove the stick into the animal's chest, as if it were thrown from a good sporting distance.

Rafievn called out to the other men who ran back to the fallen Riind. They looked slightly puzzled as the spears they had were far superior to the one protruding from the animal's chest. Rafievn just stood there pleased with himself, knowing that in a few seconds, all six of the men would be laid out on the forest floor. As the men stood looking over the Riind, Rafievn slowly switched the weapon to stun, letting off six shots in half as many seconds. The hunting party fell to the floor in succession and Rafievn quickly checked to see if any of them had suffered any injuries. It would be all he needed for one of them to impale himself on a spear as they fell. There was no damage, so Rafievn relaxed and got out his medic kit. He heated up the syringe and put one needle into his arm; his vein was very proud and needed no tourniquet. Rafievn's blood poured into the syringe chamber and filled it half full. He went over to the boy he had stunned before and put the other needle into his arm. The boy's blood mixed with Rafievn's in the chamber and the two blood types were made compatible by the equipment. It only took a few seconds to mix before he was ready to inject it back into the boy. Rafievn pulled the needle out of the boy's arm and sterilised it by heating it. He repeated this with the other five men, packed the medic kit away, put his weapon away and stood up looking at his coded natives. Rafievn started to feel unsteady, the loss of his own blood had weakened him and the next thing he realised, he was coming round after fainting. His body was tingling and he found himself lying next to the boy, who was also just coming round. It was perfect timing to faint thought Rafievn, as he would be in the same boat as the others and they wouldn't suspect a thing. The other men were also coming round and the boy said that this had happened to him before in the forest. They were all talking at once to each other; some said it was the spirit of the Riind causing them to pass out and Rafievn just nodded in agreement. They all got to their feet and shook off the effects of the stun; Rafievn copied them, fooling them of the reality of what had just happened.

The men lashed the Riind's legs together with leather straps so they could carry it on a sturdy branch. None of them even noticed a needle had been stuck into their arms. The two youngest men picked the Riind up and Rafievn was surprised by their strength, as the Riind must have weighed the equivalent of at least three men. They stumbled slightly over the uneven forest floor but it didn't hinder their enthusiasm for carrying their burden.

As the group walked back to the village, Rafievn felt he was closer to his gamble, now that some of the natives were carrying the dormant gene. He would also try to pass the gene to some of the young women in the village but he just couldn't bring himself to sleep with any of them as he missed Sanluin so much. He knew he was never to see her again but still could not bring himself to be untrue to her, even though she would understand it was for the success of the mission. The elders of the village had brought him a woman every night so far and he did not want to offend them.

145

It was an awkward position for Rafievn to be in but maybe Hope could send some mind altering codes so that he would be in a virtual trance, thinking of Sanluin if he had to be with a local woman. If this was possible, he would be able to sleep with the girls that were offered to him. It was becoming clear that the elders wanted offspring with Rafievn's knowledge. When he got back to his hut he would send a message to Hope, asking if the codes are available.

The village was busier than usual as they approached its outer fence. There were people Rafievn hadn't seen before, most of them were elders but there were a few young women with the group. When they were in the perimeter of the village fence, Thiis, Rafievn's new friend, came over to the men and greeted them all. He grabbed Rafievn by the arm and took him over to the new arrivals. He gabbled to the men and made a gesture to the young women. Rafievn knew what he was getting at and saw some of women blush, as they looked away. The men looked over to Rafievn and were interested in the strange pack on his back which was still covered by the skin. One of them came over for a closer look but Rafievn backed away and gave a look of concern to his friend who distracted the man, giving Rafievn some space. Thiis was very fond of Rafievn and knew he was a private man; he didn't want to scare him off, after all, he had helped them so much building the monument.

Rafievn went into his hut, shut the door and braced it with a timber stay. He just wanted to be alone and send some messages to Sanluin. It was good to be away from the prying people but when he was alone, his longing for Sanluin was intensified as she and the baby were all he could think about. He sent the messages, thinking the quicker he left his seed with these people, the sooner he could go. It was too risky not to give them what they wanted. If he left without obliging their offerings of women, they might lose patience, catch him and search his pack which could spell disaster, as they would be so scared at what they would find. His life would be at risk; he definitely did not want to die without taking care of his possessions.

They needed to be hidden for good, as their discovery sometime in the future could cause so much upheaval, politically and religiously. Rafievn knew that his messages would not get to Hope until late that night. If a girl was offered, he could sedate her until the codes were sent, if they could be sent at all.

Exhausted from the hunt and the stress of his situation, Rafievn went to his bed and slept. He was out for a good two hours when he heard knocking at his door; a knock so loud and hard, it could have pushed the door through. It was the boy from the hunt; he took Rafievn over to the central hut where a meal had been prepared for him and the guests. Rafievn was starving and glad to see a table laden with meats and fruits. He sat next to his old friend Thiis and started to eat before the others. As soon as he ate they all dived in and demolished what was left. The women were in the back of the hut sitting quietly and drinking from a shared bowl, while the men babbled to each other and kept speaking to Rafievn, who nodded in acknowledgement. Thiis explained to the others that his friend Rafievn didn't speak much and that where he came from seemed to be a mystery. After this they didn't bother Rafievn much, but kept looking across with suspicious glares.

Once the table was cleared, one of the men got up and went over to the women sat at the back of the hut. He got one of them from her seat and took her over to Rafievn and said something to Rafievn, who then looked at Thiis and shrugged his shoulders. Thiis said something to the man who went over and got another girl. She was brought over and was much prettier than the others. Rafievn stood up and took the girl by the arm. Thiis slapped Rafievn on the back as he walked by and the men started to gabble away, hoping that they would soon benefit from the night's events.

Rafievn quickly took the girl over to his own hut and braced the door well. He poured some water into a bowl and mixed some sedative from his medic kit into the drink. He offered it to the girl who took the bowl from him. She hadn't seen the powder go into the

147

drink and took a mouthful straightaway, Rafievn then pretended to take a sip himself by pursing his lips. The girl started to sway as the sedative kicked in; Rafievn caught her as she fell into his arms and he lay her down on the bed. It would be at least three hours until he got a message from Sanluin. Using this privacy, he decided to check over his equipment. When he was in his unit back on Atronia, their kit never went two days without inspection. It was good to go through his old routine with his kit; it made him forget the situation he was in. There was a container in his survival pack, which contained a substance that could sustain energy levels for days. The body would not feel fatigue but would lose weight dramatically. An overdose of this would not induce death but eradicate all feelings of pain, whilst also giving the most amazing boost of energy the body could handle. Rafievn looked at the container knowing that he would need it for the gamble he was willing to take. Every piece of kit was meticulously cleaned and checked.

Time passed, and then the communicator buzzed into life with a message. It was news that would make the local people happy if the girl was fertile, but Rafievn was still tinged with guilt about the whole situation. Sanluin's words of love and encouragement made Rafievn feel a bit better. He sent back a long and sensitive message, telling Sanluin that he loved her with every ounce of his soul. He then put the sensor to his temple, activated the codes and allowed his mind to be filled with the presence of Sanluin. It was just like in a dream but a hundred times more realistic, he could even smell Sanluin; it was an amazing sensation to feel so close to someone who wasn't even there. Rafievn still had his eyes shut but when he opened them, to his amazement he saw Sanluin's face, as if she stood in front of him. He took the sensor away and slowly the image diminished along with his thoughts of her. It took a few minutes for Rafievn to come to his senses. He sat down and came off this massive high of almost being with Sanluin. The sensor on the communicator was still connected by wire but could be disconnected and work by remote.

He would need to do this when he slept with the girl but knew that his hair would cover the sensor on his temple and not be visible.

The night had cooled considerably outside but the hut still retained the day's heat. Rafievn took his skins off and was surprised how much he was starting to smell like the locals. He also noticed that he had only four mouthwash tablets left, but took one anyway for the girl's sake, even though her breath would probably be as bad as the other womens'. When she came out of sedation he would make the girl take one of the tablets too, to be fair to himself.

One more hour passed and the girl started to stir, Rafievn went over and offered her some water without any added chemicals. She drank eagerly from the bowl and Rafievn offered her the mouthwash tablet. He showed her how to take it and she swished it around her mouth. Her eyes widened as the tablet frothed in her mouth; years of plaque were dissolved as the substance killed off the bacteria and there was so much froth, it spilled out of her mouth. Rafievn showed her to spit and she copied him by spitting the lot on the floor. She rinsed her mouth with water and felt her teeth with her fingers, rubbing her tongue across her smooth teeth. The girl muttered to Rafievn; she was saying how good it felt now that all the fur had gone from her mouth. Rafievn just smiled and went over to his cordless sensor and set the codes again. With his mind filled by thoughts of Sanluin, he lay next to the girl and took off her clothing. Her body was taught and young but had never seen a razor; all this slowly disappeared as the vision of Sanluin fell into his eyes. Rafievn kissed the girl with hesitation, but even this was just like kissing Sanluin. He eased himself on top of her and she responded by wrapping her legs around him. The young woman felt the full force of Rafievn's loaded loins. The mind alteration allowed him to orgasm over and over well into the small hours. Finally he rolled back on to the bed, totally exhausted from his performance. The girl was bathed in sweat and full of Rafievn's seed, which would find her fertile eggs. She was left trembling by the onslaught from Rafievn.

As Rafievn removed the sensor from his temple, he felt terrible feelings of guilt flood over him; he wanted to be a million miles from that bed. Never in his life had he felt so untrue to anyone, as well as himself. The deed itself was totally falsified by the images of Sanluin but now back in reality, the dark and dirty feelings were only too real. Rafievn got up from the bed and dressed into his skins. He gathered his pack together and headed straight for the river where the stones were being hauled onto the land; he wanted to wash his body, hoping it would also help to cleanse his memory. As he was walking past the monument, he remembered how he eradicated the mens' memories before and realised he could eradicate the evening's events from his own head. First, he would wash his body thoroughly, then he would clean his mind.

It was early morning as Rafievn reached the river. The log rails waiting patiently for the next stone were snuggled in the damp grass; cobwebs were visible as the early morning dew hung delicately on them. The water was very still, not a ripple on its surface, only vapour rising. Rafievn stripped naked and dived straight in; once again, he felt the freshness of the water wash over him. As he came to the surface the cool morning air made the water feel much warmer to his skin, so he just held his head above the water. Rubbing his body and ridding it from the sweat of the girl and himself, made him feel better. He couldn't help thinking of Sanluin and what she was doing at this very moment; he thought back to their swim on the islands when they first landed. He started to swim up stream, imagining that Sanluin was with him and must have swum for at least fifteen minutes without realising the time, before heading back before anyone came across his kit. The swim back was quicker as he swam with the flow of the river.

Once dried and dressed in his skins, he got out the communicator and set about the memory eradication. He set it to erase the previous ten hours, from just after the feast. With the sensor pressed to his temple, Rafievn set the programme with slight anticipation, as he had never done this before to himself. His mind went blank for a moment. He set the programme and his vision blacked out for a split second, he then re-focused even though his eyes were still open. Rafievn looked around and wondered what he was doing by the river. He saw his kit and tried to think why he was sat by the river so early in the morning with his communicator out and the sensor to his head. What had he done to get here? This was bizarre he thought to himself. He thought back to the last thing he remembered; it was having a meal with the elders in the central hut, there were strangers as well as a group of young women. Before then he was hunting with the men and he had injected them with the dormant gene. He took his thoughts back to the hut but wondered why all of a sudden he had come to the river. How did he get there? Rafievn's memory was a complete blank just as he had programmed it to be, but it totally confused him, as he had no idea how he had got to the river. He put it down to sleepwalking; something he had never done before but it was the only option to keep him from going mad trying to remember. Looking at the communicator he saw that it had been set to memory erase. Did he erase his own memory, he thought to himself? If so, why did he do it? This was the side of memory eradication that can drive someone mad. He packed away his kit and walked back to the settlement trying to forget the problem with his memory.

Ashait got up and prepared a breakfast of bread and oats, mixing the oats with goat's milk and then heating it on the fire. Cinciev woke to the smell of the cooking.

"Why are you are up so early?" he asked Ashait, still yawning.

"I have to go to work. I will find out about the Hareem; there is a delivery of sandals that has to be ready in two days and I will ask if I can take them myself. Come, eat your breakfast you need to keep your energy up," she said with an amorous look in her eye. Cinciev ate every scrap in his bowl and looked forward to going out that day, as he would understand the banter of the local people with ease. Ashait kissed him on the head and left for work. Cinciev took out a tablet to wash his mouth and teeth, dressed and packed away his kit. He took only his communicator, so that he could scan some of the writing carved into the walls of the great buildings.

As Cinciev stood near the doorway of the house, he was amazed how he understood what the local people were saying. Although he was billions of miles from Atronia, the way people were talking could have been just like a busy street in his home city, Leetyi. They were just going about their every day business. Cinciev was ear-wigging what two women were discussing; how they both found one of the shop keepers very attractive, saying they would quite happily leave their husbands for him, if it were possible. Cinciev laughed as he heard the gossip. Nothing seems to change with humans, even when they are from different planets.

He walked into the morning sun, which was pouring over the roof of Ashait's house; come midday the front of the house would be too hot to touch. Cinciev casually strolled through the town much slower than usual, as he loved to hear what was going on in the town. It must be classed as a city he thought to himself, by the amount of buildings, especially the massive pyramids and the Iaan. Cinciev decided to walk north along the river; he hadn't been that way yet as he was unsure of the area but with his understanding of the new language in his armoury, he was much more confident. About a mile downstream he could see a jetty with many boats moored up to it. They were all preparing for a voyage, so Cinciev put a spring in his step to find out where they were going. As he got closer he saw nets being loaded into the boats and some of the crew inspecting them for damage. The smell of the fish was very strong and Cinciev wondered how the sailors stomached it in such close proximity all day. The boats were primitive but well built, their joints well crafted and the boats looked like they could handle quite heavy seas. Cinciev remembered from when he was looking down from Hope, a large sea to the north. That must be where they were heading, as plenty of provisions were also packed away. One of the crew acknowledged Cinciev while he was looking in the boat.

"Will you be fishing for many days?" asked Cinciev.

"We will be gone for about a week depending on the catch," the man replied. His skin was very dark, weathered by the sun, but his body was young by the look of his taut skin over his lean muscles.

"Do you take passengers on any of your trips?"

"Only if they pay well and don't get in the way," said the fisherman, as he hoisted the boat's sail.

"I will see you again sometime; take care on the trip and good luck with the fishing." Cinciev walked back off the jetty and watched the boats prepare to depart. The boats rowed out clear from the jetty and then pulled the rigging to catch the breeze that was blowing south-easterly, perfect to carry them to the sea. The sails made that satisfying sound, as the wind blew them taught and the oarsmen drew in the oars as the breeze fuelled the boats. Cinciev thought back to when he sailed; the feeling of being thrust over the waves by a strong natural power was so exhilarating that he decided he would definitely sail with the fishermen one day.

He sat and watched the boats until they were out of sight. He couldn't help thinking how Dr Viuuv felt when Hope took off. It was very odd to have travelled on the most advanced ship ever built and soon to travel on one of the earliest ever built; a privilege he would have of being the only person of two planets and billions of people to experience. Cinciev walked back through the town and wondered how Rafievn was coping. It must be such a strain to know his child would be born without him being there or ever being able to see it. He would send Rafievn a message later to see how he was.

Ashait was busy at the sandal shop finishing off the order for the Pharaoh's court. She worked with great skill and speed and was highly valued by her employer, who was a large lady to say the least. She had taken over the business after her husband died and had stayed married to the art of making sandals and other leather goods since then. Her name was Affradees and she had known Ashait and her family for years. Ashait knew that she would let her take the delivery to the court without any questions.

When Ashait arrived home Cinciev was already home making supper. He had bought some Faiis and vegetables with freshly baked bread. He was boiling the Faiis and vegetables to make a broth.

"That smells good Cinciev, what's the occasion?"

"I just wanted to show my appreciation for your kindness."

"That's OK, Cinciev, only I have never felt this way about anyone before. The first time I saw you, I knew there was something different about you, not to mention how handsome you are."

"That first night, there was a young girl with you but I haven't seen her since."

"Oh, that was my niece, she lives two days away up the river with her parents; she often visits when they come to the city. Anyway, tell me what you have been up to today? Did you find the local people interesting, now you know what they are talking about?"

"Yes, and I went down to the jetty where the boats moor up when there not out fishing. I talked to one of the crew and asked him if he took passengers. He said he would at the right price."

"I would love to pay for you but it might cost more than I can afford Cinciev."

"I sailed a lot before and I could go along as one of the crew. They might give me a job if they think I am any use."

"I will miss you too much, they go for two weeks sometimes."

"I will only go on a short voyage with them, that is if they will have me." Cinciev went back to his cooking as Ashait laid the table and washed from her day's toil.

"How did you get on with the delivery Ashait? Will your boss let you take the sandals to the court?"

"Yes, that was never going to be a problem, I know Affradees too well. She would do anything rather than visit the court with those 'whinging whores', as she puts it. We will take them in two days time, so we will have time to make you look like an old maid by then."

"Well, I look forward to that Ashait." Cinciev took the cooking pot to the table and dished out the broth. They ate two helpings each and then discussed how they would get into the court.

The seasons were on the change, early autumn was just around the corner in the north and Sanluin still hadn't ventured outside Hope. The days were growing longer as the Antarctic summer approached. Nn had been out hunting sea birds, which Hope had processed and broken down into food paste. The foods contained better protein than the synthetic foods developed by the nano boxes. This would be essential for Sanluin and her baby. Hope had taken scans of the foetus and it was in good health but still too young to determine the sex. Sanluin was coping well considering the situation. Hope and Nn gave her plenty of support but she still felt this gaping chasm of loss for Rafievn. All she could do was to keep strong for Rafievn and send him positive messages. All this was to ensure that the dormant gene got passed on, as this would, with luck, lead to their discovery sometime in the future and the possible chance to save Planetician from the same fate as that of Atronia. Sanluin started to have morning sickness; the retching was terrible and could be avoided with medication but Sanluin wanted to experience everything that her baby would bring. It made her feel closer to Rafievn for some strange reason. The pain in her heart was eased by the sickness; it took her mind off dwelling too much on the loss of Rafievn.

As the days passed she concentrated more and more on the baby. All she had ever wanted was to be loved and in a secure family. Sometimes, thoughts of self-pity came into her mind but the fact that she and Rafievn had experienced something no other person had ever experienced before, put her thoughts into perspective. They had reached a place and felt freedom that could only be dreamed of. It hadn't lasted long but the memory of their time was full of such quality that it was enough to last a lifetime. Sanluin sent Rafievn a message, as she wanted to know all he was doing; she asked him for his picture, even though it would be of a bearded and rugged native by now. She wanted to see him in his skins and would imagine herself stood with him in the same attire.

Looking out of Hope's Bridge windows, Sanluin saw the sun lighting up the snow as it sparkled with the thousands of tiny lights that had enchanted her the first time she saw it. She would go out again but not yet; something so peaceful had taken Tehkin and she still hadn't gained enough confidence in the white wilderness. As the door of Hope opened a gust of icy wind blew in and sent a shiver over Sanluin's body, it was Nn coming in from clearing the build-up of snow around Hope's stabilisers. The blast of cold took Sanluin back to Tehkin's icy tomb, making her curl up on the chair and hold her legs tight to her chest for comfort. The door closed as Nn entered the ship and the cold air slowly warmed, as the haunting thoughts left Sanluin's mind.

"How long will it be Nn, before we will be covered in snow?"

" It will take some time as we don't know what the average snow fall is, we will have a much clearer picture this time next year." Another year Sanluin thought, could she cope? She had to she thought, the baby will be a few months old by then and Rafievn must see a picture of his child, it was the least she could do for him. Sanluin went into the pod room and lay in her pod. She set her communicator to read her memory of when she was on the beach with Rafievn. The communicator would then play it back to her, almost as vividly as if she was actually there. She closed her eyes and waited for the blissful and erotic memories to flood her mind.

As Rafievn approached the monument he saw the workers toiling away with the stones; they seemed to work much quicker than before and there was much more noise about them. Maybe it was because their old thug of a foreman was dead? The men acknowledged Rafievn and smiled as he passed them, which made Rafievn feel good about himself however, he wanted to be alone for a while. He had been to the south of the monument and now wanted go to the west, where the ocean was. He remembered observing from Hope that the ocean to the west went straight down to where Sanluin was; if he could see the ocean he would feel closer to her. By the scale of the land he calculated that it would take him a good week to get to the ocean, as it must be nearly 40 miles. A break from these people would do him good, so he decided not to waste any time and head off that day. Before he left, he went to the settlement and tried to tell Thiis that he would be gone for some time but would be back to see how they were getting on with the monument. It was hard-going explaining to Thiis but eventually he got through. Rafievn ate well before he set off and took as much food as he could carry. He didn't want to be hungry if the hunting was dry.

It was midday when Rafievn left the settlement and as he walked by the last hut, a young girl looked at him with a very warm look in her eye; little did Rafievn know, it was the girl he had erased from his memory from the previous night. She felt a physical urge for him but didn't know what to say. She folded her arms and held her own body as Rafievn had done the night before yet wanted him to make her feel that way again, a way she had never experienced before. Rafievn walked away puzzled by the glancing encounter. He had walked far enough away from the village so it was safe to put his boots back on. He removed the skins he had fashioned for shoes and put on fresh socks and his comfy boots. It was luxury for his feet, which had been damp and sore from the skins for so long. He could walk much quicker now not feeling every stone in the ground.

As Rafievn walked past the trees, he noticed something different about them; they were changing colour very slightly and losing their leaves. The season must be on the change he thought to himself; the temperature was still warm enough to be bare-chested in the day but it was getting colder at night. He didn't want to be away from the village if the weather got really bad, as his kit could only take so much of a battering before it would start to get damaged. He would reach the ocean and stay there a few days, returning to the village before winter set in.

Rafievn covered a lot of ground before nightfall; he set up camp and ate well before reading any messages. He was pleased to hear from Cinciev but couldn't help be envious of him, as he had met someone he cared for, whilst he was never to see Sanluin again. The people where Cinciev was seemed much more sophisticated than the people Rafievn had encountered, but apart from all their faults, they had given Rafievn shelter and food, as well as offered him women for his trouble. Rafievn was just glad he had never accepted any of the women, as he couldn't bear to be untrue to Sanluin. He read Sanluin's message and replied by thought as it was going to be a very long message.

After two days hard trekking, Rafievn came to high ground; the land to the south was quite flat and the ocean could be seen in the distance. The water looked very grey, this was because it was estuary water, carrying silt from the banks. He had seen no other people for the two days he had been on the go, but could see smoke coming from a few settlements in the distance, on the edge of the hill. He decided to head north, as he had made good ground and there was plenty of time to get to the ocean. The walk took him to a cliff edge that formed a gorge, which meandered its way down to more low and level ground. The height of the cliffs in places must have been at least 400 feet. He sat by the cliff edge and looked out to the estuary, which was on the move constantly from the tide. The readings of this area from Hope had shown that the tide had a speed of 12 knots, which was much stronger than any on Atronia. Picking up a stone the size of his fist, Rafievn hurled it over the edge, listening for it to land. The stone smashed on the rocks below and echoed around the walls of the gorge. He wondered whether this would be a good place to take his gamble, then again, no place would be good for the gamble he was willing to take.

There was plenty of Hunnit around, so before setting off

hot steaming skin.

"How does that feel?" he asked, as he tied the leather lace. The girl stood up and walked towards the window, her buttocks were perfectly shaped and smooth. The maid only just pulled the comb out of her hair in time as the girl stood up. The light from the setting sun shone between her legs as she moved her feet in the sandals. It looked very erotic, but Cinciev stopped staring so as not to upset Ashait. The girl walked back and sat down.

"They are very good old woman, now take them off, I want to return to my bath."

"As you wish, and my name is Affradees." Ashait quickly apologised for Cinciev to the girl, saying that Affradees didn't mean to be rude. Ashait nudged Cinciev with her elbow. Cinciev looked at the floor, as it was the only safe haven for him. They were fitting the sandals for over an hour and it was hard going, being spoken to like dirt but Cinciev didn't seem to mind too much. When they were finished they went back to the hallway where Tooru offered them supper as it was getting late. This was an ideal opportunity to get into the kitchens. Ashait and Cinciev followed the maid into the kitchen and sat at a table that was laden with food.

"Who is this food for?" Ashait asked.

"It is for the girls, they are very fussy you know, sometimes I just feel like giving them what normal people eat. Still, it means I get to eat what they get, which isn't too bad. Take what you want, there is plenty more." Ashait and Cinciev tucked in, they were very hungry from the day so far. Tooru sat down, sighing from a long day.

"I won't be able to keep this up for much longer, my legs are too old for this work," said Tooru.

"We will take the food through to the girls if you want to rest, you go on home and sleep," replied Ashait.

"That is kind of you, just lay it out in the next room when you are finished. To save you going back through the main gate, the deliveries come through that door which leads to the back gates, it will save you some time as the guard won't be at his post and he won't be in any rush to let you out."

"You are too kind Tooru, we may see you again sometime. Good night," said Ashait as Tooru gathered her bags and left.

"This couldn't have worked out any better Ashait."

"No it couldn't Cinciev. You have feasted your eyes as well as your stomach." It was reassuring to Cinciev that Ashait was jealous, even though she said that she loved him every day.

Cinciev got out his medic kit and mixed a sedative with the wine and water that was in jugs on the table. Ashait started to take the plates of food into the next room; it was decorated very ornately and the furniture was of the highest quality. She had never seen such a room. The table was carved from stone and looked like it was carved from one piece. She put the plates down and went back to fetch the rest. When she entered again two of the girls were looking at what was on offer. They looked up at Ashait.

"So you cook as well as make sandals, what talents you have," said one of the girls in a condescending way.

"I am just helping out the maid, she was very tired," replied Ashait with a bowed head.

"Bring the wine next, we are desperate for a drink."

"As you wish." Ashait fetched the wine with a grin on her face. When she returned, the rest of the girls had turned up for supper. They all went for the wine first and picked at the food like peacocks choosing only the finest seeds. They got through two large jugs, which were both laced with the sedative.

"How long will the drug take Cinciev?" whispered Ashait.

"Only a short while and they will be sleeping like babies." Cinciev got out the syringe for mixing the two blood types just as Rafievn had done a few weeks earlier. He tested the equipment and set the mixing codes. Quietly, he looked into the dining room and saw that the girls were all sitting down looking very drowsy, one by one they dropped off to sleep where they sat. He quickly went in and started to pass on the dormant gene; it took about forty seconds a girl, so within 15 minutes the whole Hareem was carrying the gene.

Ashait cleared away the kitchen and waited for Cinciev. He walked into the kitchen and sat at the table with the needle still in his arm. He pulled it out and took some energy tablets, which were the last lot in his rations. This gave him the boost he needed, as he was feeling very weak.

"Are you alright Cinciev, do you want a drink?" asked Ashait.

"Please Ashait, but not the water, it has the sedative in it." Ashait poured some fresh water from the vat and handed it to Cinciev, whose colour was returning to his face. They made their way out of the building the way Tooru had shown them. It was pitch black outside, the only light coming from the oil torches by the gate. This gate had a smaller door within, but it opened with ease. They were both out of the court and the mission had run without a hitch. Relaxing, they walked back to Ashait's house where they collapsed on the bed and slept well into the morning.

Rafievn woke to a fresh morning; he was a couple of days from the monument and wasn't looking forward to a winter of damp skins for shoes. He decided to cover his boots with new skins; at least he would have some comfort for the winter. The clouds were high in the sky as Rafievn walked briskly in his new skin covered boots, the thought of a dry-footed winter and the glorious autumnal weather had given him a lift. He gazed across the landscape, mostly covered in woodland and thought how it would change as the centuries went by. If the future of Planetician were going to be like the past of Atronia's, there would be much bloodshed in these lands. He just hoped that war or disease wouldn't wipe out the dormant gene. The gene would be resistant to most diseases but there could be a chance that it may not be able to cope with every disease it might encounter. The future chances of the mission being any sort of success, definitely lay with the Gods.

Rafievn constantly had a visual thought of Sanluin in the

back of his mind, of her warm and safe inside Hope, nurturing her pregnancy. His mind couldn't help but look in on them every so often. When the baby was born he decided he would travel back to the gorge and stay there until he was ready to take his gamble. He only hoped that Sanluin would understand his actions and maybe follow him. It would be a very hard decision to make but they would only prolong their pain of separation, which was definitely guaranteed if they stayed where they were. His earlier feelings of mild happiness soon left him, as he marched on not looking where he stepped and into a dark, lonely, desperately cold winter.

The weeks passed and the snow had built up to the belly of Hope. Nn, who had cleared the snow from her stabilisers, was now clearing it from her underside and had built a wall of snow circling Hope. In time this would slowly become a cavern to enclose Hope from the outside world. Sanluin was heavy with child and the only real connection with Rafievn was the pregnancy, as all other was through the screens. She was so desperate for him now, not for her sake or for the baby but for the sake of Rafievn, who had deteriorated, not physically but mentally. His messages tried to hide his feelings but Sanluin picked up how deep his depression had descended. She just hoped that the coming spring would lift his spirits, so that he could experience the feeling of being a father with a positive mind. The baby would be born in five weeks if all went to Hope's dates.

The winter in the north had been exceptionally miserable. It hadn't been that cold except for a two-week snap of snow and frost. It was a refreshing break for Rafievn, who had been the lowest he had ever been in his life, to see the crisp snows and frost. This enabled him to experience what it was like for Sanluin. Where she was the summer was coming to an end and the very short days of the Antarctic winter approached. Sanluin told Rafievn how the baby kicked and wriggled; she was in such an awful position knowing how eagerly he wanted news of the baby, while appreciating how much it would upset him.

Cinciev had sent a message to Hope that Ashait was pregnant and guessed the baby would be born in midsummer. He said how hot the summers were and how Ashait would struggle with the heat. Sanluin was so pleased for him, knowing that his wife on Atronia could not conceive; it was one of the reasons she left him. He deserved this good fortune, which also meant there was another generation carrying the dormant gene. Ashait had heard news that some of the girls in the Hareem were carrying the Pharaoh's children, which made Cinciev very happy considering all the effort and acting he had done to make it possible.

Rafievn had been out during the winter with hunting parties to keep himself busy. The work on the monument had slowed considerably and only a few gangs went up to the monument when the weather was fine to dress the stones for fitting the following spring. The weather was starting to break and signs of spring were starting to show. There were small white flowers in the woods with heads that drooped downward. Rafievn would love to pick some for Sanluin but could only send her a picture of them. He was looking very different now with a fully-grown beard that covered his angular features, and he smelt like the natives and longed for a wash in the river once it got warm enough. His teeth had not been properly cleaned as his tablets had run out months before; he had only picked at them with fish bones to get the meat out, but was glad that he hadn't suffered any dental problems, as he was out of painkillers as well.

Lying on his bed, Rafievn woke to bright beams of sunlight finding their way through the walls of his hut, they were like the slim tentacles of some eager mass of light wanting to flood the darkness. He got up and wandered outside. It was the best day for weeks, as well as the mildest. He wanted to wash so badly he decided to go to the river and try the water. Not bothering with any food, he gathered his pack, which he had constantly checked to enure the skins covered it, and made his way to the river; it was only the night before that he had sent Sanluin a message telling her how desperate he was for a wash. It looked like she answered it for him with the fine weather that seemed to wash over the damp settlement with a burst of freshness.

As he approached the river he noticed three stones moored up ready for their final part of the journey to the monument. Thiis had managed to tell Rafievn that they were brought from many days away, from where the sun went each night. The stones were always

however, would benefit humans in the long run.

Renut and Luta had pulled the nets in and the mass of fish made the water boil with their captured struggle, their scales catching the sun and reflecting it back, like millions of stars packed together. Taita grabbed a leather bucket with holes in the bottom for water to escape, and pushed it under the writhing bodies of fish. A strong rope was tied to the sides of the bucket and the eyelets were reinforced with metal rings. Taita pulled the bucket out of the throng and poured the fish into the hull of the boat. The fish slapped about on the planking, their mouths gasping. Renut and Luta tied off the ends of the net and sorted the fish into bags that had been woven from reed. They gave each fish a sharp knock on the head and slipped them into the bags. Captain Thanus was counting each bag as it was stored out of the sun. Sweat poured from the face of each man and Cinciev fetched them water as they toiled; it took over an hour to bring the catch in before the men sat down, exhausted from their work.

"That's the best catch I have ever had," Captain Thanus said, as he looked at the mass of bags stored in the hold. "We can go back early as there is no more room on the boat for any more." Cinciev was glad to hear it knowing Ashait would be pleased to see him back ahead of schedule.

"Before we set sail, we will celebrate our good fortune and the ingenuity of our guest." Captain Thanus reached into his chest and pulled out two jugs of wine. "I was saving these for later but we might as well drink them now, as we are heading back." He passed one to Renut who took the jug and drank from it straightaway, the red liquid running down his chin and mixing with the sweat that glistened on his bare and hairless chest.

"Here Cinciev, take a swig, you deserve it," Renut said handing him the jug while wiping the wine from his chin.

"Thank you." Cinciev drank the wine as Renut had done but wasn't ready for its raw strength and as he moved the jug from his mouth, he gasped and coughed.

"Not to your taste?" laughed Renut.

"Not what I'm used to Renut, but not too bad." Cinciev passed the jug to Taita who swigged away and then showed his inexperience of strong alcohol by the squinted expression on his face. Cinciev felt his stomach battle with the wine; it took him back to his youth when he first had a drink.

It was late afternoon and the breeze had picked up a little. It still blew in from the west, so getting back would be an easy affair. The heavy cargo made the boat react much more slowly, as Captain Thanus turned it round. Luta pulled the sail into the wind and lashed it down ready for the voyage home. The extra weight in the boat added to the ballast; the ride was smooth but the wake behind the boat was much greater. Taita and Luta prepared a fire in a small stove and started cooking a couple of the fresh fish. They had jugs of water nearby, just in case the boat suddenly listed and the fire from the stove spilled onto the deck.

The darkening sea finally swallowed the sun, the fish Taita was cooking simmered away in the wine and herbs that sent mouth-watering aromas into the air. When cooked, the fish tasted delicious and the crew had their hunger quashed by Taita's expert cooking that he had learned from his mother. Captain Thanus settled down in the hull of the boat next to the spare masts that had been untied from the stern of the boat. He was snoring away in no time, as the unexpectedly long day had taken its toll.

Ashait had stayed up late into the night worrying about Cinciev. She hadn't been alone for months and now that she was pregnant, it made the loneliness worse. Unbeknown to her it would only be a few more days until Cinciev would return. He woke just as dawn was breaking; he had slept like a baby, the gentle rocking of the boat acting like a child's cradle. He looked towards the bow of the boat and was surprised to notice that land was still a few hours away. The breeze in the night had dropped considerably and the rowing of Luta and Taita was much slower due to the heavy load.

"Cinciev, shall we relieve the two rowers for a while, they look exhausted?" offered Renut, as he hopped down from the rudder, which was tied off to the stern braces.

"OK, Renut. Let's show them how it's done!" Cinciev took the oar from Taita, who quickly went to the rudder and assumed the role of captain. Cinciev sat on the rowing bench that had been warmed by Taita and started to row. He wished he hadn't been so cocky, as the rowing turned out to be very hard work and his hands were soon starting to blister. He looked across at Renut who was pulling easily on his oar. His body movement was programmed to move perfectly with the oar and his leathery hands showed the handle no mercy. Through gritted teeth Cinciev carried on, his pride overcoming the agonising pain. Captain Thanus woke and stood up, stretching his back, which clicked and crunched as he moved it.

"Good morning lads," he said, looking round the boat. "I see that my retirement might be sooner than I had expected; Taita is at the helm and we have a new oarsman and fisherman, who from the look of things, would rather fish than row?"

"You're right about the rowing Captain, my hands aren't used to this, I haven't rowed for years," replied Cinciev through gritted teeth.

"They will get used to it, just grin and bear it Cinciev," said Renut, showing Cinciev the palm of his hand while rowing with just as much ease one-handed. The water from the mouth of the river was mixing with the sea and the oar was being pulled in Cinciev's hands, as if there were someone on the other end. This made the blisters hurt even more but Cinciev carried on. The mouth of the river was closing in on them from both sides and Cinciev thought how he was once again in crocodile country; the safety of the quay was a magnet to row harder.

Captain Thanus was in a very relaxed and optimistic mood, as this new style of fishing would swell his wealth considerably. He tacked back up the river, taking advantage of the wind that had picked up from the southeast. It was just what Cinciev was praying for; as the wind caught the sails he and Renut pulled in the oars and stored them on their brackets. Renut got up, fetched a jug of water and poured it over his body, rinsing the sweat from his pours. He drank the remainder and then refilled the jug from the keg.

"Do you want water Cinciev?" Renut filled the jug as Cinciev was stretching backwards, his back ached so much he feared it would snap. Cinciev's blistered hands stuck to his tunic and when he pulled them off the fabric, bits of skin hung from his palms, as the fabric had more purchase on the skin than his hands did. Renut could see the pain in Cinciev's face and held the jug to his lips. The water was cool and overflowed from his mouth, dripping onto the deck that was already dampened by sweat. The journey back up river would take two days but this would give Cinciev time to recover from the marathon row he had just endured.

Three days had passed since Rafievn left the monument and still there was no news from Sanluin. Rafievn hadn't travelled as far as the last time he'd made the journey as he had taken a different route. He decided to camp by a stream where it had formed into a small pool on its way to the river and decided he wouldn't move until he got word from Sanluin. Rafievn washed in the pool, which still held in it the cold from the winter. Dressing in fresh clothes for the first time in months lifted his spirits, but the lack of news from Sanluin worried him immensely. His reflection in the water was unrecognisable once the ripples had flattened. He reached into his pack and found a razor that hadn't been used since he was on Hope. On closer inspection he saw that the hairs caught in between the blades were not his, they belonged to Sanluin. It hit him that this was the only physical presence he had of Sanluin, like an unexpected punch. Part of her was with him and in any normal situation he would not even have noticed, but now it meant so much to hold even a minute part of the most important person in his life. He tapped the hairs from the razor into his hand and felt them with the tip of his finger. Though short, they were still soft and with the utmost care he sniffed the hairs to get the faintest smell of her, closing his eyes as if he was with her again; he was on the beach where they had caught the fish and remembered holding her head in his hands and stroking her hair. With a rush of uncontrollable emotion he started to cry, the tears falling onto his palm and swamping the tiny fair hairs. His tears saved the only part of her from blowing away. Carefully, he got out his medic kit and put the mixture of hair and tears into a sealed container used for drugs and only once they were safe, could he wipe his swollen eyes with the back of his hand. The container held the two of them safely together and was now the most precious item he had ever possessed.

Suddenly, his communicator buzzed into life with a message from Sanluin. Grabbing the sensor he placed it to his temple and replied to her as he read the message. The message read, 'My dear Rafievn, so sorry for not being in contact recently but I had to have some time to think; it is not like I am short of time but what I have thought about needed some very deep and careful thought. I haven't told Hope about it but then again I wouldn't need to, as Hope can pick up my brain signals and know what I am about to do before I even do it. From your messages I know that you can't go on for much longer; your pain being so much greater than mine, as very soon I will have our baby to help me.' The words cut deep into Rafievn's heart. 'Please hold on until the baby is born, I need you to be there for me even though it is just through a screen on our communicators. The baby will be soon. I am having small contractions but there is nothing to worry about; Nn has been programmed to be a midwife and he is monitoring the baby every second, he even tells me when I should rest if the baby gets slightly stressed in my womb. Yesterday I went out onto the snow for the first time since Tehkin died. Hope has snow up to her belly now and Nn is steadily forming a wall of snow and ice around her. We will be completely covered in a few years so

193

no one will ever find us until the dormant gene is activated. Cinciev has got involved with a fishing boat and will hide his equipment at sea in a stone coffin. He seems very happy with Ashait. I found it hard to accept this at first, as we are separated but he should have our best wishes for the future. I will be in contact very soon, but don't panic if there is a delay as I might be busy having our baby. Take care my love, Sanluin.'

Rafievn went on sending his message by thought for ten minutes. He was so pleased to hear from her and the fact that he found some of her hairs in his razor made him feel the closest he had felt to her for months. This gave him the strength to carry on and he felt much more confident that the gamble wouldn't be the end but the start of a new beginning. It was the first time that he felt his gamble was the right thing to do, and not an easy way out. The next days' walks were a mix of spring showers and hot sunshine, the woodland and meadows were bursting into life and the smell of this new beginning lifted his spirits. Every time he thought of Sanluin he held the drug container tightly, as if he were holding her hand. From her last message he knew that in time he would be with her again, but not in this life.

Cinciev was stood on the bow of the boat as she slowly turned into the quay. There were only two other boats moored up and the crews off them had packed and secured the sails, and were either in for repairs or the catch had been poor. Cinciev threw the bow rope onto the quay and hopped off the boat just as she was about to dock. He secured the rope, as the weight of the boat creaked the fibres and he squeezed out what moisture there had been in the rope. His blistered hands were now bandaged up and although it was painful, he still managed to handle his chores. Cinciev waited on the quay as the stern came round, and Luta secured the ropes to the timber trunks that made up the main structure of the quay. Jumping back aboard he gathered up his belongings and went over to Captain Thanus.

"What do I owe you for the trip Captain?" asked Cinciev, while reaching into his money pouch.

"It is I who should be paying you Cinciev. It could take us as much as four separate trips to catch that amount of fish; this one is on me. If you want to come again, just ask and you will be welcome."

"Thank you very much Captain." Cinciev held out his hand and shook the Captain's hand firmly, forgetting his blisters. He winced in discomfort as the Captain's grip was just like Renut's but Cinciev didn't show his pain.

"See you all again soon I hope," Cinciev called out to the rest of the crew who were busy readying the boat to be unloaded. They called back and said their farewells as Cinciev jumped back on the quay and headed home to Ashait. Apart from his hands, the trip had gone according to plan and it wouldn't be long until he could off-load his belongings, which were a weight around his neck having to watch them constantly and trust they were never stolen.

Sanluin was getting more and more contractions but Nn was monitoring the pregnancy constantly and she hadn't gone into labour yet, but it wouldn't be long. She was constantly cleaning Hope; it was her nesting instinct. Nn could clean but she refused to let him, so he just helped her and kept out of the way. Nn had converted the sick bay to the birth room and Hope had set new programmes that would direct Nn through the whole birth. Dr. Viuuv had yearned for a grandchild so he had prepared for this if ever Sanluin fell pregnant. It would only be the synthetic copy of Dr. Viuuv that would ever see the baby but at least it would be something for him, as by now he had been living with the Dooduin in the northern steppes for months. The journey through space and the hyper sleep suspended the crews' life but the people they left behind carried on ageing. Sanluin never thought of her father ageing, as he was so well and healthy when she had left; that was what she had locked in her mind. She would never see him deteriorate with age.

It had been a couple of months since Sanluin had been

outside Hope and she felt that she needed the fresh air, equally the gentle exercise might bring on the birth. She changed into her thermal suit, which had been renewed by Hope to fit her new shape and then opened the door to the outside. The build up of snow Nn had formed around the perimeter of Hope dampened the usual blast of icy cold air. He had cut a corridor to the open vastness of snow that was downwind from the gales blowing in off the sea; the same sea that had been forced miles away due to the expansion of the winter ice sheet.

Sanluin stepped out of the perimeter snow, walked to higher ground and looked out to the sea that was just visible on the horizon. The water was reflecting the grey clouds, which seemed to hang heavy in the sky, giving a sharp contrast to the brilliant white that stretched from her feet to the horizon. The picture in her mind was the shape of the island where Rafievn was, knowing he was making his final journey. She did not feel sadness any more but slightly relieved, knowing that his pain would soon be over. Although she had never shown it to Rafievn in her messages, she too was in just as much pain, the baby had just distracted it but the intensity was there every time she let her thoughts dwell on the situation.

Sanluin had decided that she would follow Rafievn, not directly after the baby but in her own good time, as she knew Rafievn would be waiting. She walked a little further on the snow and the usual squeaking beneath her feet reminded her of the last time she was out in this untouched wilderness. She wondered if this would be the last time she would ever venture outside, as the baby was due any minute. The journey that brought her to this place had been so long, but the last few months had been filled with all the events of a lifetime. Her time spent with Rafievn was too short but she was grateful for the intense love they shared. Their situation magnified their love, as they had experienced the discovery of another planet, identical to their own but the balance tipped only too soon with their separation. The job of passing on the dormant gene to Planetician's native people and the responsibility they owed them, had parried the initial shock. It was only now, with time to dwell, they felt sorry for themselves but soon the baby would keep their minds busy. It would be the start of the end for them, but their choice to try and be together had given them fresh hope. Never before had they thought of ending their own lives' but the love they had for each other was so strong, it outweighed the option of living apart.

She thought how much in the coming 4,000 years Planetician would change. She would be preserved in her pod but what would the reaction be by whoever found her? It seemed the fate of Atronia would benefit this beautiful planet, where human beings were having a second chance to get evolution right. Hope and her crew were the connection between the two planets, as well as messengers with a warning for a humane evolution, rather than one that would blindly slide into its own destruction. When Hope eventually got discovered, the people who would find her would have such a burden placed upon them that it would change their lives' beyond any stretch of their imagination. During the time Hope had been stranded in the southern ice cap, she had assessed the situation and knew what needed to be done to stop the future people of Planetician slipping into the same trap that Atronia's people had. It was inevitable they would develop the same technology that had been developed on Atronia but Hope had the advantage of time, and Sanluin's baby would be an essential part of the blocking gene, which would have to be developed.

Sanluin turned to walk back to Hope when suddenly her waters broke and her suit was flooded with the liquid padding that had protected the baby for the past nine months. No sooner had she looked down to see the flood and the melting snow by her feet when Nn was there to help her back to Hope. He knew from the monitoring that her waters were going to break, so she was never further than a few seconds away.

"Nn," Sanluin said instinctively and looked up to see Nn

holding his hand out to her.

"It won't be long now but lets get you inside Sanluin, take it easy." Nn had spoken in her father's voice, which was reassuring but she was still swamped with fear, as she knew that childbirth could be very painful. Hope had all the necessary equipment to make the birth completely painless but she wanted to feel the birth; it was her way of feeling closer to Rafievn, as numbing the birth would distance her from his only physical presence left with her. Her feet squelched in her boots as she slowly walked back to Hope, with Nn helping her stop from slipping all the way. Her waters puddled where her feet had stepped in the snow and the freezing temperatures had frozen the first signs of a birth by a human being on another planet. The footprints would be frozen in time, lying hidden in the layers of snow; a discovery that would be connected to Hope, which would be fully operational, except for the fact that her time in the air had died along with Tehkin.

Safely back in Hope, Sanluin changed, washed and padded for the remaining waters, which seemed to trickle out relentlessly. She walked around the ship waiting for the next stage of the labour. She wanted the real contractions to start when suddenly she realised she hadn't told Rafievn. She went to send a message to Rafievn and told him that it would be very soon that he would be a dad.

"It could be hours until you go into full labour so try to rest; the birth room is ready for you, just relax, everything is in hand." Nn's calmness in the situation was just what she needed. The next few hours passed and Sanluin was glad to read a message from Rafievn who was almost in a trance-like state thinking of her going into labour. He was being mentally torn to pieces but knowing that Sanluin was in the capable hands of Nn, who posed no jealousy for Rafievn as he was only a droid, helped him keep his sanity.

The only other time Rafievn had witnessed childbirth was when he and his unit were on exercise in one of the more desolate, northern regions of Atronia. The unit had come across a small group of Dooduin people, one of the only remaining nomadic people to exist on Atronia. The Corporations ignored their existence, but these people represented the only chance Atronians would have when the virus swept through the nano-beings and food production ceased to be viable. The Dooduin would be the sole survivors and anybody they came across would adopt their way of living, surviving off the land, just as they had done for centuries.

It had been midwinter when Rafievn's unit came across the Dooduin camp; they would have passed it by but the cries of a woman giving birth, gave reason for them to stop. The cries were so loud that Rafievn had thought someone was being tortured and he had gone into the camp to investigate. The circular huts in the camp were made from animal skins and enabled them to be packed away and carried by Lactte, and a type of Seeor. Rafievn had called through the skin-door of the hut in the rough tongue of the Dooduin and a young boy, whose face was wrought with fear and as pale as a full moon had appeared at the door. Inside the hut was a man bending over a woman, writhing in agony and the crying of a newborn baby was drowned out by the woman's shrieks. Rafievn had called to his medic who raced over to the hut and they both entered, seeing the man in tears as he realised he was losing his wife because of the birth. The medic had quickly injected the woman with a nano-code programmed to identify any malfunction with the birth. The Dooduin people are a tough breed and her strength had carried her through long enough for the nano-codes to take effect. Within the hour she was stable and the haemorrhaging had stopped and as night fell silent, the gentle suckling of the newborn, feeding greedily on her mother's rich milk, was the only noise to be heard. The father had given Rafievn a shaped bone, carved from an Iaan, who roamed the northern wastes. It was a sacred item, as these animals were never hunted and represented the most valued gift a Dooduin could offer. It was thought that Iaans carried powers from the spirit-world and if a man killed one, his family would be cursed forever; this bone must have come from an animal that had died of natural causes. These Iaans were also as white as snow; you could walk by one without even noticing it was there in winter. Rafievn had accepted the gift and left the family with a healthy new baby who would carry on the Doodiun's survival. He walked away from the hut knowing that he had helped a group of people who only took what they needed and needed what they took from the planet; it was the nearest perfect balance that human and nature could achieve.

Coming out of these thoughts, he remembered the bone was in his kit and frantically went through his pockets until he found it. In the same pocket was a drug, only to be used as a last resort for survival. He put the drug back and held the bone tight, hoping the spirit would see Sanluin safely through the birth of their baby, even though it was a spirit from another planet.

The contractions came more and more regularly, causing Sanluin so much pain. She walked round and round Hope trying to ease her discomfort. Nn was sat patiently monitoring all her functions; her heartbeat and stress level, as well as the baby's heart, oxygen and stress level. They were both doing well considering Sanluin was going through the labour with no other human contact on the ship. Nn was some comfort to her and maybe she might have felt closer to him, but he was only a droid. What she didn't know was that Nn's synthetic brain was a replica of Dr Viuuv's own brain. It was the only way that Dr Viuuv could be with his daughter and be as close to her as when she was on Atronia.

Three hours had passed and Sanluin was sweating profusely; Nn was dabbing her head with a damp cloth while following her round Hope. He tried to persuade her to lie down but she still paced the ship in the same pattern; out of the birth room to the Bridge then into the galley, where she would drink some water and then back to the birth room. Nn had taken on the full role of midwife and felt the dilation of Sanluin's cervix. She was already 20mm dilated and the head of the baby was very close to the opening of the cervix.

For her first baby it was a very good labour and it wouldn't be long before Sanluin would have to start to push really hard to get the head past the cervix.

She clambered up onto the bed that Nn had converted in the sick bay and gripped the handles as another contraction wrenched her body in agony. Nn was by her side, content with progress as the monitoring was showing the normal levels of stress for this stage of birth. If Rafievn had been there it would be a different matter and he would probably be getting in the way, with his natural instinct as a father. As with most young men present at a birth, they tend to hamper matters, rather then help proceedings. Nn was the perfect person to be there, he was neither male nor female but the mixture of the two. Sanluin was oblivious to all of this as the pain that ripped through her with every contraction overwhelmed her. More and more often the contractions came, and the shrieks from Sanluin echoed around the ship. Nn remained as calm and supportive as ever. He could see the baby's head squeezing through the stretched flesh of Sanluin's vulva; it was a wonder it didn't tear under the pressure. Then, with one more push the head popped through and the tiniest hand pressed to the baby's left cheek.

"The head is through Sanluin, keep pushing and the body will follow soon enough." Gasping for breath and pushing once again the rest of the baby slipped out into the hands of Nn. Sanluin flopped back on the bed exhausted, her sweaty hair and skin sticking to the sheets.

"You have a beautiful baby girl Sanluin." Nn gave the baby a little tap on the back and she started to cry in short bursts, the noise of her baby numbed the pain Sanluin was feeling. Nn cut the umbilical cord, clamped it and then wrapped the baby in a clean sheet, placing her carefully in Sanluin's arms. Sanluin was so full of emotion, tears were running down her face and adding to the already soaking pillow. Her baby was so perfect; she studied her features with wide eyes, unable to blink, which stopped her crying for a short time. Then she thought of Rafievn and immediately she was sobbing uncontrollably again. Nn checked that the remainder of the afterbirth had come out and scanned for any haemorrhaging; there was none, and neither were any stitches required. Nn fetched Sanluin a high glucose drink, which she drank with great pleasure; the sweet liquid replenishing her spent energy as it flooded her stomach.

"Try the baby on your breast. She should be hungry." Sanluin lifted the baby's tiny head, which was covered in the finest of blond hair; it was slowly drying and coming unstuck from the scalp like the drying wings of a newly hatched butterfly. The baby latched onto Sanluin's nipple, which oozed with her rich colostrum; the baby's sucking action making delicate slurping noises as she fed. It was a beautiful feeling for Sanluin who was also glad of the release of pressure. Nn looked at mother and baby and thought Dr Viuuv would be proud. He then remembered he was the copy of Dr Viuuv, so he took the role of grandfather and even though he could not feel anything as a machine, he felt responsible.

"She is so beautiful Nn, she is the first Planetician to be born with parents from another planet. She is so pure Nn, what shall we call her?" Nn thought for a while and then looked out to the Bridge to the white mass that surrounded them.

"She can be called Sno, baby Sno; if you like it Sanluin?"

"I love it Nn. Baby Sno it is. Quickly, get me the communicator, I want to tell her father."

Rafievn was sat waiting for any news; he knew what Sanluin was going through from the time when he had been with the Dooduin people. He could imagine the shrieks echoing around Hope as he nervously clenched the communicator in his sweating hands. It buzzed suddenly and Rafievn nearly dropped it, as he desperately fumbled the keys for the message. Rafievn was totally oblivious to the dawn that was nearly breaking and the early morning bird song filling the air with its melodic din; all he could hear were the memories in his head of childbirth. Suddenly the words came up on the screen. 'My dear Rafievn, we have a beautiful baby girl. I have called her Sno; she is so perfect. I can't imagine what you must be going through but please be as happy as I am; my heart burns with pride but also for you to be here to hold her.' The message went on as Rafievn's tears fell to the screen of the communicator. He was so happy and proud but could feel the huge sadness build up in the back of his mind, he knew that the only chance he would have to be with them would be in another dimension, and that was not guaranteed. He still had to hide his kit, which would keep him busy for a few days while he conditioned his mind that his soul would soon be leaving his body. He tried not to think of the reality that he couldn't hold his baby or kiss Sanluin. He looked at his inevitable suicide as the start of a journey to be with them. This thinking slowly turned the dark view of death into a chink of light that would end his pain and hopefully take him to his family.

It was now time to hide his kit. He had seen some large boulders that looked like they were deposited by glaciers thousands of years ago; this was just the spot where his kit would probably never be found. The surrounding land would most probably be classed as a nature reserve or used as farmland. Similar types of wilderness on Atronia had stayed free from major construction work; Rafievn just hoped this spot would stay free from the buckets of excavating machines. The boulders had been deposited in such a way that allowed the earth beneath them to be dug out. Rafievn would have to brace the boulders with small tree trunks while he excavated the soil from underneath. His plan was to burn out the bracing, allowing the boulders to fall on top of his kit. He would then cover the tops of the stones with soil and in time grass would grow, leaving them there as natural as if nothing had ever happened.

Rafievn set to work using his Luuse alloy folding spade, its edge cutting through the turf with ease. It took most of the day to dig around the boulders and he was starting to feel very weak from the strenuous work. It was then that he remembered the energy drug; taking it would give him a massive energy boost. Knowing that his time was coming to an end, he would ration it until he needed the overdose that would numb his pain from the encroaching suicide. Taking the small container from the pocket on his arm, he poured some of the powder into his palm and with a slight hesitation, knowing that this was definitely the beginning of the end, he licked the powder, tasting its bitterness. The bitterness caused his mouth to salivate, which helped to wash the taste from his mouth. The energy rush was immense and his whole body wanted to explode into any sort of exercise. He started to dig with a frenzy of flying earth and dripping sweat; his muscles felt no lactic acid build up but kept pumping like well-oiled machines. He had dug down and was waist high with the level of the ground; both edges of the spade were sharpened so it could be used as an axe, making light work of felling the young trees dotted around the surrounding area in small clumps.

By the end of the day most of the bracing had been complete and Rafievn used the waste timber for a fire. The sap from the freshly cut timber bubbled out from the end of the logs, as the Hunnit he had caught, dripped its fat onto the fire. He looked into the flames thinking deeply about his child and how Sanluin must be feeling, his face hot from the fire. He had already conditioned his mind to what he had to do and this had numbed his feelings a little. His thoughts had taken away the comedown from the drug and suddenly he felt exhausted, before he knew it he was snoring away under his bivouac.

The following morning started with the buzz of his communicator, it was a message from Sanluin. After reading it Rafievn sent her a reply and also sent a message to Cinciev telling him that he would be leaving. He wished Cinciev happiness for his future with Ashait and the children he would have, and also thanked him for the support he had given him over the months they had spent on Planetician. It wasn't until the following morning that he got a reply back from Cinciev.

Cinciev felt helpless and also a slight tinge of guilt that he was with Ashait and that he had access to sea-faring boats but none that could carry Rafievn to Sanluin. It was possible that he could reach Rafievn but then what? See Rafievn go through even more pain. It would be torture for him and this helped Cinciev accept the realisation that what Rafievn was going to do was the only option. Cinciev sent a message of support to Rafievn and also a reminder of what they had achieved as humans for another human race; the possibility not to make the same mistake people on Atronia had. This was testament to them and they should be proud of the unselfish way they had behaved on arriving on Planetician.

Rafievn read the message and felt a huge sense of responsibility to the people of Planetician, although he had successfully fulfilled his task of passing on the dormant gene and was now about to do something just for himself, he knew he was leaving after doing his best for the future of the planet. What he didn't know was that his own offspring would help complete the monument he had also helped with, but more importantly, his and Sanluin's child would become the only human available for Nn to test an airborne genetic code, which would guarantee the survival of the human race on Planetician. His love for Sanluin gave the whole mission its success but this would only become apparent when in 4,000 years time, the people of Planetician would not be able to upgrade themselves with a genetic code, as it would have been blocked by a code developed by Nn thousands of years earlier in a space ship cocooned in ice. Baby Sno would be the guinea pig that would allow the blocking gene to be developed. Rafievn and Sanluin would never know this but, as Nn was soon to be in sole charge of the mission, the fact that he had no emotional feelings for a human only a programmed responsibility to help guarantee their survival, gave the roots of survival the best chance.

The morning was still but the air hung clean and fresh as Rafievn drew in a large lungful of air that was to be his last taste of the worlds he had known. He still had to complete the hiding of his equipment but most of the work had been done the day before. He had enough of the drug left he needed to take the leap from the cliff edge. He felt at ease with his ensuing suicide; it was a strange feeling for him to be so comfortable with death as he had never experienced even slight depression. He had valued life so much and could not understand why a person would choose to take his or her own. But here he was, close to ending his to be with his loved ones; maybe that was what made the whole situation so normal.

He looked at the huge stone he had braced and the pit he had dug beneath it. There were just a few more hours of digging to complete the task and then it would be down to potluck if it would ever be found. Rafievn dabbed some more of the drug onto his finger and rubbed it on his gums, the surge of energy was instant and he quickly got to work in the pit to maximise the effect of the drug. His body had already lost much of its fat stores and he was becoming leaner by the minute.

Sanluin was feeding the baby when Nn came in from scraping the endless barrage of snow from Hope's hull; the blizzard, which had been blowing relentlessly for two days, had a vicious howl that scared Sanluin but the love and warmth from baby Sno kept her calm.

"Are you hungry Sanluin?"

"Yes Nn. Can you get me the meal we had when we arrived on Planetician? It was the fish Rafievn and I caught."

"Yes Sanluin, it shouldn't take too long." All the new types of food they had eaten were examined by Hope and the molecular structure copied, to produce an endless supply of meals for Sanluin.

The same system was being used on Atronia but the virus would wipe it out, causing massive starvation across their world. Hope had all the possible virus codes locked well away from any of the systems on the ship.

Sanluin ate the meal; it took her back to when she first tasted it, on the windswept hillside on the first islands they had landed. She remembered how Rafievn had cooked it in the moss and how full of life he had been. She felt almost guilty for the way he felt now; it was his love for her that had driven him to the desperate fate he had chosen. Sanluin looked down at Sno sleeping, and thought how hard it will be for her to follow Rafievn, but she knew the time would come. She sent Rafievn another message and then lay next to Sno. Soon they were both in a deep sleep and Nn covered them with a quilt, made from the copied down from the sea birds he had caught.

Standing in his pit Rafievn was now a good foot below the surface, he had excavated at least eight tonnes of soil and stone. The supporting struts were holding the two large stones well and Rafievn started to gather his kit and put it in the pit. He had just picked up his communicator as it buzzed with a message from Sanluin. He read for at least ten minutes as Sanluin spilled her heart out to him. There he was, feeling so close to her but the physical distance was so far that his fate seemed to draw him closer to the suicide he was now more ready to take than ever. He sent a message back to Sanluin, it was only a few minutes long but the words would last until Sanluin was ready to join Rafievn.

Rafievn threw the communicator into the nest of timber from the pit's edge. It clattered its way through the tangled sticks and lay on top of his pack. He turned to the fire he had burning whilst he had been digging and picked up two large branches burning ferociously as the wind blew through them. It was then he remembered he had some of Sanluin's hair, mixed with his tears. He threw the branches back in the fire and scrambled into the pit. He cleared the branches from his pack and searched for his jacket with the drug container in one of the pockets. Ransacking his jacket he found the container and slowly opened it. The tiny hairs were there; he tapped them into his hand and clenched his fist tightly. He was holding a part of Sanluin that he would take with him to the end. He covered his kit again and climbed out; picking up the burning branches, while still clenching the hairs, he walked back to the pit. Hot embers fell and some landed on Rafievn's feet but he didn't flinch as his flesh blistered and burned. Rafievn looked once more at his only contact with Sanluin and felt so glad to be holding a part of her. He threw the branches into the pit, which exploded into a flurry of embers and crackles, as the small twigs instantly caught alight.

The day was drawing to a close as the fire grew, until it warmed Rafievn so much he had to step back. The struts were now well alight as the flames wrapped around them, eating their timber and turning it into a bellowing smoke that stained the underside of the stones black. Naked and now totally alone, Rafievn watched as the struts gave way and the huge stones crashed into the pit sending a blast of embers towards him. He didn't move as his beard singed, caught by the flying embers. Smoke filled the air, forcing Rafievn back until it cleared. He took some more of the drug and started to cover the stones, which lay in their new position as tombstones for his kit, a little proud from the surface of the ground. Using the shoulder blade bone of an adult Riind as a shovel, Rafievn had the stones covered in under an hour. He wasted no time and walked towards the cliff edge, which loomed dauntingly, a gaping chasm to the north, and prepared himself to die.

The remainder of the drug was in his clenched hand, as he had thrown the container into the pit. Looking skyward he thought of Atronia and her fate. He still had very strong feelings about Dr Viuuv's decision why only Tehkin could fly Hope but what is done is done. Standing at the precipice Rafievn looked down to the rocky gully below, he could just make out the rocks that littered the ground. This was to be his final resting place but only for his physical being, as he knew his spirit would have much travelling to do. He put his right foot right on a slab of granite that overhung the edge of the cliff and took large steps back. He wanted to time his run up to the millimetre so he would clear any jutting rocks as he fell. He was thirty strides from the edge and took a deep breath before taking the rest of the drug. His palm was clammy and it caused the powder to clump together; he licked it with feelings of apathy but for the chink of light that he would hopefully be with Sanluin and his baby. The energy rush was so great that it made his heart palpitate wildly.

Rafievn started to run, taking in huge lungfuls of air as he accelerated. Not once in his mind was there any notion to stop; he felt he was leaving an existence, which was only going to degrade him to the point where his cowardice would leave a beaten soul. The realisation that he was beating this fear spurred him on and just steps from the cliff edge, his heart started to give out but his momentum kept him going. He managed his last step, which slapped his foot on the granite slab, where just minutes earlier he had placed such a tentative foot. Launching his body into the black gaping gorge his heart finally packed up; the drug blanked the pain and his mind drifted into a soft, warm place where he saw Sanluin waiting for him with her beautiful smile. Rafievn's body hurtled to the ground, as the wind rippled his loose skin that had developed from the massive weight loss due to the drug-fuelled digging. Sickening thuds, followed by the clatter of dislodged stones were the last physical sounds from Rafievn on Planetician. His body lay broken and bloodied between two rocks that slowly turned red from his leaking corpse.

Sanluin sent message after message but to no avail, she knew Rafievn had gone but didn't want to accept it. She had not broken down yet, as she was still in shock but knew her grief would soon pour out. She contacted Cinciev who sent words of encouragement and sympathy, but she felt in her heart that her own time clock to suicide had started to tick. Baby Sno suckled hungrily, oblivious to her mother's grief; even this closeness did nothing to help her sorrow.

Weeks had passed since Rafievn's death and Sanluin felt more and more hollow and cold. Her grief was eating from inside and she knew she would soon have nothing left. Nn had taken more and more care of Sno and there was a bond developing between them, easing Sanluin's guilt of slightly neglecting Sno whilst she was swamped with grief. Sanluin never thought she would feel this way about anyone, even more to her surprise was that she felt a strange distance from Sno. She couldn't understand why this was but slowly she seemed more comfortable with the way Nn took care of Sno. It should have made her feel tinges of guilt but she felt none. She put it down to her broken heart and dived back into her world of grief.

The weather outside had been very severe and snow was starting to bridge the wall that had been built by Nn. Nn started to form the roof of the snow cave as the prevailing wind blew more and more material in from the sea. Nn was constantly monitoring Sanluin, just in case she did anything rash to herself and Sno. Nn needed Sno; she would be the link for the super airborne code that would be developed for when Hope was to be discovered. Sanluin sat in Rafievn's seat, her glassy stare looking nowhere but deep into her memories of the time she had spent with Rafievn.

Nn was feeding Sno, who looked upon him as a father figure since Rafievn's death. Nn could sense that Sanluin was ready to follow Rafievn and had prepared the necessary injections. She hadn't eaten in days and her face had started to look sunken and drawn, her beauty still shone through but was just a fraction of what it had been.

"Sanluin you must try to eat something," said Nn as he put his hand on her shoulder.

"I can't Nn, I just don't want to go on anymore." As she answered, the conviction in her voice told Nn that she was ready to go and meet Rafievn. "You will take care of Sno won't you Nn? She sees you as a father, she feels so secure with you."

"You won't have to worry about anything, Sno has everything she will need with me, I will let you prepare yourself in your own time. It might be a good idea to eat something and try to brighten yourself up, you should see Rafievn looking your best."

"You're right Nn, can you make me the fish again? I will go and shower." Sanluin felt a great weight lift from her shoulders, as she knew Nn was supporting her in following Rafievn. She got up and went to shower, thinking of how she had first showered with Rafievn. The hot water rinsed away all the depression and all of her negative thoughts and she was soon lost in the memory of the loving embrace with Rafievn when he had first held her.

"Sanluin," called Nn, "your food is ready." The call had woken her from her thoughts, which were warming every corner of her body. She called back.

"A few more minutes Nn," and she went back to her erotic thoughts as her hands felt their way around her body, just as Rafievn's had done.

Sno was sitting in her chair, her bright little smile completely unaware of the situation that her mother was in. Sanluin went over and kissed her, the same way she had done when Rafievn was alive. Nn put the food on the table and Sanluin ate with an appetite that had been missing for so long. Her spirits were high, even though she knew her end was close. She had decided that her time to leave would be on her birthday. It seemed an odd choice for a time to die but what time would ever be appropriate for such an act. She spent every second being positive and close to Sno but involving Nn all the time so that the infant would feel as close to Nn as she was to Sanluin.

As her birthday approached, her feelings were still as clear as ever and she didn't feel any sadness that she was going to leave her baby. It was as if she had woken up from a nightmare and was now ready to take on the day, which up to now had been a distant horror.

Sanluin had been so oblivious to her surroundings when she was in the depths of depression; she hadn't noticed that Nn had been working on new genetic codes. He had designed a code specifically for Sanluin, as he could not bear to see her suffer anymore. The code was put into the water she drank and over time was designed to alter her thoughts, so that suicide and leaving her baby would not be a problem for her. The code had alerted Nn just before it triggered Sanluin's thoughts to be different and this is when he suggested she should look her best for Rafievn. The experiment had worked perfectly, but it was for the good of Sanluin who was falling so deep into depression that it would have been cruel to let it go on any further. The code even blocked out Sanluin questioning her own mind, so that she was happy to go along with her fate. She wouldn't have had the strength to do it alone. Nn had picked up these messages from the electrical impulses in her mind and this is when he designed the new codes to help her climb out of depression and face her destiny to be with Rafievn.

Nn had prepared Sanluin's pod. He had connected all of the life support system to a preservation liquid so that Sanluin would be kept perfectly preserved. When Hope was eventually discovered her beauty would be there for a distant descendant of Rafievn's to see. It was as if Nn wanted to see Sanluin and Rafievn reunited in person. Sanluin had been with Sno constantly for three days and she had followed Nn all over the ship.

"Nn can we go outside when the weather clears, I want to

show Sno Planetician before I leave?" asked Sanluin.

"That will be fine. Let me get some clothes made for Sno and then we can wait for the appropriate time," replied Nn.

"Thanks Nn," replied Sanluin holding Sno up to the widow of Hope and showing her baby the tunnel through the snow and ice that Nn had built. The tunnel led to the vastness of the southern ice cap and the blizzard, which blew relentlessly from the sea causing the opening to get blocked. Nn cleared it daily, which also added to the length of the tunnel. Sanluin had only ventured outside once since the death of Tehkin but wanted to show her daughter the reality of a planet that would sustain life. Nn came back into the galley holding a tiny one-piece suit.

"Try this for size, it should be a good fit as I scanned Sno only the other day," said Nn, passing the suit to Sanluin. Sanluin put Sno down on the table and dressed her in the suit. It fitted perfectly and Sno seemed to like the secure feeling of being in a warm body even if it was one made of fabric from synthetic fibres, and down collected from the sea birds. The three of them in their thermal suits went to the door; as it opened a rush of freezing air spilled into the ship. It took Sanluin's breath away as she walked steadily down the steps, holding Sno tightly, with Nn following close behind. The sound of their footsteps in the snow took Sanluin back to the time when she went out to look for Tehkin but she was not afraid anymore. Her grieving had finished for the old pilot but was replaced with the immense loss for Rafievn. She still couldn't find it in her heart to feel a loss for Sno, which worried her a little. Nn was picking these thoughts up and slowly changing Sanluin's thoughts by the day and soon she wouldn't even question why she was sensing no guilt for leaving Sno to live on her own with Nn. The cold wind cut into Sanluin who held Sno close to her chest and Nn stood behind them both, trying to protect them from the icy gusts.

"I still can't accept that things have turned out this way Nn." Sanluin's voice was carried away with the wind but it did not matter, as Nn could understand her by her thoughts. Nn had no words for her but put a reassuring hand on her shoulder. He knew she was at her end and walked back into the ship. Sanluin stood there looking out into the frozen waste holding her baby and saying her goodbyes to a natural environment for the last time. Sno started to cry from the cold and Sanluin took her back to the ship. She handed Sno to Nn and went to Rafievn's seat at the Bridge, she sat there for the rest of the night falling in and out of sleep, still dressed in the thermal suit.

When morning came Sanluin had fallen asleep in the chair and Nn came into the Bridge with Sno in his arms. The sound of Sno woke Sanluin and she got up and took hold of Sno.

"Mummy has to go today my little Angel but Nn will look after you, so there is nothing to be afraid of." Sanluin said the words with no sorrow in her voice, as the codes Nn had been administering had taken away all her sadness of leaving her baby. Sno looked into her mother's eyes and smiled, completely oblivious to what her mother had said. It wouldn't take long for Sno to forget her mother and she would be totally reliant on Nn who would replace her as the parent.

"I am ready now Nn, but let's wait for Sno to have her sleep. Will that be OK?" asked Sanluin.

"That will be for the best Sanluin. Will you want to change out of your thermal suit?" replied Nn.

"Yes Nn, I will put something different on after I shower." Sanluin handed Sno back to Nn and went off to wash and change. Nn prepared some food for Sno and also made some for Sanluin in case she wanted any. He wasn't sure if she would have much of an appetite before her leaving. All the preparations were complete for her death and all Sanluin had to do was to lie in her pod and go off to sleep when she was ready. Two hours had passed when Sanluin came into the galley; Nn was stunned to see how beautiful she looked. She had colour in her face for the first time in months and a vibrant fresh looking young woman who had looked that way when her lover was alive, had replaced the pale gaunt complexion.

"Sanluin, you look beautiful. Do you want some food?" Nn was pleased to see her looking her old self as he offered her the meal he had prepared. She sat down and ate her meal in silence, only the noise of the cutlery disturbed the silence. The meal was prepared with a final code added so that Sanluin would be totally ready for her death, with no thoughts of doubt. She went over to Sno and picked her up, stroking her fine hair as she held her close to her chest. Mother and daughter walked around the ship going into each room. The Bridge held a special memory for Sanluin, as it was where she had held Rafievn's hand as they touched down on Planetician for the first time. She sat in his chair and told Sno how she would one day see her father. Sanliun held Sno tightly as she knew she was soon to be with him. Nn had also administered codes in her food so that Sanliun totally believed that she would see Rafievn after her death. All the time Sanluin was sat in Rafievn's chair Nn was sending a message to Cinciev telling him that Sanluin was very close to leaving. He told him that all was well with Sno and that he needed her to test the super airborne code that would be used in the future.

Sanluin held Sno until she was in a deep sleep and then got up to go to her pod. She lay Sno down in Rafievn's pod and covered her with a blanket; she gave her daughter one final kiss before lying in her pod, which was next to Rafievn's. Sanluin lay on her back looking across at Sno, as Nn put a needle into her arm and injected her with the fluid that would send her off to sleep. She didn't even flinch as the needle pierced the skin. The liquid flowed into her veins as Sanluin looked at her sleeping daughter, there was no remorse or sense of loss but a reassuring warmth that Sno would be well looked after by Nn. Slowly Sanluin's eyes closed as she fell into her final sleep in the living world and taking with her the lasting view of her beautiful daughter. Nn let her go into a deep sleep before altering her brain functions to shut down; she would be clinically dead but her heart would still function, so that when the preserving fluid was

215

administered it would be pumped to every part of her body.

Nn worked methodically, only looking fleetingly at Sanluin as she slowly crept towards her death. The ship fell into silence bar the sounds of Sno sleeping. Nn wanted Sanluin to meet Rafievn again but that would never be known; it was the gamble they had both taken, as their love was so strong.

The Last Tronion

Cinciev received the message from Nn and needed to be alone with his thoughts, he went up to the gully where he had stayed the first few nights after he was dropped off by Hope. He sat looking across to the pyramids knowing that he was the only living person from Atronia on this new planet. He suddenly felt very alone, even though he was with Ashait and his child. The people from his own planet were all gone now; only Nn, the droid and Sno, who was a Planetician were left. He knew that Nn would complete the super airborne codes and then send Sno off to be with her parents. He couldn't help thinking how the poor child living on Hope was being used for a scientific test to help save the future inhabitants of Planetician. Rafievn and Sanluin's sacrifice to be with each other was dwarfed by the sacrifice of their child who would be the link from Atronia's mistakes to the silent solution for the people of Planetician.

Nn had explained to Cinciev how the airborne code would work and how it would inoculate the whole of Planetician's inhabitants in the future. It would be an inoculation, not from a normal disease but one of the oldest plagues known to man, the plague of greed. When Hope was due to be found and descendants from Rafievn and Cinciev were stood inside Hope, the airborne code would be released from the ventilation system and inhaled by everyone there. The code would be designed to prevent any upgrades to the human body and mind, as Planetician would have evolved enough by then to develop its own nano-technology. Once the people had inhaled the codes in Hope, their spread to the wider world would begin. Every time one of the coded people exhaled or passed water, the code would spread. It would get into the planet's hydro-cycle and atmospheric systems, spreading so rapidly that every person on Planetician would have the codes in their system within five years. Even when the scientists were ready to try and upgrade people, they would be blocked by Nn's code each time. There would be no way around it; humans would always be humans with all of their imperfections, perfections and different talents. With a bit of luck the lives of Tehkin, Cinciev, Rafievn, Sanluin and Sno would have not been lost in vain. They may not have lived out their lives how they had planned but their love for humanity and respect for fellow human beings, even though they were from another planet, would have saved the lives of billions. There could be one thing that would unblock the super code but that would be locked deep inside Hope. It would be all the possible nano-codes, including viruses and every possible variation that could be programmed. It would be the Pandora's box for the basis of life itself. Nn would have worked for years developing the different codes, creating just one master code that could block any that could be programmed by future scientists from Planetician.

Looking to the north Cinciev knew it would soon be time to hide his kit at sea; the stone coffin was ready, he just needed to speak with Captain Thanus about another voyage. Ashait was keen to see Cinciev stop worrying about his kit so it would be good to see the back of it, even though it was full of such wonders. They couldn't afford for it to be found, and the sooner it went the better so they could carry on their lives without fear of being found with such a mind boggling hoard.

Cinciev thought how the future of Planetician would pan out, what would these people eventually call this planet? There was so much history to elapse until the discovery of Hope. Would Hope ever be discovered? That would be the most difficult predication. When Hope and Nn were ready to activate the pulse from the probe on Planetician's moon, would there be any descendants carrying the dormant gene left within the 100-mile radius of the original co-ordinates? All these factors needed to be in place for there to be any chance of their mission being a success. Cinciev knew that bloodlines of people on Atronia had stayed in one area for centuries. This gave Cinciev some optimism for the future; he just couldn't help wondering how the people who were going to be activated by the pulse were going to react. They couldn't just suddenly say that there was a spaceship buried beneath the ice in the southern ice cap. He remembered from one of Nn's messages that they would appear to suffer some sort of break down and experience vivid illusions of what had happened since their coming to Planetician. All this was still a very long time in the future and something that Cinciev had no more responsibility or control over. His future was now planned out with Ashait and his baby, and the burial of his kit at sea was now the last part of the mission. It was a mission that started with no overall plan, as they had never known what to expect since leaving Atronia. The only factor that linked any of the missions together was the fact that they were human beings who had discovered other human beings on another planet, and wanted to pass on their knowledge of previous mistakes made by one human race to another.

Cinciev walked back to his new life, which lay in the shadows of one of the wonders of this new planet. He knew that these massive structures would be dwarfed by the discovery that will one day be made in the distant future.

Nn had removed all of the preserving tubes from Sanluin's arm. She was now perfectly preserved with the full beauty that had shone from her when she was with Rafievn on the first islands they had visited. Her pod closed silently and the air inside was slowly removed and replaced with an inert gas. Sno was still sleeping in her father's pod as Nn went straight to work on the airborne codes. It would take months of testing before he could try anything out on Sno because she was too young at the moment, she needed to be walking.

Over the next couple of years Nn perfected the codes and Hope was completely buried beneath the snow that would form into ice over time. Nn had to keep Hope close to the surface of the ice so that her discovery would be penetrable from above, with manual digging if need be. Nn knew that Planetician would develop satellite technology, which would be able to detect Hope beneath ten foot of ice. He altered the ship's Luuse alloy skin so she couldn't be detected from space or by sonar. This protective guard would disengage when she was due to be discovered, so that any salvage or search crew would find her.

Three years after the passing of Sanluin, Nn carried out the same procedure on Sno. She was the link that had made the airborne code possible and it now worked without a flaw; Nn had no more need for the child. He knew that her existence on Hope would be no life for a human, so putting her to sleep and sending her to her parents was the only option left. Hope was now in complete silence from any human activity, it would be nearly 4,000 years before any human would set foot in Hope again. Nn would scrape ice from the ceiling of Hope's tomb and pack it beneath her stabilisers, keeping her close to the surface, ready for her detection.

Present Day

The decades and centuries slowly rolled by with all the history unfolding on the surface of Planetician, just as it had done on Atronia. Wars came and went and along with them super powers, only to be replaced by other countries and dictators with their own ideas of domination. The dormant gene had survived these culling periods, as well as diseases that had reared up, killing millions. Not only had the gene spread to many descendants, but some still lived close to the stone monument in the northern islands, which were now part of the British Isles, called Stonehenge. The Pyramids of Egypt had descendants living in their shadows as well. Both of these people were the carrier of an alien gene that would change their world for the better and it was only a matter of days now before it would be activated.

Nn was making final checks to the probe on the moon, which had sat patiently waiting its orders. The probe had been in suspension until now; its batteries only charging themselves with enough power to receive any messages from Hope. It had now opened up a larger solar disc, using the moon's gravity to help charge the gravity cell, as it needed much more power to send the pulse that would activate the dormant gene. The pulse worked by sending an undetectable radio signal to start the activation process. The carriers of the gene would feel nothing at first but as the brain started to be contacted, they would fall into a Hypo-manic state. It was a risky way to activate the code, as humans can react very differently to manic episode. Nn checked the power in the probe's batteries and it showed it was ready to send the pulse. He didn't know if there were any people within the range of a 100-mile radius of the Pyramids or Stonehenge, but now was the time to send and find out.

The Carriers

Bill Thompson was thirty-two and had been working and living in the south west of England since 1986. He had been working in the construction industry since school and had been looking to get out of the game for years, but nothing came up. The chance of a pub was a possibility and he was sure it would be his ticket out of the building industry. What he didn't know, was that it would only be a matter of hours until his life would change forever. He had the same blood as Rafievn flowing through his veins and with it the gene, which was ready for its awakening. A bolt from the blue would take him away from building sites sure enough, but it couldn't be further from running a pub.

The road to Weston was damp and filling with the morning traffic. Bill and his mate Nick were due to fit a ceiling in a bank re-fit for their boss Des, who was one of the better guys to work for. The sea-front at Weston was empty but for a couple of dog walkers who were wrapped up from the chilly sea breeze. Bill pulled into the street where the job was and spotted a café, which was a very inviting sight at this time of the morning, with the weather so cold and damp. He pulled over and Nick hopped out and went straight for two teas, his shoulders hunched under his hoody and hands fisted into his jean pockets. Just as Nick came out with the teas, Des rang to re-route them to Salisbury as a job needed to be finished as a team of three had not turned up. Another hour plus in the van was better than working over the top of every other trade in the bank re-fit. Jimi Hendrix's 'Cross Town Traffic' blasted out from the radio as Bill started the van and Nick got in.

"Change of plan mate, we're off to Salisbury to help out for a few days."

"OK dude, here's your tea."

"Thanks."

The sun had risen over the bustling city of Cairo, the markets full of traders and the tourists looking and haggling for bargains. Falima Barhoud was still in her apartment, ready to take another group of tourists round the ruins of the Sphinx and then on to the great Pyramids. Little did she know that Cinciev had walked that very route 4,000 years earlier and just like Bill, within a few hours her memory would start to fill with every part of the Mission which took place so long ago. She took one last sip of her coffee and left the apartment with the thought of another hot draining day in front of her. Another bunch of over enthusiastic tourists to deal with then a relaxing meal overlooking the Nile with her friend, Alishia from the tourist office. The day did not seem so bad after all, but it was beyond her wildest imagination what was going to happen to her that evening.

Bill pulled into the site entrance, which was clogged with mud; already he knew what sort of job it would be looking at the state of the entrance. He parked up and the two of them walked into the site office, kicking off clumps of mud and grit from their boots at the door. The site agent was an old school type, in his late 60s at least. He should have retired long ago but worked to get out of the house and away from the boredom that can stifle some retirements.

"OK boss? We are from Teegrid. Des sent us to help out on the ceilings for a couple of days," said Bill to the site agent, who had his back to them while he squeezed a tea bag from a steaming mug.

"What fuckin' time do you call this boys? It's nearly ten," replied the agent in a tone of voice, which was calm and relaxed for the use of language. It was the sort of reply Bill was used to from the older site agents and he knew it was a sense of humour that most people would find highly offensive, but the building game was a different industry to any other and no offence was taken.

"Didn't realise it was so late. We were stuck on the motorway; a tea would be nice though," Bill said with a smile on his face.

"You've got some neck for a young 'un - late and want tea.

223

Go on, help yourselves. Des said you were on your way to Weston when he told you to get down here." Nick didn't know that Bill knew the agent from previous jobs and was shocked by the agent's tone; he had only been working on building sites for a few months and wasn't used to the banter that came with the territory.

"Take your teas into the other room, the video for the induction is in there." The agent followed Bill and Nick into the room and switched on the TV and played the video. It was the usual health and safety nonsense that Bill had seen a hundred times on different sites and this one was just as boring. It was nearly 11.30am and rain had started to fall in a miserable drizzle as the two unloaded their tools from the van. They only needed screw guns and 110v leads for the job, which was plaster-boarding timber joisted ceilings. The agent gave Bill the drawings of the block they were to work on and had shaded the rooms that needed boarding. The ground floor had been done, so they trudged up the stairs and set up in the largest shaded room, which overlooked the road.

"Right Nick, set the leads up and I'll clear the crap from the room." The room was littered with off-cuts of timber and broken thermal blocks; some of the larger blocks would come in handy for a small hop-up, all that was needed were some scaffold planks. The scaffold was still erected on the outside of the building and a few of the planks were just the right length for what Bill needed. He pulled a couple through the window opening and set them up on the blocks, the height was just right. Bill had his pouch loaded with screws and screw gun at the ready as Nick brought in the first of the plank boards. It didn't take long before the buzz of the screw gun echoed through the semi-finished building.

Falima waved to the last tourist who was struggling to get her bulk onto the tour coach that would be heading back to one of the beach resorts. It had been a long day dealing with the constant questioning from the group, who were all from the deep south of America. They were very nice but were too much for Falima who found them too intense, and almost too nice; they dragged out every part of the tour with an abundance of intrigue that seemed almost false at times. She wiped her brow and felt the day's dust that had dried with her sweat, and was slightly coarse to her skin. A good shower before her meal with Alishia was in order. She sped off back to her apartment on her Vespa, which had been waiting patiently in the Egyptian sun.

The restaurant was only a short walk from her apartment and she was there before Alishia so she ordered drinks for the two of them. It was good to see her friend and not have to cook for once after a draining day. It would be a while before she would cook again as future events would change her life for ever.

Bill pumped in the last screw for the day, they had both worked flat out since they started and had made up for the lost time earlier in the day.

"Wrap the leads up Nick. That was a good day considering the delay this morning."

"My arms know it was a good day, they are knackered but they should still be able to lift a pint."

"We'll stop on the way back for one. I'll get them in if you sort the kit out while I go and see the agent about next week."

"OK mate, see you by the van." Just as Bill was leaving the room he spotted a date carved into a stone that was built into the wall. At closer inspection the date read 1756 with the initials RH below it. It had been a trait by stonemasons to initial and date their work, and showed the exact date of the building's construction. Bill reached into his pouch and pulled out his pad saw, he cut through the mortar surrounding the stone with ease and removed the stone. It was about the size of a bag of sugar and was white and smooth to the touch; the stone dust covered his fingertips white. He stuffed it into his pouch and went to the van; it could be a memento from the building game, especially if he was going to become a publican.

The main road out of Salisbury had road works and the

traffic was snarling up so Bill turned off towards the Plain, which would take them right by Stonehenge.

Nn was sending the pulse codes to the probe on the moon, which had plenty of power in its cells since it was reactivated. A series of pulses would emit from the probe in two-minute intervals. Nn started the first pulse, after which it would be automated for the next half hour. There would be no knowing if the operation was a success unless Hope was found. It would be a waiting game for Nn, but a few more months would be nothing, compared to four thousand years.

The eerie silhouette of Stonehenge came into view in the darkening sky. Bill looked across and thought how much manpower had gone into its construction; the generations that toiled to create such a wonder for its time. Little did Bill know that his own ancestor, Rafievn had spent time there; soon Bill would be recalling Rafievn's very actions, learning how it was really built.

The first of the pulses had penetrated the Earth's atmosphere and charged the 100-mile radius around Stonehenge. Bill and Nick had driven straight through the centre of it and the reaction deep inside Bill's genes had started. The process would be slow at first but by the early hours of the following morning Bill would start to go into a staged Hypo-manic episode. The second pulse had shot from the probe but this time in the direction of Cairo. Falima was sleeping on her couch oblivious when her reaction started, but her dreams would be altered to a reality of the events all those years ago when Cinciev was in Egypt.

"Shall we stop in the George for a quick one Bill?"

"Might as well Nick. Guinness or Dog?"

"Bottle of Dog I think, haven't had one for ages." The pub was quite empty when they pulled in but would soon fill up, as it had recently been refitted and was now a popular eatery. Bill called home, to let his wife Linda know they would be stopping for a drink while Nick went on in and ordered the beers.

"Cheers Nick," said Bill as he poured the Newcastle Brown into the glass.

"Your round, remember Bill?"

"Oh yeh, I did say I'd get them in." Bill dug out his change and sifted through it on the bar.

"What did the agent say about next week?"

"If we finish off that floor by Wednesday they will be back on track. Hopefully the bank will been finished by Kev and Neil."

"Hope so, this is not a bad job apart from the travelling, three more days is OK though."

"Yeh, another stop off here Wednesday would be sound." They finished their beer and headed home, the car park was filling up now as the hungry punters arrived.

Bill had dropped Nick off and went onto his parents' house, which he was looking after while they were on holiday. Linda had tea ready and the smell of the garlic was wafting out to the driveway. The house was a large detached bungalow with a 250 metre drive leading from road; it was the last house on the street with fields beyond.

"OK love, how was your day?" asked Linda, as she dished up the Bolognese.

"It was OK, we ended up in Salisbury to help out on a job, so we called in the George for a pint."

"I know love, you only called me an hour ago. Your daughter's in the lounge glued to Rosie and Jim. Tell her tea's ready." Bill's memory loss was a sign that the genetic code was reacting well and would soon be programming Bill's mind with details of Hope and her co-ordinates. Bill lifted his daughter off the floor and took her giggling into the dining room where the Bolognese was steaming.

Nn sat in Tehkin's seat while the probe sent its pulses. He questioned the actions he had taken all those years ago. Placing his hands on the controls of Hope and knowing all of the flight codes, he knew he could have reunited Rafievn and Sanluin. His programming had always had humanity as its primary function and his artificial thoughts had deduced that keeping Hope hidden from the people of Planetician was the only option. If the crew had re-grouped, any early civilisation would have seen them as Gods; where would they have gone? The human loss of life that would have resulted in one group of people having possession of Hope was incalculable, so the sacrifice of Sanluin and Rafievn saved many thousands, if not millions, of lives. Sno had been the key to make the super airborne code possible and this reinforced Nn's decision as the right one. Nn switched on Hope's external lights and lowered the steps from the ship's hull, opening the door to the icy tomb outside. No blast of wind from the wild surface, but a still chill crept its invisible encroaching way into Hope. Nn had scraped ice from the roof of the cavern by standing on the top of the ship. Any future visitor would have a 2 metre drop, once they cut through the solid ice roof, which was at least that deep again. The only part of the ship that touched the cavern roof were the two tail fins at the rear of the ship that were stuck into the ice, giving Hope the image of a huge stalactite, formed from the ice. Within a matter of months, people would be drilling into this cavern and Nn would be waiting with all the wonder and shock that was to change the population of Planetician forever.

Bill was having a rough night; in and out of sleep, dreaming of events that had happened to Rafievn all those years ago. He couldn't understand these dreams but fell back into such vivid events every time he went back to sleep.

It was 7.30 am and Bill had slept well for the last half hour. Linda was still asleep, so he went downstairs to make some tea. He was still confused by the previous night's dreams and apart from the journey home past Stonehenge, none of it made sense. Just as the kettle boiled the phone rang.

"Hello,'" answered Bill while yawning.

"Hello Bill," replied his Dad's voice. The line from Thailand was clear and Bill could make out the sound of lapping waves and the breeze in the background.

"OK Dad, you're on the beach then?"

"Yes, we're all OK. Mum's struggling with the heat but everything's fine. Is everything alright back at the ranch?"

"No problems here, we're all well. What is Richard doing?" Richard was Bill's brother and had been living in Thailand for the last ten years.

"He's out swimming."

"Is it an onshore wind Dad? Remember when I had that accident kite-surfing. That was an offshore, not that Rich is kite-surfing at the moment."

"No, it's a calm onshore breeze and there are no fins sticking out of the water either, so he should be quite safe."

"Have a good time Dad. Don't over do it sat on that beach."

"OK Bill, speak to you in a few days; take care."

"Cheers, bye." Bill returned to the kitchen thinking of what his Dad had said about the sharks. It was just what his subconscious needed to hear to trigger the Hypo-manic episode. The programme in his genes altered his thoughts, making him think his brother had been in a shark attack; this created the anger needed to kick-start the episode. Bill sat in the front room reeling from the shock; of what he thought was his brother's shark attack. Linda walked into the room as Bill sat there sobbing into his hands.

"Bill, what is it? Is everything OK?"

"It's Rich, he's been in a shark attack."

"What? When? When?"

"Just now. I just spoke to Dad." Before Linda could say another word Bill got up and ran to the door; it was a double-glazed aluminium framed door and Bill ran straight into it. Linda screamed out to him but Bill's mind was flat-lining on present day technology as he had slipped back 4,000 years to when Rafievn was at Stonehenge and glass didn't exist. Bill's frantic hands caught the door handle and as it swung open he ran straight outside. The events of what Rafievn had gone through were shooting through his brain in no particular order, just in a jumbled mess. The energy drug, which Rafievn had had in his kit, jolted Bill into thinking the white powdery stone, dated 1756 that he had taken the day before, was made of the same stuff. He ran to his van and went to reach onto the dash but again he hit the glass, not knowing it was there, just as a wild bird will sometimes fly into a window-pane. Bill's fist hit the glass dead square and bounced off. Bill, stunned at the hardness of the transparent material, shouted out.

"Fuck me, that's hard," but he spoke in Tronion, not English. He looked in wonder at the machine that was his van; his mind not registering what it was. The force of his fist hitting the window set the van's alarm off but Bill did not hear the noise. His torrents of thoughts were numbing some of his senses and he was in a silent world but for the sounds in his head. Linda was shouting to him from the door in her dressing gown in total bewilderment, as her husband seemed to be going completely mad. Flashing through Bill's mind now was when Rafievn ran to the monument to get his communicator. Bill sprinted down the drive to the gate and stopped suddenly, his mind in a vicious haze of past and present events that rushed into his thoughts. The hole to his left was a badger burrow; he looked and ran straight towards it. Just past the burrow was his parents' fence, he ran straight through the fence breaking the slats and tripping into the neighbour's garden, which happened to be his Auntie's property. The grass was damp and lush, and this took his mind back to when Hope first landed on the islands in the Atlantic, now the Azores, where the land was also a lush green. This is when Sanluin flew into his thoughts; getting up again and running down the garden, Bill knew that those first islands were where Rafievn and the crew should have stayed. He dived outstretched onto the lawn, the soft wet grass taking his fall. Smelling the turf and grabbing a handful of grass and mud, Bill ripped it up and looked deep into the mud in his palms and again speaking in Tronion, said how they didn't have to go anywhere, all they needed was on the islands. It was as if Rafievn was taking over Bill's mind completely but Bill's own memory kept shooting into his head.

Bill stood up and looked to where the grass ended and the road began. A car slowly passed Bill who looked in amazement at this strange object; it made no sound to Bill's ears. He recognised the driver who was a friend of his father called Tom. Bill stared at him as he went by, the window was wound down and the driver asked if Bill was OK. The moving lips were also silent, as Bill shouted to him.

"Where the fuck did you get that?" The words came out in a mix of English and Tronion. Harry's friend Tom didn't know what to make of Bill, whose shirt was ripped and grass-stained. He drove on and parked further down the road as Bill ran back off in the other direction towards his Auntie's house. Linda had run back into the house, called the police and then Kevin, who worked with Bill.

Kevin's phone buzzed on the café table.

"Kev it's Linda. Bill's gone mad. Quick, come and help me, please."

"What do you mean Linda?"

"He's just gone completely nuts. He tried running though glass doors and nearly punched his van window out."

"I'm in Bristol Linda, I'll give Shane a ring. I spoke to him just now so I know he's at home. Go steady Linda. I'll call round when I get back."

"OK Kev, thanks." Bill was running towards his Auntie's house, which was built up about four feet higher than the lawn and was heading for a flight of stone steps that led up to the patio doors. He had seen his Auntie looking out from the front room and had recognised her face but didn't know who she was. He ran up the steps in one stride and threw himself at the glass with his Auntie looking in horror, as the double-glazed units took the full force of Bill, but didn't break. He bounced back off the glass and turned to his right and saw a Police car pull up in his Auntie's driveway. He couldn't believe his eyes, not at the sight of the Police but the fact that they arrived in another one of those strange vehicles he had seen for the first time that morning. This one was a similar shape to his van that he had punched minutes before, but it had strange yet familiar text written on the side.

The Policeman in the passenger seat got out and walked steadily towards Bill, who was now face to face with his Auntie. He looked at her face confused, as he recognised her but did not have a clue who she was. Bill walked towards the Policeman who was approaching at a very slow pace. He looked at the lettering on the left of the officer's jacket and went to speak but nothing could come out. Bill was completely dumbstruck, he had forgotten his own language but knew the text to be familiar.

"Steady now young man," said the Policeman, with one hand outstretched to grab hold of Bill's arm. Frightened by the physical gesture, Bill pulled away and ran past him. The driver of the Police car had got out and blocked the way to the gate. There was a puddle on the drive and Bill saw the water, which reminded him of the swim Rafievn had had with Sanluin. He sank to his knees and patted the water looking at the drips fall from his hand. He pulled his shirt off that was nearly in rags from the hammering it had already taken, and tried to swim in the puddle. Everyone looked at Bill as he tried to swim in the puddle; their reaction was to laugh but the situation took away the humour of it. This is when Bill saw his watch and signet ring. He suddenly realised that these people who had turned up in the strange vehicle, could be a threat and might find out who he was; he now believed he was Rafievn. Bill's mind went on the defensive, so he took his watch and ring off thinking they were items brought with him from Atronia. His Auntie by this time had told the first Policeman what had happened and had gone over to Bill to try to talk to him.

"Bill calm down, these people are here to help you." Bill

looked up at his Auntie understanding her voice and feeling slightly less frightened. Again he tried to speak but only jumbled Tronion came out as his Auntie listened in surprise to the strange language her nephew was speaking. All of a sudden Bill's hearing came back and he heard the alarm from his van and a loud noise overhead, which was a 'plane above the clouds. All these noises of the present day confused Bill even more. Then, he heard a loud sound behind him. He looked round and saw another vehicle speeding towards him; it was Shane in his BMW 5 series. Shane got out and started to run towards Bill, for some reason Shane reminded Bill of Tehkin.

"Fuck me Tehkin, I thought you were dead," shouted Bill in Tronion, stopping Shane in his tracks at the sight and sound of his mate Bill. "Tehkin, will you look after Sanluin if these people take me away?" asked Bill as he pointed to Linda, who was looking on from over the fence, tears running down her cheeks as she thought she had lost her husband to this madness that came out of the blue. Bill stood up and said to the Police that his Auntie was nothing to do with the mission and not to harm her. The two Policemen looked at each other puzzled.

"Bill, what's going on mate? Let's go inside. Come on, you'll get cold out here," Shane said in a calm voice but Bill could not understand what he said.

"He'd better come with us," said the Policeman, who had been driving the car. Slowly, the first Policeman took out his handcuffs and went over to Bill.

"Come on lad, come with us, you'll be OK." Bill looked at his Auntie and then across to Linda, as he felt the cold steel of the handcuffs clasp around his wrist. Bill looked down at the strange object now joining his hands together and hesitantly walked towards the Police car where the other Policeman was holding the back door open. In desperation Bill remembered his false tooth. If he showed them this they would know he was one of them and not from an alien world, which even he was unsure of. Grabbing hold of his front tooth with both hands bound by the cuffs, Bill tried to break off his tooth. It started to loosen then came off its post. His Auntie saw what he was doing and called out for him to stop but it was too late, Bill was showing the two officers the small white tooth in his bound hands.

Bill sat on the soft material of the car seat and gave one final glance at Linda who was feeling slightly better now, as at least Bill couldn't harm himself. The door of the car shut and Bill looked around the inside as the two officers got in. The genetic codes in Bill's brain took in everything but only allowed him to realise what certain things were. Rafievn would have known what a car was, but a person from 4,000 years ago wouldn't, and this is how the codes were working at this early stage of the memory realisation. As events progressed Bill's new genetically enhanced thoughts would slowly bring Bill back to the present day but with all the knowledge of what had happened in the past.

The engine of the Police car started and it slowly pulled forward. The movement of the vehicle felt completely alien to Bill and his whole body tensed up as he pushed his feet into the foot-well, bracing himself. The Policeman sat next to him edged away and watched Bill's actions intently. He was on his guard, as he knew that a very frightened person could be very unpredictable. Shane moved his car so the Police could drive by. Bill still sat rigid in the seat as it slowly made its way to the station. Bill's Auntie had gone over to comfort Linda who was still very upset and very frightened about what had happened to her husband.

"I'm sure he'll be OK Linda. At least he won't do himself any harm in the Police station."

"I know Mary but what made him go so mad in the first place?" Linda remembered that Bill had spoken to his Dad and he was convinced that his brother had been involved in a shark attack. Linda quickly rang her brother-in-law, Richard on his mobile. Bill's dad Harry was still on the beach as the phone rang.

"Hello, Richard's phone," said Harry.

"Harry, it's Linda. Is Richard OK? Only Bill seems to think he's been in a shark attack and he's gone completely nuts over here because of it."

"Shark attack? What is he thinking? Richard has just gone to the café to get drinks and lunch. He's fine."

"Bill's just gone completely nuts. He tried to run through glass doors and he ran straight through your fence and into Auntie Mary's garden. I called the Police and they've taken him to the station."

"Oh my God Linda, are you and the baby OK? Do you want us to come home?"

"No, I'll be alright but it scared me out of my wits."

"Try to stay calm Linda. Here, I'll pass you on to Mum." Harry passed the phone to his wife and Linda told Connie the whole story. Every time the Police car went to turn or stop at lights, Bill tensed his whole body but when travelling in a straight line he relaxed slightly. The car travelled slowly the whole journey to Bath Police station. Bill looked at the handcuffs and held them up close to his eyes; he tried to look into the material they were made of and was confused how such a small piece of material could be so strong. He twisted his wrists to try and break the cuffs apart but the metal dug painfully into his wrists. He looked at the window of the car but had remembered how tough this material was and decided not to break it. The Police car was approaching Bath centre and names of shops looked familiar to Bill but he still could not understand them. They pulled into the station car park and Bill was relieved when the vehicle came to a stop. The Policeman sitting next to Bill spoke first.

"Do you know where we are Bill?" Bill listened to the familiar sounds but said nothing, as he was still dumbstruck. Then the driver spoke.

"We are just going to take you in for some questions and you can have a rest; you need it after all that running about." Bill looked at the driver and then to the dashboard of the car, which had a digital clock in the centre. The time was 10.23 am and the numbers instantly registered in Bill's brain. He blurted the numbers out in order of value.

"0-1-2-3." Then as his memory of numbers came rushing back, he called out all of the numbers he could see in the car, including the four numbers on each of the Police uniforms. Both Police officers were shocked at the sudden outburst but felt their man was coming to his senses. After Bill had exhausted all the numbers he could see, he felt slightly more relaxed and realised that these people dressed in the dark clothing meant him no harm.

The two officers got out of the car and the one who was sat next to Bill opened his door. Bill got out and looked around. The place seemed familiar but still as if it were an alien world. The officer led Bill into the station by holding his arm; other officers in the building gave them a wide birth as Bill was taken through the reception and back to the cells. They had heard from the two Police officers when they had radioed through, what sort of guest might be arriving.

Bill was taken straight to a cell; he walked in with the officer he trusted. Bill stood in the cell glaring at the walls and the strange rectangle on the ceiling, which was bright to look at. He hadn't noticed the handcuffs being taken off as this unusual surrounding of flat walls and the light-emitting object distracted him. Bill didn't even hear the officer say that he was locking the door and was going to call a doctor. The heavy thud of the door shook Bill from his trance and the realisation that he was trapped in this confined space. Instinctively he tried to get out and slammed on the door with his fists, he flew into a rage fuelled by fear of being in this box. Shouting obscenities and kicking at the walls, Bill seemed to slip back into the same frame of mind he had experienced earlier that morning. Two Policemen came straight back to the cell door and peered through the spy hole to make sure he wasn't harming himself. They gave him time to let off steam knowing he couldn't carry on for much longer before becoming exhausted, but one officer stayed, just in case.

For no apparent reason Nelson Mandela came into Bill's

head; he knew how long he had been locked up for. Bill stopped shouting and tried to calculate how long he might be in there. He had been living for what seemed thousands of years whilst Mandela had only lived for a fraction of that time, so on that basis, he calculated that he could be locked up for centuries. Questioning his own thoughts and why Nelson Mandela had come into his mind now troubled him. Deep in Bill's mind the Tronion gene was selecting some of Bill's own memory and sending it to his thoughts, which is why it chose a person who had been imprisoned before, as that reflected Bill's present situation.

Silence fell upon the cell; Bill paced up and down trying to understand what was going on. He looked at the door and saw the spy hole and looked through it sheepishly but saw only a blur. There were five small holes that went right through the door just below the spy hole; Bill could hear sounds of people talking through these holes, but still did not understand what they said. Turning back into the cell and walking towards the toilet, the smell of urine became more apparent. Bill recognised the smell and then saw where it was coming from. The toilet hadn't been flushed; excrement was floating on the surface. This was the only substance in the cell he recognised and thought how he might resort to drinking the foul water that surrounded it to survive.

Bill only recognised natural substances; all man made material was being held from his memory by the Tronion gene. He must try to make some sort of communication with the people on the other side of the cell door he thought, but still could not speak. Language was still being blocked in his mind by the gene, which was searching Bill's memory and preparing certain thoughts to come into his mind. It would be a gradual process that would be helped with the questioning that was soon to follow, by a psychiatrist called in by the police. Dr Viuuv had programmed the dormant gene to start with a reaction that would require psychiatric help, which would hopefully throw the scent off Hope being found by the governing people of whatever planet Hope had landed on. The plan was working well, considering it was devised thousands of years ago and billions of miles away.

Fatigue was enveloping Bill like a warm breeze and he sat down on a plastic coated mattress, laid out on the soiled bed. He lay down and drifted into sleep that was being controlled by the gene. Bill's dreams took him right back to when Rafievn was staying in the hut at Stonehenge. They were so vivid and so real but that was because these events had actually happened. All the events that had happened to Rafievn had been passed on to the hunters and also the girl who had had Rafievn's children, through the gene. Any event after that would not be in Bill's memory.

The sound of Faiis woke Bill; this really confused him. He knew he was in Bath now but also knew there are no sheep in the middle of this modern city. A modern city? How did he get to one of those? He had been at a settlement by Stonehenge thousands of years ago in his sleep. Bill's mind was working overtime thinking how he was going to communicate with these people so that he could see his wife and children again. Then, released from his memory was the only tune he could play on the harmonica, 'Silent Night'. He played the tune over and over in his mind and without thinking, he started to whistle it quietly to himself. Bill walked quickly over to the door and whistled through the holes in the door. 'Silent Night' echoed out into the corridor and one of the passing Policemen listened and looked through the spy hole. He saw the top of Bill's head pressed up to the door.

"Bill Thompson, can you hear me? This is PC Bill Smith, I was with you in the car and my number is 34867. Can you remember?" called the officer through the door. Bill instantly recognised the number and recognised what the officer was saying and knew he had the same name as himself. Just as suddenly as Bill's speech had gone, it came back.

"Officer Bill, can you let me out, it fuckin' stinks in here."

Bill spoke through the holes in the door and was surprised how suddenly he could speak again. Officer Smith unlocked the door and slowly opened it as Bill stood back.

"Are you back with us now Bill?" asked the officer.

"Sort of."

"Just stay here for a while and someone will be coming to see if everything is alright with you upstairs. Can I get you a cup of tea?" Officer Smith tapped his head with his finger as he said 'upstairs' to Bill, who nodded and the officer locked the door again. Officer Smith went off to report that Bill Thompson had started to communicate. The Police psychiatrist was called and would be at the station in about twenty minutes. Officer Smith returned with Bill's tea, checking through the spy hole before unlocking the door. Bill was sat on the bed as he came in with the steaming tea in a plastic cup.

"Here you go Bill, mind yourself it's hot." Bill took the tea but stayed silent. "It wont be long now Bill, the doctor is on his way." Officer Smith left the cell once more and was pleased that he had managed to bring his guest to his senses.

"OK," replied Bill, as Officer Smith left the cell. Bill sipped the sweet tea, which was another jog to his memory, as even the taste of this drink had been eradicated from his mind by the activated gene. Linda had arrived at the station with Kevin and Shane. She waited in the reception area as she was scared by her husband's earlier outburst, whilst Officers Smith and Johnson took Kevin and Shane to Bill's cell.

"He might not recognise you but he is talking again," said Officer Smith as he unlocked the door. Kevin and Shane went into the cell and were shocked at the state that Bill was in, who 'looked as if the lights were on but no one was home'. Officer Smith followed them in to flush the toilet and spray air freshener in the air, after remembering Bill's first words to him.

"Are you OK mate? Linda is outside, do you want to see her?" said Shane with slight enthusiasm. Bill understood what his mate had said but was glued to his seat, he wanted to go out and see his wife but felt too secure where he was. Kevin went over to Bill who was a man of few words at the best of times and pressed his head to Bill's, just to try and comfort him in some way. Bill felt better by the gesture but stayed put. Shane and Kevin both asked Bill one more time as they left the cell, but Bill was staying where he was.

"What did he say Shane?" asked Linda in desperation, her eyes red and puffy from crying.

"Nothing Linda, I think you had better go and see him."

"OK, but I'm still scared."

"He's calmed down now Linda; go and see him," Kevin reassured her. She followed Officer Smith to the cell and he let her in. Bill was still sat on the bed, as his wife walked to him. She was as pale as Bill, as his earlier outburst had frightened her out of her wits. Bill held his hand out to her, which she took; it still had dried mud on from his auntie's garden, as well as grazes from Harry's fence.

"Linda, I didn't think I was going to see you again, what happened?" Bill was so pleased to see his wife and went to get up to hold her. Linda was still unsure of her husband's state of mind. She told him to stay where he was and put her hand on his shoulder; she wanted to hold him, but was still too scared.

"Everything will be alright love, a doctor is coming to see you in a minute and they will try to find out what happened."

"But why are they keeping me? I have done nothing wrong."

"I know my love, they just don't want you to harm yourself." Linda was holding back her tears trying to be strong for her husband, as he looked so scared and helpless.

"Is our Louise alright Linda? Where is she?"

"She's fine. She is with Mum, but I have to get back to feed her soon. I will be in later, so don't worry about anything."

"OK, love." Linda kissed her husband on the head and their hands slowly let go of their grip as she walked away.

"Don't worry Billy everything will be fine." Linda left the

cell, Officer Smith locked the door and took Linda back to Kevin and Shane, who were waiting outside. She burst into tears as she left the station and got into Shane's car. Dr Baker passed them as they pulled out, on his way in. He was riding his bike, which was as old as the hills but kept rattling on; he was a lean man in his mid forties and wore frame-less glasses that highlighted his piercing blue eyes. Dr Baker had been a psychiatrist for the Police for years and had seen all sorts of cases but none were in the same league as Bill Thompson's case, as he was yet to discover.

He chained his bike up to the railings and strolled into the station.

"Morning Doctor," said the reception officer.

"Morning. What have you for me today then?" he asked, taking his Regatta waterproof off.

"A young man, early thirties. Went totally nuts earlier; tried to run through glass doors and swim in a puddle, and succeeded in going through a fence."

"Sounds like fun then Officer. Which cell is he in?"

"Number 5. Officer Smith has managed to talk to him. He'll take you through."

"Thank you: see you later. Oh, by the way, have you got a room spare for me to question him in?"

"Yes, Doctor. The usual, two doors up from his cell."

"Good, good,' replied Dr Baker, as he slung his leather satchel strap over his shoulder; his satchel looked as old as his bike by the hammering it had taken.

Officer Smith came into reception and took Dr Baker through.

"Were you the officer who picked our man up this morning?"

"Yes Doctor."

"How was he?"

"In a bit of a state. He seemed completely confused about what and who we were; he was very dubious of the car and broke

241

off his front tooth for some reason. He showed it to us and was gabbling away in some strange language. I've never seen anything like it before."

"By the sounds of things, nor have I. Did he harm anyone this morning?" replied the doctor, as he looked through the spy hole in the cell door.

"No, only himself by the scratches on his arms; nobody else got in his way." Bill was on the bed sleeping again, back dreaming of the events at Stonehenge, snoring lightly.

"Let him sleep for a while officer whilst I call a few colleagues. This case needs to be assessed by more than just me and next time you go in the cell, take his boots off, he could use those laces on himself or even on us."

"I will,' replied Officer Smith, knowing he should have done this already.

Dr Baker called two other colleagues and went to the room where they would interview Bill. Drs Knowles and Meacher arrived just as Bill was waking up and Officer Smith, who was keeping an eye on him, went into the cell.

"How are we feeling now, Bill?"

"Better thanks. What is happening now? What time is it?"

"The doctors are here to see you and it's just gone twelve. We have to take your boots off Bill, just to be on the safe side."

"I'm fine officer, I'm not going to do anything stupid."

"I'm sure you're not, but it's doctor's orders I'm afraid." Bill took his boots off while holding his false tooth tightly in his right hand. Officer Smith took the boots and went back to call Dr Baker. Bill sat waiting on the mattress, which he had put on the floor.

The door unlocked again and Dr Baker walked into the cell. He sat on the floor next to Bill to be on the same level as him so that he didn't seem superior by standing over him.

"Hello Bill, I am Dr Baker. Can you tell me what has gone on today?" Bill looked at his muddied hands and then his broken tooth that he was holding.

"Is everyone OK?" asked Bill, hoping that no one had come to any harm during his outburst.

"I don't know Bill, you tell me?" Bill felt unsure by the reply; was he looking for Bill to confess to something he had done without knowing? He looked at his hands for bloodstains but they were only smeared with mud, which eased Bill's mind.

"My wife is OK, she has just been in to see me. My baby is fine; I know that too, but there are a few blank spots in my memory."

"Take your time Bill, your memory will come back soon enough; I will take you through to another room and ask you some questions. There will be two other colleagues of mine there so don't feel intimidated. They are psychiatrists too; so don't hold back on anything you want to say. Do you feel up to some questions now or shall we wait a while more?"

"I feel alright to answer some questions now doctor." Bill felt very at ease with this man, he had a way of making people feel secure in his company. Bill got up and followed Dr Baker into the interview room.

"This is Dr Knowles and Dr Meacher; take a seat over there Bill." Dr Baker pointed to one of the two chairs at the back of the room.

"Hello Bill, nice to meet you." They both stayed seated and didn't offer out any handshakes; they were both very relaxed and wanted to make Bill feel at ease. The two doctors both greeted Bill at the same time; he replied with a quiet hello. Dr Knowles and Dr Meacher were sat in front of the desk both wearing casual clothes. Dr Meacher had a black basin hair cut, which Bill found very amusing as he resembled Rowan Atkinson in his Black Adder role. Dr Knowles was older than the other two but had a mop of blond hair that was greying with a vengeance. Bill sat on the chair to the right; Dr Baker sat next to him.

"Bill, the two officers who picked you up this morning have

told us what they saw and have also asked your Auntie and your wife what you did. Do you have any idea why you had this episode this morning?" asked Dr Baker. Bill thought back to the earliest he could remember and snippets shot back but not in any order.

"I..." Bill stopped suddenly and then looked at Dr Baker. "Is my brother dead? I think he has been attacked when swimming. He lives in Thailand." Bill's hands were trembling as he asked.

"No Bill, he is fine. Linda told us you thought that, but there has been no shark attack, he is fine, just a bit worried about you." Bill sighed, sat back in his chair and stopped trembling as his memory was allowed to come back to him in order.

"I woke up feeling surprisingly fresh, after a very restless night's sleep. I went downstairs, checking the baby was OK on my way and put the kettle on. There was a bottle of port on the side, so I poured a glass whilst waiting for the kettle to boil. I put some bread in the toaster, made two teas; one for my wife and one for me and then I took the tea and toast upstairs. Linda was still asleep as I ate my breakfast. I woke her before her tea went cold and the phone rang. I went downstairs to answer it. It was my Dad calling from Thailand; he and my Mum are on holiday over there, visiting my brother who lives there. They were on the beach and my brother was swimming. I asked my Dad which way the wind was blowing, he said it was an onshore, light breeze. I asked about the wind because I'd had a kite-surfing accident in an offshore wind. I then asked if everything was OK with them and we said our goodbyes. This is when I was sure that my brother had been involved in a shark attack. I started to cry and Linda came into the room, asking what was wrong. I told her a shark had attacked my brother and then I became filled with a wild anger. I ran into the kitchen and straight for the back door." Bill put his head in his hands and started to mumble to himself at this stage. All three doctors looked at each other as they stopped writing in their note pads. Bill then looked up and carried on recounting the morning's events. He spoke in fluent Tronion. The doctors were stunned by the change in dialect; none had heard such a language.

Quickly, Dr Baker got out his tape recorder from his satchel and plugged it into the mains, quietly hissing away as it recorded the first ever Tronion recording. Bill re-lived the whole of the morning's event in Tronion, as the doctors listened intently to words that had no meaning to them whatsoever. As Bill came to the end of his recollection he started to speak in English again.

"Bill, can you remember what you were saying a few moments ago?" asked Dr Baker, as he pushed his glasses back on the bridge of his nose.

"I told you what happened this morning, I left nothing out."

"Bill, listen to this for a minute." Dr Baker rewound the tape and pressed play. The Tronion came out of the crackly old speaker and Bill sat listening carefully.

"Yes, that is what I told you just now." Bill spoke in English. He could translate the language in his mind easily.

"The problem we have Bill is that we don't understand what you said on the tape, can you help us with this?" Dr Baker played some of the tape again and Bill translated the dialect.

"This is when I left the stone monument and walked to the gorge. I buried my kit, which must not be found and then waited until I was ready to see Sanluin again.

"Bill, who is Sanluin? Can you tell us about this person?" Dr Baker moved to the edge of his seat as he listened to Bill's reply.

"She is the only one left on Hope and we have both accepted that the only way we will see each other again is in the next life."

"Bill, are you Bill in this story?"

"No, my name is Rafievn. I was dropped off by Hope at the monument to study the people there. The ship's pilot Tehkin got killed in a crevasse, which left Hope stranded in the south, which is how I got separated from Sanluin."

"OK Bill, that's fine for now. Would you like to get some rest and we can carry on in a moment?"

"Yes Doctor, I am feeling tired again." Dr Baker took off his glasses and cleaned the lenses with the corner of his shirt. Dr Knowles and Dr Meacher still said nothing but smiled at Bill as he got up and was led to his cell by Officer Smith. Bill lay down on the mattress and drifted off to sleep, muttering quietly in Tronion.

"Well chaps, what do you make of that then?" Dr Baker asked his two colleagues.

"It seems to be heading in a split personality direction but the change in language is remarkable, I've never come across anything like it before," said Dr Knowles, in his strong Yorkshire accent.

"It is a very interesting interview so far, I will be keen to learn the rest of the story when our patient wakes up. In the mean time, who wants coffee?" Dr Meacher asked, as he got up from his chair.

"I'll take tea please, one sugar," said Dr Baker.

"Same here," replied Dr Knowles.

Bill's adopted Tronion gene was selecting all the information it wanted Bill to reveal to the doctors while he slept. Nearly all of Hope's arrival to Earth would be revealed, apart from the co-ordinates where Hope was. The only clue would be that it is somewhere in the southern polar ice cap. The co-ordinates would be revealed when Dr Baker believed what Bill was saying.

The rest of the day was spent with a series of twenty-minute interviews in which Bill revealed everything he was supposed to. Every detail up to when Rafievn was introduced to the girl he slept with at the monument was on tape; it was in Tronion but was partly translated during the interviews.

Ten hours had passed and Linda was being comforted by her friend Suzanne. They both worked together and had always been supportive of each other. It was 9.00 pm when the police station called Linda, they said Bill was ready to come home and had been released with no charge. Linda called Shane and they both went to collect him. The gene was allowing Bill to be his old self again. Now that the initial activation had been complete, Dr Viuuv's own thought process was working subconsciously in Bill's mind. It was as if Dr Viuuv was re-awakened in someone else's mind, not completely controlling the other person but just using them as a carrier of information. It was now a case of convincing the right people that what Bill was told to say from within by Dr Viuuv, would work and be the root of mankind's survival.

Linda ran up to Bill, who was stood next to Officer Smith on the steps of the police station and threw her arms around him. He hugged her firmly back.

"The doctor said you're feeling better now but need to rest and slow down a little?" Linda spoke, still hugging her husband.

"OK love, I will. Come on let's go home." Shane was waiting in the car. Bill and Linda both sat in the back.

"OK mate, feeling better now? asked Shane.

"Yes mate. That was a funny old day to say the fuckin' least," Bill replied, looking at the station as Shane drove away. Bill knew what had been said in the interview room but was slightly reluctant to tell anyone else; he would tell Linda later but when they were on their own. Dr Baker had arranged for Bill to spend time in a mental health clinic, as he was unsure of Bill's state of mind. Dr Baker believed that Bill was suffering from a serious manic episode and bi-polar disorder but the change in language and the story was an added ingredient in this case. Bill needed a lot more observation so that Dr Baker could evaluate the situation in its entirety.

All beds were taken at the local National Health Institute, so he was lucky to get into a private clinic through the NHS. Dr Baker had spoken to Linda about the clinic and reassured her it was the best option in this situation. She agreed straight away; she just wanted her husband back to normal. Bill stayed very quiet that evening, letting Linda do all the talking and agreed with her that the stay in the clinic was the best option.

It was a long time before Bill drifted off to sleep; he kept turning the thoughts over and over in his mind, questioning the story that had suddenly entered his head. It was strange how he was at complete ease with the situation; he should have been in a state of shock but Dr Viuuv had taken care of all the after-effects of the awakened gene.

Falima Barhoud had told the same story in Egypt through Cinciev. She was now being cared for in a private clinic on the edge of Cairo. The doctor was a Dutch woman called Trudi Van Teller. She had been working in Egypt for two years and was as intrigued by Falima's episode as much as Dr Baker was with Bill Thompson's. Falima had not had the same outburst as Bill but had stayed in her apartment, until her friend Alishia, found Falima curled up on her couch muttering away in Tronion. Alishia had called the doctor who in turn referred Falima to Dr Van Teller. Dr Van Teller was keen to find out more about Falima's story, which she had told in a strange language. She would soon be shocked to find out that a very similar story had been told in England by someone Falima Barhoud had never met before.

Shane and Kevin took Bill to the Priory Clinic on the outskirts of Bristol the following morning. Linda still didn't have her full driving licence and was grateful to Shane for being her husband's taxi driver; Kevin was also a great, but silent support.

The day was fresh and cold with clear blue skies and Linda sat in the back of the car with Bill, as they drove up the long private road to the Clinic. The Clinic was set in its own grounds and had once been a large private house, funded by the slave trade that had fuelled Bristol's economy during the 17th and 18th centuries. Shane parked the car and went to the boot to carry Bill's case.

"How do you feel Bill?" Linda asked. Bill sat and looked at the stone building with its large front door and symmetrical façade.

" I feel OK. I am looking forward to seeing Dr Baker again, he makes me feel comfortable about the whole situation."

"Come on mate, your hotel is waiting," said Shane in a comical voice. Bill did not mean to ignore the humour but walked up to the door as Shane and Linda followed. Kevin waited with the car and turned it round in the car park. The front door was unlocked as Linda reached round Bill to open it. The reception was furnished quite extravagantly and Bill was impressed by the amount of money that had been spent; he felt that his case was worthy of the best treatment. The reception desk was on the left side of the room and a plump lady was perched on her stool with bi-focals resting on the end of her nose. Linda, Bill and Shane went over to the desk; the receptionist's head was buried in a book by Wilbur Smith and she hadn't seen the new guests arrive.

"Hello, my name is Linda Thompson. My husband Bill is booked in to be assessed by Dr Baker."

"Oh hello there, I didn't see you come in, nothing like a good read to take you away from the day. Now, let's see, Bill Thompson." The lady tapped away on the keypad with her sausage-like fingers whilst looking at Bill over her glasses. "I've got you Mr Thompson. If you take your bags and go through the door on my left you will come to another reception where one of the nurses will take care of you. Can only Mrs Thompson go with you at this stage please, your friend can wait here."

"Good luck mate," said Shane, as he passed Bill his case and went over to one of the leather couches. Bill led the way and walked down a long corridor, glazed on one side. The well-kept courtyard was still powdered in a light frost, as the sun was unable to penetrate due to its low position in the winter sky. Another set of double doors led to the second reception that was manned by two nurses. They were both sat behind the desk as Bill and Linda approached. The atmosphere was very calm and there was a radio just loud enough to hear classical music playing. The older of the two nurses got up to welcome the new guest to the clinic.

"Hello Mr Thompson, we have your room ready. Would you and your wife like something to drink?" The nurse made Bill and Linda feel very welcome; it was like being checked into a hotel, not a mental health clinic.

"Oh, tea would be nice, both with milk and sugar please," replied Linda.

"My name is Helen, I'll show you to your room," said the nurse, as she walked round from the reception. Bill and Linda followed the nurse down a corridor, which had rooms on either side, they were numbered and some had the doors ajar. Bill could hear other patients in these rooms and he wondered why they were in the clinic. His room was the last on the left and looked out onto the courtyard.

"I'll let you get settled while I go and fetch your tea." Helen quickly checked the room was OK and went off to make the drinks.

"Well Bill, this seems very nice, you were lucky to get in here; the nurses seem very nice too."

"I wonder when Dr Baker will come and see me again?" Bill sat on the edge of the bed and looked out to the courtyard wondering what would happen next. He knew what had suddenly entered his head was very real and it had to be investigated. One thing that Bill couldn't understand was how at ease he was with what had happened. It was all so natural to him, he felt that he was part of a chain yet to be completed; his goal now was to try and link the chain. Bill was given a strong cocktail of drugs to combat his diagnosis for a manic episode. The anti-psychotic drugs and sleeping tablets knocked him out and he was under observation for the night. Linda left the room where Bill sank into his drug-induced sleep and headed for the exit. Shane drove her home and offered to take her in the following day. Linda appreciated Shane's offer but felt in too much debt for his kindness, so declined. Linda's Mother, Cathy had been looking after Louise who was sleeping soundly, oblivious to the day's events.

"Is Bill OK now Linda? What are they going to do with him?" asked Cathy.

"They have sedated him, and will keep a close watch over him for the next few days," replied Linda, who then broke down into tears as the stress of the day hit home. Cathy comforted her daughter in the same way as she had done when she was a young child.

"I'll stay here with you tonight Linda, you get some rest and don't worry about a thing. Everything will get sorted out, just give it some time."

Bill had been evaluated by a number of nurses and doctors and was still on his dosage of drugs, which made him feel rotten. His confidence had completely gone because of the anti-psychotics and he felt constantly drowsy. Even his speech had slurred and his eyesight had gone blurred. Dr Baker hadn't been in to see Bill but was due the next day. Bill counted the hours, as he felt Dr Baker would reduce his drug intake. He drifted off into another drug-induced sleep where dreams were void and his mind became immersed in a black hole of nothing. Bill woke to the sound of shoe soles crushing the short bristles of the floor tiles in the corridor. The night observation nurse left his door ajar. Clumsily, Bill reached for his watch and could make out the time was 9.30 am. He lifted himself slowly from the bed and let his legs fall to the floor. The carpet tiles in the rooms were the same as in the corridor and Bill's feet felt the fibres bend beneath his weight. He made his way to the en-suite toilet and was surprised how yellow and pungent his urine was; it must be the drugs he thought to himself. The shower seemed a good option, so he turned the mixer lever to about halfway on the narrow red arrow. Bill cleaned his teeth as he waited for the water to run at an even temperature.

Dr Baker stared patiently at the traffic lights, waiting for them to change colour; he was trying not to rush, even though he wanted to. His new patient was waiting, and from the first evaluation at the police station, Dr Baker was eager to delve deeper into the mind of Bill Thompson. It made such a change from sessions with the various addicts, be they dependent on drugs, alcohol, gambling, sex or depression, they were usually quite similar.

Bill lay back on the bed wrapped in the clinic's bathrobe; his body steaming from the hot shower felt fresh and clean. Bill's mind was still a blur, with the racing thoughts of 4,000 years ago but his ability to function on everyday tasks was more stable. He thought about how he had just showered, but the day before he wouldn't have even know what a shower was. A knock at Bill's door took him from his thoughts.

"Hello Bill," came a soft voice from one of the nurses. "Dr Baker is here, are you ready to see him?"

"Yes, a couple of minutes while I get dressed," he said, as he sat up and looked for his clothes.

"I'll give you a few minutes and send the Dr on down."

"OK," replied Bill. Dr Baker was asking the night staff how Bill had been through the night. They told him that Bill had slept well for the whole night and that they wouldn't get any trouble from him because of the amount of drugs he had been given.

Bill was dressed and looking in the mirror when Dr Baker knocked on the door. Bill went over to the door, still slightly shaky on his feet, and opened it to see Dr Baker, who was now a reassuring sight that filled him with confidence.

"Feeling better Bill?"

"Sort of, but the drugs are making me feel uneasy and shaky."

"That's normal Bill. Shall we go to another room to chat? It's a bit stuffy in here."

"Yes, that's fine by me." They walked up to the reception and went into one of the consulting rooms, which had a desk and leather clad chairs.

"Please, take a seat Bill and get comfortable. Would you like a drink?"

"Oh, tea please." Dr Baker opened the door slightly and asked one of the nurses to bring in some tea.

"Right then Bill, let's go back to yesterday and go over what we talked about at the Police Station. You told me about how some sort of space ship landed on this planet around 4,000 years ago and that the crew of the ship got separated; can you remember this?"

"Of course Doctor. The ship is called Hope and is hidden under the ice in the southern ice cap. The pilot of the crew had fallen through the snow into a crevasse and died, leaving the only female member of the crew stranded with her baby. The other crew members were in the north, one in Stonehenge and the other in Cairo. They were dropped off there to evaluate the people and to see which ones they might settle with." Bill went on to describe the whole mission, up to when Rafievn had last communicated with Sanluin. Dr Baker was still amazed, not only by the story but the exact way in which Bill recited it again. Not one flaw, not one change and told as honestly if it were true.

"OK Bill, that is exactly what you told me yesterday but do you think it is slightly strange that you should be coming up with a story like this?"

"I do a little, but it feels so normal to tell you. I feel that this really has happened in the past and that we should try to find the ship; I know the co-ordinates, so we could try." Dr Baker looked at his patient who seemed to be totally in control, but was he seriously thinking of trying to find a space ship in Antarctica?

"Look Bill, what we will do is let you get some more rest and hopefully we will sort this out in a few days. I don't really think there is anything in Antarctica and you will start to realise that this is part of some strange activity within your brain." Dr Baker wanted to say this sort of thing had happened before but could not lie, as in fact this was the first case he had ever come across.

As Dr Baker drove home he played the tape of the interview with Bill. Every detail of the story was word perfect and told as if it was the absolute truth. The whole incident was burning into his mind so he decided to call Dr Meacher, who was always keen to compare cases using various websites. Dr Baker was not one for new technology but was about to give in regarding his latest patient. Dr Craig Meacher's flat was clinically pristine, nothing was out of place; it had the house-proud bachelor feel written all over it. The study was of the same standard except for the full waste paper bin. Dr Baker pulled a chair up to the side of Craig's and watched as the process of getting on to a website began. The dial up was taking its time, reinforcing Dr Baker's doubt of this latest technology. Craig Meacher clicked away to Dr Baker's silent impatience.

"Here we go, the latest posts of strange bi-polar cases." They read through the cases to themselves; the only sign from Dr Meacher was enquiring if his colleague had finished reading the page. Nothing came up from any of the comparisons they could find but it was early days and some cases might not have made it to this new comparison network, especially if psychiatrists were of the same ilk as Dr Baker.

Bill Thompson had now been at home for a week and was itching to get back to work and earn some money. He was self-employed and not working meant no income. He was advised to rest but felt he was fully in charge of his mind and thoughts. He still had the story as fresh as it was the first moment it had been activated but he had a strong yearning to get to the bottom of the episode. Every time Dr Baker phoned, Bill expected him to say, go and find this ship. Unbeknown to Dr Baker, there was a thought process being assembled in his own brain to persuade him to go along with the whole story and each meeting between the two men added to this process. It came from when Rafievn had injected himself with the dormant gene and wasn't anything Bill said to Dr Baker; it was in the very air Bill exhaled.

Falima Barhoud was still in her apartment and being assessed by Dr Van Teller; these two were in exactly the same situation as Dr Baker and Bill Thompson in England. Compared to Dr Baker, Dr Van Teller was much more adept and au fait with the Internet and had posted Falima's episode on one of the websites Dr Meacher was looking at. It was only a matter of time until the two identical stories would collide in the eyes of a trained psychiatrist. It wasn't only Dr Baker who was being persuaded in believing Bill's story but Belinda Thompson was also in the frame. It was all meant to happen. Dr Viuuv knew that the people who were to be reactivated by the dormant gene needed help in making other people believe in their story. The process was working well and all the people who were in personal contact with Bill Thompson and Falima Barhoud were steadily starting to believe in every word they spoke.

It was around seven thirty when Craig Meacher got home from work. His day consisted of the general assessment of his patients, a mundane and non-eventful day all in all. He started to prepare his meal when he thought he should check the Internet for any comparative cases to the one Dr Baker was involved with; he wanted to get it out of the way and then switch off from work. The computer booted up as Dr Meacher scoured the kitchen cupboard for tinned fish and pasta, a simple and quick meal. He left the water simmering as he went to the computer. He tapped away and looked for any new posts from other psychiatrists; there were six in total and Dr Meacher started to read through them as he went to and from the kitchen preparing his meal. The first four were all from UK based surgeries and showed no similarities to Dr Baker's case. Dr Meacher was back in the kitchen as the last two cases came up on the screen; Dr Van Teller had titled her case with Falima Barhoud as a 'One off case'. Not expecting to find anything interesting, Dr Meacher quickly glanced through the text. It was when leaning on the desk that his expression changed; he couldn't believe what he was reading. The whole episode that Falima Barhoud had experienced was almost exactly the same, to the last word, as what Dr Baker had told him. He quickly switched on the printer and ran off two copies.

Dr Baker was sat watching the evening news when his phone rang. He reached across and answered,

"Dr Baker."

"Dave, it's Craig. You had better come over. I have got some news for you which you wont believe." Dr Meacher tried to keep calm but his voice was not hiding his excitement.

"What have you got? Tell me over the phone," replied Dr Baker, eager to hear the news.

"I have just printed out a near exact copy of your own case; you won't believe it until you see it," replied Dr Meacher, holding the printout in his hands.

"OK, I will be straight over." Dr Baker drove just under the speed limit, which was too quick for him as he was a very slow driver. He ran up to Dr Meacher's door, forgetting to lock his car. Dr Meacher was in his kitchen as the doorbell rang clearing up the boiled-over water from the pasta that he had left on during the excitement.

"Come in David, take a seat in the study; just read this," he urged, handing the two sheets of printed A4 to him. Dr Baker read intently and was amazed at what he read. Never in their experience as psychologists had they come across two such strange and identical stories related to a bi-polar manic episode. Dr Baker looked up at Dr Meacher and said,

"It can't be, this is unheard of. We need to contact this Dr Van Teller straightaway."

It would be 1.00 am in Cairo, so Dr Baker and Dr Meacher decided to leave it until the morning, although they were both very impatient to speak to Dr Van Teller. They stayed up most of the night talking about the similarities of the two cases, unaware of how their subconscious had already been altered. The airborne nano programmes, transferred by carriers of the dormant gene Bill and Falima, had already passed into their blood stream and settled in their brain. Here, the nano programme would form a microprocessor to control an electrical current, so that from now on Dr Meacher, Dr Baker, Bill Thompson, Linda Thompson, Falima Barhoud and Dr Van Teller would be semi-controlled and programmed to find Hope. Once inside Hope, they would inhale the inoculation gene that had been designed to spread in the same way. Dr Viuuv had also programmed the nano-processors to read the minds of the carrier and eradicate their memory. It was just a matter of time until Hope was found, but it would be done with the constant assessment of who came into contact with Dr Meacher, Dr Baker, Bill and Linda Thompson, Falima and Van Teller. Nn would not know the time of arrival but Hope's sensors would pick up any movement directly above the ship and instruct Nn to flood the ship's atmosphere with the inoculation gene.

It was six thirty when Dr Meacher's alarm sounded; both men were sleeping in Dr Meacher's lounge where they had drifted off to sleep. Craig Meacher struggled from his chair and went to turn off the alarm that was buzzing away in his bedroom.

"Tea?" asked Craig, leaning on the lounge door-frame,

"Coffee please. I need the caffeine, and put two sugars in will you. Thanks," came the yawning reply.

It was approaching 9.00 am in Cairo and Dr Van Teller had been in her office for an hour going over the tapes of Falima's story. She was thinking how a trip using the co-ordinates Falima had come up with, would be possible. The processor in her brain had already convinced her the story was true and it was up to her to decide what action to take next. The phone on the desk buzzed into life as Dr Van Teller reached across to answer it.

"Morning. Dr Van Teller," came the answer.

"Oh, good morning. My name is Dr Baker, I am calling from England: my colleague and I have read your post on the Internet forum about one of your patients and we have a patient with an almost identical story. We are baffled how two people, in different parts of the world and who have never met, can come up with the same story." Dr Baker talked calmly, even though he was full of intrigue.

"Well Dr Baker, that is interesting and coincidently, I was just listening to the recording of the patient I think you are referring to. Let me play it to you through the phone; here listen to this." Dr Van Teller placed the Dictaphone to the mouthpiece of the phone and pressed play. Dr Baker's jaw dropped as he heard the story from Falima's interview, he just couldn't believe his ears. Everything was the same, the names, the places, the whole thing. This information was being picked up by the processor in Dr Baker's brain and the following actions and reasoning were being semi-controlled by the processor, or in other words, in the minute brain of Dr Viuuv. The recording ended and Dr Van Teller put the phone back to her ear.

"What do you make of that Dr Baker?" asked Van Teller.

"Uncanny, just wait a second." Dr Baker got his tape player. "Dr Van Teller, listen to our patient; we recorded this when he was taken into the Police Station." Dr Baker held the tape player to the phone and played the tape. It was Dr Van Teller's turn for her jaw to drop; she listened in amazement, as she heard Bill Thompson talk about events that had happened 4,000 years ago. The processor in Dr Van Teller's brain was working exactly the same way in Dr Baker's, with the answers ready and waiting to be sent to receptors in its host mind.

It was decided that no one should know anything about the situation except for the three doctors and Bill Thompson. Even when they were aware of what had happened, they would be controlled from telling anyone else. Drs Baker, Van Teller and Meacher talked for well over an hour about what they should do next. It was agreed they would meet up before telling Bill Thompson and that it was imperative the whole story should remain a secret for the moment.

The best way they could get to Hope was in the guise of going to the Antarctic on a salvage-search mission. The Viuuv processor decided that a light aircraft had gone down in a storm in the Antarctic and that one of the passengers was a relation of Dr Baker. A rescue mission, plus memorial service would be launched that would include all three doctors. The Viuuv processor had read the memory of Dr Baker and found an uncle of his that had done weather research in the Antarctic, which had led to the plan and would make it more credible. All three agreed with this, the only problem would be the cost of such an expedition.

The Viuuv processors knew what funds were available from the doctors and just needed to know what the cost of a salvage-search trip to the Antarctic would be to find Hope. A salvage-search company would need to be contacted and from that, finances arranged. This could be done in a number of ways, from research funding for psychology grants to pension funds and personal savings. When all three doctors and Bill Thompson got together, they could pool their resources and come up with a way to fund the expedition. When Hope had landed on Planetician, the co-ordinates were set from the islands in the mid Atlantic (now the Azores) and these were 28 degrees to the west, from the GMT meridian. Now the doctors had these co-ordinates from Bill and Falima, the mission would be able to find Hope. Dr Viuuv had surpassed himself when programming Nn and developing mind control technology, as it was not only working, it was working on another planet and with the ultimate goal of inoculation to save a human race from its own demise.

The Viuuv processors were working 24 hours a day reading the memory banks of the chosen four, scanning every detail. There should be no financial gain for anyone by finding Hope, as there would undoubtedly be a frenzy of activity that might possibly destroy the whole mission, not to mention the religious and social tremors that would be sent across Planetician. If news got out, all hell would break loose. As with the arrival of Hope, this mission was being assessed by Nn, and the Viuuv processors were planning the next phase; sacrifices might need to be made. It would be a tough decision, but some people might just have to be taken out of the equation if they thought that finding Hope could be used for their own financial gain.

The North African runway was shimmering with a heat haze as it waited for the airbus from London. Dr Van Teller was in arrivals, ready to take Dr Baker and Dr Meacher to the Holiday Inn where she had booked them a room, as it was only ten minutes from the airport. Dr Van Teller held up her card with the doctors' names on, she was in a line with other taxi drivers and personal chauffeurs. Dr Meacher was first to spot his name, as his eyesight was better than Dr Baker's. He walked over to Van Teller and introduced himself, closely followed by Dr Baker. All three got into the taxi that Van Teller had waiting, exchanging only pleasantries as they did and saying nothing about what they were there for. The Viuuv processors were controlling all this. Once in the hotel they ordered drinks and went over the arrangements for a salvage-search mission to find Hope; they were far too interested in the reason of their meeting to start any small talk.

"It's good that we have met like this. This is such a serious matter we have to discuss things in person, plus I wanted to stress the importance of it being kept secret; not to be repeated to any one." Dr Baker was speaking to both Dr Van Teller and Dr Meacher.

"Oh, I totally agree," replied Van Teller.

"Let's start sorting out what we are going to do next," said Dr Meacher. Van Teller offered to do all of the organising from her office but the other two decided it would be safer from the hotel, as it was private with no prying ears. Van Teller was to get contact telephone numbers of salvage-search teams from her office Internet connection and bring them to the hotel.

The next two days passed with phone calls to various salvage-search companies, most of whom did not venture to the Antarctic. One company from Florida had shown interest as it had worked on an old science station and was involved in its demolition, plus it was struggling financially and wanted the work. The owner was in his fifties and needed the money badly; he didn't want to see his company go bust. Dave Wheeler of D.W.S. Recoveries got the job and a deposit of $500 was wired to his office. The rest of the money would be paid in two further instalments, one when they got to the Antarctic and the final balance when the light aircraft was found. The total cost was just under $100,000 and would be a collection from the many different accounts the processors ha͎ found in the minds of its hosts.

It was agreed that Dr Baker, Meacher and Bill Thompson were to go on the salvage-search mission; Van Teller would stay in Egypt, as she hadn't flown since 9/11. Bill Thompson had met with both Baker and Meacher and was ready for the trip to Florida and from there, on to the Antarctic. There was no doubt in any of their minds and if there was, it was blocked by the processors. Bill had explained to Linda and she was fine, as she too was being semi-controlled, otherwise she would have been seen the proposal as madness. The rest of their family were kept in the dark as to where Bill would be going. They were led to believe that he had a contract working in Scotland for a month with no weekend leave, and as some of his other work mates had done similar spells of work away from home, it was believable.

Dr Meacher had set up a separate bank account that would hold all the funds for the trip and two days before they were due to fly out, the three had been to a specialist outdoor retailers to get the appropriate gear for the Antarctic weather. It was summer in the Antarctic but still bitterly cold, compared to what they are used to in the British winters. Dave Wheeler already had all the kit from his previous time in the Antarctic and he was the only outside person needed for this trip. He liked this idea as he could maximise the profits and afterwards set about starting another business near the Florida Keys. He had booked a Snow Cat with a drilling auger fitted, from the new science station that had been built to replace the one he had demolished. The 'Blue Climate' station was glad to hire it out, as it brought in extra money for them to spend on research. Everything was now in place for the trip to the alleged light aircraft's position. It was just luck that the Blue Climate was only two days travel from the co-ordinates of Hope.

Dave Wheeler was waiting at Orlando International Airport; the Virgin flight was on time and due to land in the next ten minutes. Dave Wheeler looked at the itinerary he had drawn up for the trip and noticed the co-ordinates were close to the South Pole; it would be good to go back to that region, as he had not had the chance to go to the actual South Pole during his previous time on the frozen continent.

The carousel laboured its way carrying bags, cases, prams, golf kits and the swollen holdalls of Dr Baker, Dr Meacher and Bill Thompson. They bundled the luggage onto a trolley and made for the exit. Just as Dr Van Teller had done, Dave Wheeler had his board up with Dr Baker's name on it.

"Good trip?" asked Dave Wheeler in his broad southern drawl as he reached out his hand.

"Yes, thank you Mr Wheeler, we got some good rest too."

They shook hands as Dave Wheeler said,

"Call me Dave."

The airport shuttle took them to the car park where Dave Wheeler's Dodge Ram was waiting. He put the bags in the open back of the truck as the others climbed in and drove to the offices of his company. The team had a few days rest before flying down to Punta Arenas in southern Chile, where they would change planes and go on to the Antarctic.

It was early morning as the sun split the Antarctic sky; the four engines of the Dash Seven spun the props, pulling huge spirals of air through them. The Dash had already stopped for fuel at Rothara and was now on the last run into Blue Climate; the vastness of snow with the distant peaks of Mt Kirkpatrick and Mt Markham, spiking through the ice crust was a sight that few had seen from Planetician. As well as Dr Baker's team, three scientists were travelling with them, to replace a team already in Blue Climate.

The plane started to drop in altitude as the gentle thuds of air turbulence cradled the craft. Excitement was building inside Bill and the two doctors, never having seen this frozen wilderness before. The other passengers had all experienced its staggering beauty and considered it as work, however, the best possible kind of work. The airstrip was lined with bright orange markers that headed straight for Blue Climate. Great clouds of fine powder snow bellowed up and swirled in circular shapes off the tips of the wings, as the plane landed and even though the airstrip was well maintained, the landing was much bumpier than any tarmac equivalent. The ski skids attached to all polar planes, were not needed, as fresh snow had not fallen for a while. One of Blue Climate's service personnel guided the plane to its parking bay, and then jumped on a skidoo pulling a sled to collect the luggage. The pilot got up from her seat and made her way to the door; there were no flight personnel on this trip. She opened the door and the Antarctic wind blew in, freezing the moisture in her nostrils instantly, as she breathed in the fresh air.

"Have you guys got the kettle on? We're parched," shouted the pilot to the guy on the skidoo, whose face was covered by the coat's hooded snorkel. Her voice had that slightly stern, ex-service tone, from her time as a reconnaissance pilot for the Royal Navy on the Ark Royal. The driver put a thumb up in answer to the kettle question and the pilot nodded in return. Another body came over to the plane, pushing boarding steps that slid on the hard packed snow, up to the open door of the plane. Even though the fur-lined snorkel covered his face, his portly build was recognisable to the pilot. It was Phil Turner, who was like the general go-fer at Blue Climate and for whom nothing was ever too much trouble. He fancied himself as a scientist but just lacked the necessary 'grey matter'.

The inside of the station was not made for luxury but was very clean, practical and everything worked. It was ten years since Dave Wheeler had been involved with the demolition of the old base and the maintenance team had kept the place in tiptop condition. Phil Turner showed the salvage-search team to their rooms; there were two separate rooms, with a set of bunk beds in each. The itinerary was set for one night at the base and then off in the Snow Cat the next morning. They should be at the co-ordinates of the supposed 'light aircraft' by noon the next day where they would set up camp. Bill Thompson was in a room with Dr Baker, whilst Dr Meacher was sharing with Dave Wheeler.

Soon after arrival, all four were sat at the table in the canteen, listening to the din of excited scientists' chatter about ice core readings, atmospheric gasses and other topics connected to the global warming phenomena. But was this phenomena or farce, as no one collective had definitive proof? Politicians however, loved the subject, as it gave them opportunities to create new businesses to support this notion, that in turn made them look like 'job creators', and 'guardians' of the planet and of mankind. What they failed to understand is that Earth or Planetician, had been through all sorts of climatic changes in its natural history; landmasses raised and lowered themselves and sometimes sea levels had nothing to do with it. Ice ages had come and gone, warm periods had done the same, but these 'gravy-train creators' did not exist when these past events had taken place and didn't really need to exist now, striking fear and guilt into the population of Earth or Planetician.

"These guys live well! Better than the food ten years ago," said Dave, as he picked up his knife and fork ready to devour his pile of Bolognese, garlic bread and peas.

"They do, but then again, we didn't know what the cuisine was like in the past," replied Dr Baker.

"Oh, it was garbage back then, it was the lure of decent food that helped speed up the demolition process," replied Dave, as he spoke behind a huge fork full of spaghetti.

"What are these Snow Cats like to travel in Dave?" asked Dr Meacher.

"Not bad. These ones are bigger than the ones you get on ski resorts, they have more seats in them. We should be fine," replied Dave. "Now, if you don't mind..." he continued as he held his garlic bread in one hand and another huge twist of spaghetti in the other. The others got the message and carried on with their food. Dave Wheeler was obviously a great food lover and didn't like to be disturbed too often whilst eating.

"OK guys, fire away with your questions," said Dave as he wiped his mouth with the paper serviette. The questions came in thick and fast about the following two days. By the end of the meal they were all beginning to feel the strain of the journey and overall excitement of the trip. They turned in and settled down for the night.

Alarms were not needed for the wake up call; Bill had been showered and dressed for the day since very early. The sky was cloud free with the November sun shining very brightly and unworldly; the temperature was a warm minus eighteen. Bill went onto the canteen for breakfast and sat with Phil Turner, who told him everything he wanted to know about Blue Climate. The other three soon joined them. Dave Wheeler went over the details of the Snow Cat with Phil, as it was a newer model, powered by a Mercedes six-cylinder engine. Tents for the team were packed, along with all the other provisions they would need. Dave Wheeler typed co-ordinates of their destination into the Sat Nav, which was positioned next to the hours meter in the cab; a speedometer was not necessary, as the top speed of the Snow Cat was about 25 mph, which was perfect for the flat terrain around the pole. Most other Snow Cats only reached 20 mph; these slower models were used on the steep ski slopes around the world.

Bill Thompson sat next to Dave up front, with Dr Baker and Dr Meacher in the back. As the Mercedes engine fired up, a red direction line lit up on the Sat Nav screen. A blue line was also on the screen and this moved according to Dave's driving. He had to get the blue line on top of the red line, as this would then point the vehicle in the right direction. The tracks of the Cat threw up cuts of snow as it travelled at top speed in the direction of the light aircraft that was really Hope. The drone of the engine allowed for conversation but it was a strain to keep up, so most of the journey was spent in silence. None of them had brought any type of iPod, Dr Meacher was dozing off in 'nodding dog' style, which Bill and Dave found very amusing and Dr Baker was reading books on mental health, whilst scribbling down ideas for a book of his own. Meanwhile the Viuuv processor was filtering all this detail and information, to ensure that the whole episode would never be known to the wider world. There was enough fuel in the tanks of the Cat for one day and the rest was stored in fuel cans strapped to the rear of the cab. Two hours into the journey and the bladder strain was beginning to tell. Bill tapped Dave on the shoulder.

"Dave, any chance of a toilet break?"

"Yeah, no sweat man," replied Dave as he let up on the accelerator. The Cat slowed pretty quickly and Bill hopped out. He didn't expect the blast of cold air, as the wind had picked up since leaving Blue Climate. He grabbed for his zip on his coat and pulled it right up to the end of the snorkel and turned away from the wind. He walked to the back of the Cat and relieved himself, while leaning on the drilling auger.

It was nearly dusk when the last of the tents were set up and all four gazed at the view of the sun kissing the horizon, knowing that it was only one more day until they got to their destination. Dave Wheeler saw 'dollar bills' and the other three saw what was to be the changing of mankind possibly forever. Nn was picking up the vibration of the Cat's tracks and knew by its constant direction that it was heading straight for Hope. The ice cavern started to flood with the inoculation vapour and lights from Hope's hull lit up, albeit very dimly. Sanluin was perfectly preserved in her sleep casual, with Sno alongside her.

Nn looked at Sanluin's beauty and remembered how she had prepared herself to look her best for Rafievn in the next life. Nn decided to keep her beauty private from the inevitable visit form the newcomers. He sealed off the pod room and went to the bridge area to assess the next steps of the mission. Sno had been three years old when Nn had laid her to rest. She had been used for testing the inoculation vapour and other mind-altering experiments. They were harmless experiments but had to be done, so that Hope's future visitors would be programmed with the correct information to secure the future of Planetician.

"We should be there in two minutes," said Dave, leaning across to Bill.

"OK, Dave. Did you get that, guys? Two minutes," replied Bill, turning to the two in the back of the cab, who gave a 'thumbs up' sign and started to put their gloves and thermal hats on. The weather outside had really picked up and snow was peppering the windows of the cab. Dave let off the throttle and slowed down as he approached the co-ordinates of 87°south 178° west. The Sat Nav gave out a short bleep, as Dave brought the Cat to a standstill.

They all climbed out and looked around at their destination.

The snow was about a foot deep of pure powder before it hit the hard pack below, creaking underfoot, just like polystyrene rubbing against itself. The Trans-Atlantic Mountains rose up to the east with the start of glacial landscape just visible and were the same undulations that had taken Tehkin 4,000 years earlier. By now the glacier would have crushed him and taken his body out to sea; a sandy bed his final resting place. It was the one part of the mission that was out of Nn's control but there was a very slim, almost near impossible chance that Tehkin's remains and clothing might one day be found.

Dave put up the largest tent first and set up a small kitchen inside, with a stove for boiling water and thermal boxes to keep their food packs in, to stop them freezing too much. He started to boil some water, which was frozen slush from the water tanks; he had to shake the tanks to break the ice up. It was a race against the elements and the 35° below weather, seemed to be winning. The other three huddled in the tent as the steam started to raise the temperature slightly. Dave put the boil in the bag food into the water and imagined what the smell would be.

"OK guys. Whilst that's cooking let me show you how this baby works," said Dave, as he patted the auger drill that hung on the back of the Cat. There was a small fibreglass case bolted next to the auger and inside was the remote for operating the system; it was connected to the rig by a flexi cord, similar to that used to attach an old telephone hand piece to the body.

"This baby can cut through six foot of ice, so finding your plane should be easy; the coastal area of this place gets between 500 mm and 1,000 mm of snow per year. Your plane went down in 1978, so that's 33 years of snowfall. We are quite a bit inland and allowing for blizzard drifting, plus the protection from those mountains over there, we should be around the six-foot mark. We can go deeper if it is less compact but that we will find out soon enough. Now, who's hungry?' Dave put the remote back in the fibreglass case and went back into the temporary canteen. The other three looked at each other and nodded to follow Dave.

Fed and watered or as highly caffeined as Dave was, they set about drilling the first of the exploratory holes. Dave lowered the auger bit to the snow until the weight was off the hydraulic arm; he then started to drill slowly, so that the bit had time to bite into the snow. It cut in like a sharp wood bit into soft pine. The snow spewed out as the bit spun and Bill Thompson cleared it away with a snow shovel, which had been strapped to the side of the Cat's cab. He did this instinctively, as if he was back on a building site.

It was only a few minutes before the auger had nearly disappeared and the whole rig seemed to drop suddenly. Dave stopped drilling, pulled the bit out of the hole with the arm and got on his belly to look down. He was inhaling the inoculation gene immediately, as it bellowed out of the hole with the faintest updraft, carrying powder snow into the air. There was a black void below, with just the slightest haze of light coming from Hope's hull.

"Bingo. We must be right on top or maybe behind the wing. When the plane went down she must have made a pocket of snow and this is that little cave," said Dave with the excitement of a ten year old. Bill went over to the hole and looked in, the other two leant over Bill's shoulder cautiously. Dave had already repositioned the rig so that he could cut another hole but still be half way into the first one. He did this so that there would be enough space to get a man down by rope.

The drill started again and Bill did his clearing work, some snow went down into the ice cavern and landed on Hope's roof, it slid off and onto the floor, which had been recently chopped and roughed by Nn to give the visitors some grip to walk on. Dave stopped the drill once more when it had cut through.

"Dr Baker can you get the rope from the cab? You can go in and lay your uncle to rest once you're down there, I will be in the tent to give you some time on your own," shouted Dave over the howl of the wind. He pulled the drill back up and went to tie the rope to the Cat. The rope had knots tied every half metre or so to give purchase when gripping.

"It's all yours guys," said Dave handing the rope to Dr Baker.

"Thanks Dave, you've done very well," replied Dr Baker.

"Hey, no sweat man."

"OK. Who's first?" asked Dr Baker. Bill took the rope and threw it down into the figure of eight shaped hole. He then got on his knees and shuffled towards the hole backwards; the rope went taught with his weight and he slowly disappeared. It was a drop of about eight feet to the roof of Hope, which left two foot of rope to spare. Bill's feet were flailing in the air as he found the Luuse alloy. He got his grip but still held the rope tightly until his balance was fully settled. He reached into his pocket and shone the light across the length of the ship and even though the processor in his mind had prepared him for this moment, it still took his breath away, as he stood there in complete amazement. It took a few moments to sink in before he called up to the others.

"Send another rope down and then yourselves," cried Bill.

"Stand back," came the answer, followed by the thud of the coiled rope. Bill quickly tied them together; he felt the rope tugging as one of the doctors descended into the cavern. Bill could tell it was Craig, from his blue clothing and shone the torch on the rope to help his descent. The light also caught the roof of the cavern and Bill could make out what looked like scrapping marks in the ice. It was from Nn's toil all those years ago.

"OK Craig a couple more feet," said Bill reassuringly. Craig was stunned at the sight.

"It's true Bill. It's true." Craig put his hand to his mouth and looked round the cave, noticing how Hope's tail fins nestled into the roof of the cave. The rope started to tug again as Dave Baker came into the silence whilst Bill and Craig were still taking it all in.

"Look Dave, look where we are!" Craig said in excitement, as he shone the torch round slowly. Dave was in awe with the reality of it all. All three had their hearts thumping in their chests with a feeling of extreme excitement mixed with intrigue.

"Come on, let's get below her," said Bill. He grabbed the extended rope and walked backwards towards the port side of Hope, taking tentative steps as the ship's body steepened. Bill's feet lost their grip and he slid out, banging into the side of the ship, his elbows and knees taking the full force of the hit. After a few short moments he started to lower himself down to the icy ground, which was ten feet to the floor. Finally he was on his feet and he let go of the rope and instinctively walked to the lights of Hope's hull. The boarding steps were out and the door was open, with light pouring gently from her that seemed to pull Bill towards it. Bill hadn't heard the calls from the other two who were making their own way down, both having slipped on the hull and feeling the thud against Hope's body. Craig and Dave saw Bill looking into the light pouring from Hope and rushed over to take a look. Bill was still gazing into the ship as he started to walk up the steps into her becoming the first human to make contact with a craft from another planet.

Snow and ice fell from Bill's boots as he climbed the steps; he was inside now, still in complete silence. Dr Baker and Dr Meacher slowly followed, taking their hoods and hats off as they did. Bill had already removed his and held his thermal cap in his hand. They were in the Bridge area of Hope and the screen was lit up, the same screen Sanluin had sat in front of when she had woken from hyper sleep. Bill went over and sat down, he started to read the Tronion text to himself. Dave Baker went over to Bill and looked over his shoulder.

"What does it say Bill?" asked Dave. Bill looked back at Dave to speak but found he needed to clear his throat first.

"It re-affirms what I told you in the interviews at the Police Station," replied Bill.

"Type in a question, anything. How about, 'what do we do now?'" suggested Dave. Bill tapped away on the keyboard; he knew the keys as if it were a 'qwerty' keyboard. The answer came back.

'You don't need to do anything, apart from never letting anyone from your planet know the co-ordinates of this place. The reason for this ship being here is now complete; you just have to get back to your civilisation and carry on with your lives.'

Bill stood up from his seat and looked at Craig Meacher who was ashen white, his mind had started to think of profiting from the find but the processor had spotted it and was causing a fever instantly. Craig Meacher would not make it back to Chile alive.

"Are you OK, Craig? You look awful all of a sudden," asked Dave.

"I'm fine, just shocked by it all, don't worry about me," replied Craig. Then the sound of boots came up the boarding steps; it was Dave Wheeler, he was even more ashen than Craig but not from thoughts of profit but absolute shock of what they had found. He was stumped for words; nothing came out as he entered the Bridge area.

"We couldn't tell you Dave, it would have ruined everything, but now you know you must keep this secret; secret from yourself if you can." Unbeknown to Dave Wheeler, Nn was stood right next to him, he had a camouflage suit on, which was 4,000 years more advanced than Rafievn's and his invisibility was almost perfect. Nn released a vapour for Dave to inhale that would manipulate his thoughts without needing a processor, whilst in the meantime it would start building one in his mind. Nn did not want any more deaths, Craig would be enough. The doors to the rest of the ship were shut off and the Bridge computer shut itself down; Nn was now in full control. Dave Baker reached into his pocket for his camera but found that it was smashed from the impact on Hope's hull.

"Damn it," he said to himself. Slowly the lights inside Hope dimmed and the only source became Bill's torch.

"I think this ship is trying to tell us something, we had better get going," said Bill nervously. They all turned and walked out of the ship; Nn was already at the top of the rope and out of the hole.

The others started to climb back up the rope and had to take their gloves off to get a grip on the knots. All four had been inoculated and one fatally. Nn placed himself in the cab of the Cat behind the seats; there was just enough room. Bill came out first followed by Dave Baker and then Craig Meacher, who were starting to struggle with his breathing as they went over to the tent and started to pack things up. No one had any appetite for food; the processors were telling them to get back as quickly as possible. While in the Cat's cab Nn read the minds of the other four and planned his next steps in getting the right information to the most important and powerful people on Planetician or Earth.

The Snow Cat turned on the spot and headed straight back into its old tracks; nothing was left behind. Nn waited an hour and then sent a message to Hope. Her stabilisers retracted into the hull and she started to heat up. Ice started to melt causing Hope to slowly disappear down into the ice. Nn had chosen a lake, which lay 15,000 feet beneath the ice cap to be the last resting place for Hope. Planetician or Earth as it now was, knew it as Lake Vostok, the largest sub glacial lake under the surface of Antarctica. Hope had the ability to dismantle itself in case of future discovery but this was not the same for Cinciev's, Rafievn's or Tehkin's kit.

Viuuv

The wind blew in from the south with a thudding constant force; it was not too strong to be a problem for the Dooduin who were setting up a new hut. The hut had been dismantled and brought down by packhorse from a hunting trip two months to the north, where the summer fishing was plentiful. The lifestyle of these rugged people had not changed for centuries; they did not need any of the technology which had become the nemesis for most of the population of Atronia and subsequently been destroyed. The Dooduin knew the collapse of their fellow inhabitants civilisation would force these desperate people north and were safe in the more remote northern steppes, free from a mass struggle to feed off the land. The southern areas of these harsh lands were littered with the skeletons of people who had once lived in decadent luxury.

Far in the distance, the meandering valley carried the eerie noise of helicopter blades. They cut through the clean air and bowed, as the craft twisted up the valley. Viuuv rose, his head knowing that this sound carried with it one of the most powerful men on Atronia, whose global empire had collapsed like a pack of cards. Viuuv had been with the Dooduin for nearly two years and had grown a long grey beard, with hair to match and knew that Aliik would not recognise him. After all, Aliik had been meeting with a synthetic copy of Viuuv for years, while the collapse was occurring all around them. Atronia had descended into chaos since the virus had wiped out nano-technology. Some people survived but billions had starved, killing each other for food. Viuuv had settled with the Dooduin many months before the collapse, after Rafievn had asked them to help Viuuv when he arrived. They were only too glad to welcome the new arrival into their village, as they were indebted to Rafievn for his help in delivering a child many years before.

As the helicopter hugged the hillside of the valleys, the whipping noise of the blades undulated, according to the land's natural acoustic reflection. Viuuv got up from his bed, which was not that different to the one Rafievn had slept in near the monument on Planetician. He walked to the door of his hut and watched as the young men on horseback turned to guard it. Viuuv was not afraid of Aliik but knew that his bodyguards would be armed. Aliik was only in this part of Atronia because the Dooduin had land rights to areas that harboured oil. It was an old and redundant fuel when nano-technology had reigned but was now in very high demand. The reserves would last for centuries for the amount of vehicles left on Atronia and Aliik owned over 70 per cent of those reserves.

Only a few miles from the Dooduin camp lay a redundant oil station, which had once pumped millions of barrels of oil; it was now in the safe hands of the Dooduin. They did not need any oil but an agreement was set up many years before, giving the Dooduin full rights and control of the well. It allowed the pumping of oil in return for millions of acres of land for the Dooduin to live their nomadic existence. It was a good deal and now completely safe, as the people who had set it up and signed all the rights, had perished in the collapse, only the like of Aliik and a few thousand others had managed to survive. Most of the other survivors had moved to areas of Atronia where the temperature was warm all year round and hunting was viable. It was an instant step back into the past for them, as they had become totally dependent on the technology, which had once supported their luxurious lifestyles.

The guards for Viuuv were snipers, positioned high up in the pine trees, which towered around the area cleared for the helicopter landing. They were harnessed to the trees by leather straps so that their arms grasped the rifles in a lethally accurate way. For weeks these snipers had practiced shooting at targets from high up in the trees, particularly when the wind was blowing so they would be able to compensate for the trees swaying, more accurately.

It was still windy but only slightly and this added to the snipers' confidence. The tops of the trees started to bend under the down draft of the helicopter blades, the snipers held tightly to their rifles and hoped the leather straps would hold well. The machine slowly dropped and hovered ready to land. The two head leaders of the Dooduin and Viuuv were ready to meet the unwelcome guest. Viuuv had briefed the snipers to open fire on armed guards if there were any. The blades came slowly to a whining rest as the doors of the helicopter opened revealing Aliik, who was instantly recognisable to Viuuv, cowering under the blades even though they had stopped. He approached the small 'welcome' party and as Viuuv predicted, three armed guards got out of the rear doors, and one from the front who had sat next to the pilot. The pilot stayed seated, the mirrored visor reflecting the sunlight. Aliik's plan was to negotiate for the oil well but if the deal seemed out of his reach, he had told his guards to take out the Dooduin leaders. Each guard was armed with a semi-automatic machine gun and had 500 rounds each. Aliik told his men to stay close by but not to enter the hut. Viuuv and the two leaders went into the hut followed by Aliik.

The small fire at the edge of the hut crackled in the stove, cushions were placed down as seats and fresh tea was simmering away, ready for the meeting. No word was spoken, but the taller of the Dooduin made a gesture with his open hand for Aliik to sit. Aliik sat and the other three sat opposite him. Viuuv was nervous but pleased that Aliik had not recognised him. He was dressed in the traditional Dooduin clothes and his face was dark and aged from the northerly exposed climate.

"Well gentlemen, shall we get straight to the point?" Aliik's voice was like poison to Viuuv's ears, as he knew how he had treated Sanluin.

"You want our land for the oil; you have nothing to give us but trouble. The well is broken so you won't get any oil," replied the smaller of the Dooduin.

"You can move your camps anywhere, we won't be in your way. I can give you weapons and ammunition for hunting, make your lives easier. Don't concern yourself over the well," said Aliik with optimism.

"We don't want an easy life, we love our life just as it is. You have nothing for us," replied the taller Dooduin in an aggressive tone.

"You with the long grey beard, what is your view? You seem to be the oldest," responded Aliik in an impatient way, looking straight at Viuuv. Viuuv knew that the moment he spoke Aliik would recognise his voice instantly. What would his reaction be? Would he either respond in shock or run for the door of the hut? Whatever the reaction, if Aliik's guards moved they would be shot instantly. A silence descended in the hut, the tension rose in Viuuv's heart, as he remembered how Aliik had sent hundreds of people to their deaths. But this was close, this was raw and for the first time gunshot would end human life and it all hinged on Viuuv's inevitable reaction. These thoughts shot through Viuuv's brain, his eyes piercing into Aliik's pathetic face. The hate he had for this man was unparalleled. Viuuv held no more, he burst his lips and spoke, the words flew with poetic, cutting accuracy. Aliik eyes opened, he was stuck for words as it was only a week ago he had spoken to Dr Viuuv in his secret offices in a bunker below the Siuunc Corporation Headquarters, Viuuv was clean shaven with a pale complexion at the time. How can this be the same person?

"Viuuv, it can't be, I saw you only a week ago." As Aliik spoke he reached for his waist belt, the button for help was just below his thumb. Up in the pine trees, the snipers had not rested their predatory stare on their targets, rather like an Iaan crouching in long grass waiting to pounce, their leather straps creaking quietly with each gentle sway of the trees. The wind had now dropped to a slight breeze and a wry smile crept across the faces of the snipers as they knew their accuracy would come into play by nature's kind action.

The beep came through to the ear-pieces of Aliik's guards

and immediately they moved, shots came down in an almost simultaneous burst before some of the guards had time to even put their first step forward. All four fell to the ground, machine guns still locked in the safety position. Birds flew from their perches in the surrounding trees, their flapping wing sound mixed with the diminishing echo of gunfire. Aliik's body jerked at the sudden gunshot fire but the Dooduin sat still unmoved by the events. Viuuv got up slightly shaken but relieved that it was all over; he walked to the stove and poured some hot tea. With his back turned, Aliik slowly reached for a gun in his coat pocket, whilst Viuuv turned without thinking and threw the hot tea into Aliik's face; it was an instinctive reaction that saved his life. Aliik shrieked out in pain, as the two Dooduin leapt from their seated positions and disarmed him. It was all over in a flash, the gun was wrenched from Aliik's hand and one of the Dooduin flicked out the magazine to render the weapon safe. Aliik, still screaming in pain, was bundled outside the hut with his hands tied behind his back face down on the ground.

Viuuv came out of the hut and signalled to the helicopter pilot. The door of the helicopter opened and none of the Dooduin guards even flinched, as the pilot took the helmet off and long, auburn hair came flowing from its protective prison. The pilot was Aluciuun, Viuuv's partner for the last four years; she had met Viuuv just after Hope had launched and had been part of the whole set up since. She placed her helmet on the seat of the helicopter and rushed over to Viuuv. They embraced and she felt the tremble of shock still quaking through his body from the recent events.

"Are you OK my love?" she asked, looking deep into Viuuv's eyes.

"I am now you are here. I thought we would never make it, as I know what sort this scum is," Viuuv replied, looking scornfully down at Aliik who was still held down on the ground. Aliik did not know that the pilot knew Viuuv but was now shouting obscenities to Aluciuun who took Viuuv over to the helicopter. Viuuv was glad that he had not explained anything to Aliik, and knew that the questions would harass Aliik's brain as he struggled for survival. It was an extra punishment and was effortless to enforce.

The two Dooduin followed them over and Viuuv thanked them for all they had done. The Dooduin had their instructions as what to do with Aliik and the snipers who were in the trees were already setting about the task. They had seeors ready and Aliik was being helped on to one with his hands still bound. Two other snipers mounted their steeds and steadily trotted off, heading south. They were to travel for three days and then let Aliik free to fend for himself; it was a fitting punishment for the most selfish and greedy man on Atronia. He had manipulated people for years to amass his power base and untold fortune but now he was on his own with nothing but nature, which he had completely ignored as a life provider. His efforts to survive would be tracked by the two snipers until his slow and starving death. In the mind of Viuuv it was a person that Atronia was well cleansed of.

As Aliik was led away through the trees Viuuv and Aluciuun sat in the helicopter with the switches turned and the blades slowly starting to turn, ready to travel the two hundred miles north to a station set up by Viuuv. The station was a receiving point for any messages sent from Hope and also stored enough fuel until the oil well was ready to pump and refine.

Viuuv had now secured his future in the safe haven of the steppes with the protection of the Dooduin, as well as full control of reconstructing Atronia. He still had to receive the news which awaited him about Sanluin and the rest of Hope's crew, but he would soon have the knowledge that two civilisations were to flourish without the invisible harness of greed and the ultimate temptation to abuse the most perfect technology. The helicopter lifted off the ground and blew freshly dug dirt, covering the shallow graves of Aliik's guards. It was Dooduin tradition to bury the dead where they fell in hostilities and no time was wasted. The dead guards' weapons were strapped to a pack-seeor and taken to the Dooduin camp.

Aluciuun flew low as they headed north, the sun setting to the east shone through the cockpit giving it an amber glow. Viuuv's thoughts now centred on what news he had from Hope. All sorts of possibilities went through his mind, every possible 'what if' as he put it. He knew that Nn would assess the situation and then plan the next step as if he was on the distant planet himself. Viuuv knew that the distant planet existed and that it could sustain life but he had told no one, not even Aluciuun. His silence had nearly driven him crazy but his faith and love of nature had held him strong. His resolve was strengthened by the fact that no terrorist had wiped out the technology, nor had it been man-made by a competitive corporation; the technology had seemed to wipe itself out. It was as if nature itself had taken matters into her own hands.

The thudding drone of the helicopter sent Viuuv off into a doze and he dreamt of Sanluin. His daughter who had trusted in all that her father had told her. She could have had any riches she wanted but stuck to her father's vision of a collapse and possible new start for her. She was willing to give her life and this is what woke Viuuv, as he now wept at the thought of Sanluin possibly not making it. He felt strong emotions for the other crew members but his feelings for his own daughter were so strong that those other feelings paled into insignificance. He was warmed slightly that Rafievn and Sanluin were to fall in love; they would experience pure love away from any distraction that had blurred billions of other couples' emotions throughout Atronia's history. So much pain had driven through Viuuv's heart but he knew he could handle any news. He had Aluciuun's love and now the full understanding of the power of nature, her raw and just actions. After all, she had decided to cleanse her skin of a human parasite, which had lost its way and ignored the very lifeblood that once spawned and supported it. Time was now once again the distance between the truth and realisation of what had happened over the last five years. A new world might lie in Viuuv's control or maybe there would be nothing, no other civilisation. Either way the truth was not long off, as it was getting colder, the further north they flew.

Viuuv knew that the future inoculation of Planetician would be created from the very science that could implode on itself. The inoculation on Atronia was very different; it was a new belief in that mother nature was the one and true God. The surviving people on Atronia accepted that their own talents and natural given gifts were a balance that was meant to be. Once again the written word would carry these messages as they had done before, but this time round there would be no argument as with previous philosophies and religions. This time, pure hard fact and proof had enlightened people with what was a real God or power.

It is the whole, the everything and everyone that was made up of nature's products and cells. All was this power, nothing was less or below or above, equality had risen from centuries of hierarchical division based on ancient beliefs.

A new respect fell upon Atronia and its people; a blanket of complete understanding.

It had been two years since Dr Viuuv and Aluciuun had arrived in the northern recovery station; Viuuv had finished grieving for his daughter and was at complete peace with himself and his conscience. After all, he was responsible for many deaths but none had hurt so hard as the passing of Sanluin, who had given her life for the survival of a new civilisation.

Viuuv was now in his late sixties and had what life he had left in front of him, rebuilding Atronia. He had the perfect chance to set up his projects where people could live a self-sufficient lifestyle with the benefit of no ruling power but nature herself. Small pockets of survivors had been contacted and helped, in setting up their own projects; they had solar, wind and geothermal power, and Viuuv was working on sailing ships with gravity cells fitted if the wind dropped. The future people of Atronia would want for nothing, they just had to learn to survive off the land again. There was no rush anymore, no deadline to keep or company profits to bolster. It was a place where everyone relied on everyone else, no one was above anyone else by material wealth, some just had more knowledge and experience, which was passed down to the younger generations freely, guaranteeing the survival of Atronia's people in as perfect a balance as could be with nature.

Viuuv would look out over the oceans and think of all the other surviving groups dotted around Atronia. They were creating a heaven on earth, or as it suddenly dawned on Viuuv, that earth was heaven, it had just been man that had created the rat race, the stress, the wars and the greed. Now global sharing of a planet had prevailed and the occupiers had learnt the hard way, total respect for nature and its fruits. It was not the inventions and creations of man that had brought a near extinction of man but the greed of man.

Reports were coming in from the pockets of survivors on Atronia that the eco-system was stabilising and firing back into life with a vengeance. It was as if nature had hibernated as her habitats' were raped for her last remaining minerals. This warmed Viuuv's heart immensely as he thought all might have been lost. The old fight between good and evil was really sharing versus greed. Greed had finally been beaten and a new dawn had begun.

All of the messages that came from Hope had kept Viuuv informed of Nn's actions, he knew that the dormant gene had been developed and that it was only a matter of time until Planetician was inoculated.

From the information sent from Hope, Viuuv knew that fossil fuels would be burnt for energy production and industrial use in manufacturing. This would raise questions amongst the leaders of Planetician about possible global warming. Nn was programmed to get projects, which would have worked on Atronia to the governing bodies of Planetician; they were simple but effective solutions. Atronia's rulers often debated whether their climate was getting warmer because of their carbon output, whilst some said it was the sun getting hotter during its solar cycles. Either way, the easiest remedy was to put deep space solar parasols into space so that shadows were cast over the polar and equatorial regions of Atronia. Atronia's rulers blocked the idea, as too much money was to be made in flood defence and city relocation, and many of Atronia's politicians were corrupt, being in the pockets of the big corporations.

One idea that was used was the protection of rainforest. Huge areas were burnt for farming Lactte but the concentration of this farming solved the problem. Huge sheds were erected, which allowed the local farmers to still make a living from their land but without destroying the valuable rainforest. The forest replenished itself and the yield per acre was massively increased. A sea level reduction idea was also blocked but would have kept raising sea levels at bay. Viuuv had suggested that flooding of dried up water tables beneath deserts with seawater and then constructing very large membranes over the top of the saturated desert would cause condensation of the salt water. As the water filtered through the sand, salt would be reduced and as it condensed further, salt would be filtered off. The fresh water would need to be used to irrigate new plant and forest life, so that the moisture was held on the land and not let back into the hydro-cycle. Again this was blocked, as other profit was more important to the corrupt politicians. It would be easier for Nn than it was for Viuuv, as Viuuv had not developed the mind changing processors that Nn had done during his 4,000 years on Hope. All Nn had to do was get to the civilised parts of Planetician and put these ideas into the heads of the right people. It would be done in the same way as Bill Thompson's exhaled breath had transported the processors to Dr Baker and then on to Dr Meacher.

Nn's ticket to Planetician's cities was only a few months away and his development of camouflage had improved greatly since Rafievn had worn his. Nn had also altered his mass and density so that his footsteps in the snow would show much less than his actual weight; he did not want his coming party of humans to see that owner-less footprints were following them.

Planetician

One who is versed in the science of planet Earth if mankind is to ever answer the question as to where we came from and where we are going, the survival of planet Earth must be at the forefront of everything we do.

Translations

Nelb - lamb

Tocoot - coconut

Soilhs - dolphin

Riind - deer

Deiis - spider

Tanoos - bananas

Faiis - sheep

Neaak - snake

Seeor - horse

Seppas - apples

Yinea - hyena

Hunnit - rabbit

Paais - grapes

Suugs - dogs

Seiis - flies

Ceook - chicken /cockerel

Leeps - gooseberries

Iaan - sphinx / lion

Barcee - king cobra

Lactte - cattle /wildebeest

Luuse - metal ore alloy from the Atronia's moon

Leetyi - Cinciev's home city on Atronia

Doodiun - Nomadic people on Atronia

Pyeet - city on Atronia, of ancient origin

Ciption - dark-skinned race from Atronia

Sillion- white-skinned race from Atronia

To my wife Sam

There is, in some people's lives a very special person; sometimes we don't even realise it properly until an event happens and they are there in body and soul supporting in every way. I am very lucky to have such a person, who was more than there for me. She was there for my children, who were very scared and confused at what had happened to their dad whilst also being scared to bits herself, but holding very strong for her family. It was her maternal instinct and her love for me that gave her the strength to cope with such a disturbing experience.

I was on the inside of my manic episode but Sam, my wife saw it all first hand from the outside, trying desperately hard to understand what was happening. It was not until three psychiatrists had interviewed me on and off for hours that she was told what had actually happened to me. For weeks afterwards she supported me every day as my depression and complete loss of confidence really kicked in. I remember the mornings being the hardest; sometimes crying in her arms as I felt like a small boy on the inside but was a thirty-two year old man on the outside. She pulled me together with relentless love so that I could face another day at work.

To dedicate Hope's Truth to her is the least I could do, because without her this book would have never been written.

Love you Sam, xx

To my children

I can't imagine how a young mind would evaluate what happened to their dad. I wanted to be strong for them but I was trembling inside, confidence gone and depression creeping in like the darkening of the winter days. Their innocent faces looking at me, smiling, they saw their dad who to them was the same, but to me I was full of emptiness. Their hugs and love pumped emotion through me, and

287

my tears fell in guilt as I was not able to be there for them as I was before. Time has healed and again, now I feel so strong for them, I can be their mountain and their shelter. To say 'I love them' is too small, the feelings I have for them, the words I have not looked for as they would not do my feelings justice either. They are simply my magic.

My Mum and Dad, Pearl and Richard. I love you both very much , thank you for your unwavering love and support for all of my years.

To my mother in-law Carol, who is always a great support to me but more so for Sam as she took the full force of my bi-polar 'trips'.

Dick and Jane Barrow, my in-laws, always there if needed no matter what.

Vicky and Lee Matthews. Nick and Nikki Fuller. Suzanne Benjamin

Thanks also go to the following people, in order of appearance during my bi-polar episode:
Shane Davis (Lightyear), Kevin Brain (Brainy), Dave Kipling (Kips), Alan Greenwood (Ali G), Mark Mcguiness (Maccer), Nicholas Charles Fuller (Charlie), Mark Jones (Boner), David Frank Lindsay (Bug), Michael James Dixon (The Amber Flash), Andrew John Hays(Gomez), Simon Pritchette (Snitch), Adam Harvey (Tank), Owen Neil (Bobang), John Tavener (Tavsy) and these two special people who I hope will read the book from their spiritual resting places, Vincent Seagar (Vince), David Smith (my dear cousin).

TRICORN
BOOKS